THE AMERICAN S
COLLECTION 4: THEIR BLUE-
COLLAR GIRL

Dixie Lynn Dwyer

MENAGE EVERLASTING

Siren Publishing, Inc.
www.SirenPublishing.com

A SIREN PUBLISHING BOOK
IMPRINT: Ménage Everlasting

THE AMERICAN SOLDIER COLLECTION 4: THEIR BLUE-COLLAR GIRL
Copyright © 2014 by Dixie Lynn Dwyer

ISBN: 978-1-62740-674-1

First Printing: January 2014

Cover design by Les Byerley
All art and logo copyright © 2014 by Siren Publishing, Inc.

Printed in U.S.A.

PUBLISHER
Siren Publishing, Inc.
www.SirenPublishing.com

DEDICATION

Dear readers,

Please enjoy the fourth book in my new series The American Soldier Collection: Their Blue Collar Girl.

Sometimes life throws you some unexpected things. Even at such a young age, Lori pulls through for her sister and nephew. Scared, unable to do the normal things a teenager does, she becomes an instant adult, provider, protector, and ultimately, a hero.

A bond between sisters is strong. A bond between lovers, powerful. Pulling from both of those sources makes Lori a heroine to respect and be proud of.

Thank you for purchasing this book, and may you enjoy this story of self-sacrifice, determination, and the power of love.

~Dixie~

THE AMERICAN SOLDIER COLLECTION 4: THEIR BLUE-COLLAR GIRL

DIXIE LYNN DWYER
Copyright © 2014

Prologue

Lori Ann began placing the red floral cushions on the chairs she just purchased at a local outdoor furniture store. Her sister Maggie thought the color was too bold. Lori didn't care. All she knew was that the colors were bright and uplifting and that was exactly how she felt today.

The last moving box was unloaded, items placed in their specific locations throughout the dining room, and the empty box sat on the porch floor next to her. New Orleans was now their home. She pulled the remaining tags from the last and largest cushion, tossing them into the empty box and placing the cushion on the chaise lounge.

"There! Now doesn't that look perfect, sis?" Lori asked Maggie.

"I guess so," was all Maggie said as she continued to look outside watching her four-year-old son Ben play on the swing set that came with the house. By the end of the summer he would be turning five and ready to start school in September. Maggie and Lori had moved around so much in the past four years, out of pure fear. They made the decision to finally settle down, stay put for a while and let Ben have a permanent home. He was going to start kindergarten, make some friends and perhaps join "Just for Fun Baseball."

"Why are you so quiet, Maggie?" Lori asked, taking a seat on the rocking chair next to her.

Maggie slowly turned toward her sister. She was worried. Lori could tell.

"What is it?"

"We're finally settling down, Lori. This is going to be our home." Her eyes filled up with tears.

"I know, sis, isn't it great! The landlord said we can do anything we want to this place. We can color the walls with polka dots or some wild and crazy color like raspberry hot pink or something," Lori added excitedly. Maggie giggled.

"You're crazy, Lori, you know that?" Maggie's smile appeared and disappeared like the click of a camera. Now she looked emotional.

"I…I would have never survived all these years without your help….I love you. You know that, right?"

Lori smiled.

"Yeah I know that, Maggie, and I love you, too. We're sisters and I'll always be here for you." Lori leaned over and hugged her sister.

"Mommy, come push me!" yelled Ben from the swing set and Maggie jumped up and headed out. The porch door slammed closed.

Lori watched as Maggie gave Ben a hug and began pushing him back and forth on the swing set. Inside the house the phone began to ring and Lori headed toward the kitchen to answer it.

The new refrigerator would be delivered tomorrow. The balance was due and the warehouse wanted to know which credit card to charge the purchase to.

"We'll pay cash upon delivery or a money order. Which would you prefer?" Lori asked the customer service rep and they tried to get her to give a credit card number. She refused and said she was told she could pay by cash or money order. The customer service rep said a money order would be fine then gave Lori an approximate five-hour window for delivery. As she hung up the phone, she laughed a little. She knew that by not using a store credit card the sales rep probably missed out on offering Lori extended warrantees or extra packages the reps are trained to try and sell a customer.

Lori and Maggie were too smart for that. They hadn't used credit cards in over four years. They didn't own any and they refused to leave any kind of paper trail or any means of being tracked down.

Lori opened the small compact refrigerator door and grabbed two Snapple iced tea bottles and a Grover grape juice box for Ben. The phone rang a second time and Lori put down the drinks to answer it.

"Hello…Hello…" Lori repeated into the receiver but no one responded. Instantly, she got a bad feeling then pushed those feelings aside trying to convince herself that there was no need to worry. She walked outside carrying the drinks and told Maggie about the two phone calls.

"I'm sure it was nothing, Lori. It's a new number and we're bound to get some prank calls or people dialing the wrong numbers."

"You're probably right," stated Lori as she opened up Ben's juice box and handed it to her nephew. She loved him so much and acted more like another mother to him than an aunt.

Ben was a blessing in many ways. Every day he seemed to learn something new. Watching him do so helped to keep Lori focused on ensuring his safety and his right to a safe and loving life.

Lori couldn't believe that five years had passed. She was only sixteen years old when she left home with her sister Maggie, who was twenty-one at the time. It broke their hearts to leave their family and friends behind but Maggie's and Ben's lives were in jeopardy, and if they were to survive, they needed to stay on the run. Their mother Diana and father Lou had moved around a little as well. They were now living in a small town in Houston, Texas. They hoped to someday visit them but felt it was still too risky. Not with that madman loose and out of control.

Derrick needed serious help. With his parents in denial, covering up his abusive behavior and lies, there was only one choice, and that was to run.

Lori recalled being scared out of her mind but she would do anything for Maggie…anything.

Lori watched Maggie push Ben on the swing. One day it would be safe enough to meet up with their parents again. She had dreams and moving around so much was beginning to take a toll on her. Despite being twenty-one she felt somewhat older. It was probably all the stress of providing for a family in every aspect of the words. Even Maggie had dreams and one bad decision changed all that.

One day they would be free. They could see their parents, pursue their dreams, and all the fear and danger would be behind them.

* * * *

John Luke came out of the back kitchen at Casper's to find Lou and Diana sitting at the table in the corner. New to town, and originally from New York, they were cautious in making friends. They were a very nice couple and stopped in once a month or so for lunch. They were quiet and it had taken him and his wife Eve months to get them to engage in conversation. Once Eve, Jasper, and Davie got a hold of them, they were inviting Lou and Diana over for dinner and family barbeques. They had become close and considering that Gunner, Garret, and Wes were involved in law enforcement and ex-military types, Lou and Diana confided in them about their daughters.

"Hey, Diana, Lou, what's going on?" John Luke asked as he shook Lou's hand hello then leaned down to kiss Diana on the cheek. She smiled and blushed which earned her a roll of the eyes from her husband Lou.

"I didn't know you two were coming in for lunch. I would have made sure that Jasper sent out today's special for you to try."

"Aw that's awfully nice of you, John Luke. We kind of decided last minute to head out here from the ranch. How are Gia and your sons?"

John Luke smiled wide. He loved talking about his family. He felt kind of badly that Lou and Diana couldn't have their daughters, Maggie and Lori Ann, come live with them.

"They're doing great. Keeping busy. We're all hoping for some grandchildren to spoil soon."

"I hear you there. It would be wonderful to see our grandson. One day, I suppose." Diana lowered her head as she stared at her clasped hands.

"I'm sorry, Diana. I wish you would allow my sons to help you out. I'm certain with their connections, they could get those two girls of yours and your grandchild home safely to you both."

"We can't take the chance. We explained it before," Lou said.

"He's got connections, too, and the girls are simply too scared to trust anyone."

John Luke felt both sad for Lou and Diana and angry at the way the system allowed abusive men to get away with criminal behavior just because of family connections.

"Well you let me know if you change your mind. I'm going to go check on your lunch orders. I'll be right back."

John Luke headed into the kitchen. He saw Eve, Jasper, and Davie and told them about Lou and Diana.

"I wish there was something we could do. It's seems so unrealistic that two young women and a child have to remain on the run in hiding from some abusive man and his domineering, wealthy family. Why don't laws apply to people like that?" she asked as she shook her head and wiped down the counter.

"It has to be pretty bad. They explained the situation and I for one think it best if the girls remain in hiding. Perhaps they won't have to for too much longer," Jasper said then gave his wife Eve a hug.

John Luke shook his head in annoyance and prayed that the two women could come home to their parents sooner rather than later.

* * * *

Lori looked out across the yard and watched Ben. He surely was a blessing and the one amazing miracle that came from such a tragic, abusive relationship.

Maggie met Derrick when she was seventeen. Lori remembered how excited her sister was. Maggie had a crush on him big-time. He was a handsome, rugged, bad-boy type that all the girls wanted to date. He chose Maggie and the sparks were flying between them. While she attended community college, he worked with his father and uncle as a correctional officer at the county correctional facility. After they were dating for a year, Derrick started to become abusive and Maggie was too scared to tell anyone. Derrick had just proposed to her on her twentieth birthday, and they decided to wait until she was twenty-one and at least finished a year or two of college before getting married. During that year he continued to control Maggie, pulling her away from her family and controlling every move she made. Maggie confided in Lori and Lori convinced Maggie to leave Derrick and break things off before they became worse. Unfortunately Derrick and his family were well known in the community and there was nowhere to turn for help. Derrick convinced Maggie that he would change and that he loved her more than anything and she believed him.

As Lori recalled those days of denial and fear, her heart clenched with trepidation. As far as Lori was concerned, Maggie and Ben weren't safe until Derrick was either behind bars or dead. But the man seemed invincible, especially with all the family connections.

She remembered that one fateful night that proved Derrick's capabilities and evilness. One night, in an intoxicated and abusive state, Derrick forced himself on Maggie, they had unprotected sex and she became pregnant. Only Maggie, Lori, and Derrick knew the truth, and as their families celebrated the news, Lori and Maggie planned their escape from the small town in upstate New York.

Lori and Maggie's first attempt failed as Derrick and his friend Jed caught them before they could cross the border into the next state. They both suffered the consequences and Maggie nearly lost the baby after Derrick roughed her up. Still no one came to Maggie's aid and Lori came up with another plan along with her mother.

Maggie was six months pregnant and Lori was nearly seventeen years old when they escaped from Derrick and his family. Those first three years away were intense as they moved from town to town and Derrick continued to follow them just missing them, sometimes by a day or so.

They never stayed in one place too long and it had been a good two years since they heard anything from Derrick or his family. Maggie and Lori kept contact with their mother as they called from pay phones and sent pictures or letters from towns they were passing through.

They spoke to their mother a year ago, and she said Derrick was back home in New York, working at the jail again and seemed to give up hope of finding Maggie. He would harass their mother Diana, every chance he got when he first returned home. But soon he stopped and seemed to go about his life again.

Maggie and Lori made the decision to finally settle down now that Ben was almost five and starting school. Lori attended the local community college during the day and worked weekends. Maggie took Ben to and from school during the day and worked nights. It was tough but at least Ben always had someone with him.

One afternoon, months ago, their mother Diana called saying that Derrick had gotten into some trouble. He had been drinking a lot lately, got involved with another woman who he beat up pretty badly and the local police were on to him. It didn't matter who he was or what family he came from. He was out of control, lost his job at the jail, and one night got into a bar fight with another local guy named Ted Duncan. Derrick was drunk and started a fight with Ted. Ted apparently put Derrick in his place and knocked him onto the floor with one punch.

Derrick waited for Ted to leave the bar later that night and he jumped him. Diana told her daughters that Derrick killed Ted Duncan and was on the run. He was a wanted man and all surrounding police departments were looking for him.

"Oh my gosh, I knew something like this was going to happen, Lori. I just knew it. What are we going to do?" Maggie asked her younger sister Lori, who always seemed to stay in control despite her younger age.

"We'll be even more cautious than usual, Maggie. He doesn't know where we are unless someone leaked the information to him. I told Mom not to let Uncle Jack know. He has a big mouth and drinks too much," stated Lori as she tapped her fingers on the kitchen table.

"Should we call the police? Tell them where we are and that he's probably coming after us?" Maggie asked.

"What, are you kidding me? They can't protect us from him. Besides we took off with you carrying his child. With the people his family knows we'll wind up in prison and he'll wind up with Ben and everyone feeling sorry for him. They'll blame his actions on us."

"You think that could happen, Lori?"

"It wouldn't surprise me at all. We need to keep hidden and keep Ben safe. He's our top priority, sis. He's our son. Yours and mine," stated Lori, and Maggie knew it was true. Her sister Lori loved Ben as if he were her own. The bond between them was strong and there was no way she would ever let anything happen to him.

"Okay so let's make some changes with our schedules. I'll wait outside the school every day to make sure I don't see Derrick."

"That's a good idea, Maggie. He may try to kidnap Ben. He's not thinking with a straight head. He's on the run from the police and he's already killed a man."

"Oh my God, Lori, what are we going to do?" Maggie asked as she began to cry. Instantly her sister was at her side pulling her into a hug.

It was funny how different their personalities were. Maggie was average, about five foot six with short blonde hair and blue eyes. She was preppy looking, wore hardly any makeup, and showed her emotions. She practically wore them on her shirtsleeve. Lori always knew what her big sister was feeling and what she was going to do. She was predictable.

Lori on the other hand had long golden-blonde hair that fell halfway down her back and had beautiful dark, jade-green eyes. Green eyes that hid all her emotions, dreams and desires. She held her wants and needs in life deep within and always put her sister and Ben first.

Lori was unpredictable, petite at five foot three, but filled with strength, self-confidence, and self-assurance. She was forced to grow up fast and take responsibility for herself, Maggie, and Ben. Maggie would have never been able to do any of this on her own. She knew that and continuously thanked Lori for it.

"We'll get through this, Maggie, and Ben will be fine," Lori told her sister and they planned their schedules.

* * * *

A week had passed and there was no sign of trouble as Lori prepared to leave for work one early Saturday evening around 4:00 p.m. She planned on calling Maggie every two hours until 10:00 p.m. Then Maggie would call Lori until she left the restaurant at 2:00 a.m. It was a routine they would stick by until Derrick was caught.

Lori got busy waiting on tables and missed calling Maggie by fifteen minutes. She ran to the phone the second she got a chance and gave a huge sigh of relief at her sister's voice. Maggie said everything was fine and Lori went back to work. It was a busy night and Lori hustled to get as many tables as possible and receive the best tips. Her family relied on it and it was a great form of income for them.

In the midst of clattering glasses, cleaning off tables, loud laughter, and excitement, Lori finished up her last table of the evening. She was exhausted and glad she didn't have the late shift tonight.

"Hey, Lori, why don't you come have a drink with us before you go home?" the bartender Jack asked and Lori declined as usual even though there were some rather good-looking men at the bar. If she were a normal single twenty-one-year-old woman, she would be dating right now, having a good time, and perhaps tossing responsibility to the wind here and there. But that wasn't her life. She had responsibilities and she needed to get home to them right now. Every minute that Maggie and Ben were out of sight caused her worry and anxiety.

"No thanks, Jack, I can't tonight. I've got plans early tomorrow morning," she lied to him and Jack smiled a disappointed smile as well as the others at the bar.

She did kind of have plans tomorrow, the same plans Monday through Sunday. Her 6:00 a.m. four-mile jog was her scheduled appointment. It was what kept her in shape along with the one hundred crunches she did first.

Lori headed home in the beat-up light blue Ford Tempo Maggie and her picked up in New Jersey at a local gas station. It was reliable and didn't draw too much attention to them unless it stalled at a green traffic light. She pulled into the driveway and noticed the kitchen light was on. She figured Maggie was waiting up for her again and was unable to sleep.

Lori was surprised to find the side kitchen door unlocked as she pulled the key back out of the doorknob and entered.

"Someone keeps calling the house, Lori," Maggie told her sister as Lori entered the house.

"Is that why you have the door unlocked?" Lori asked, sounding a little annoyed that her sister didn't lock it.

"I just unlocked it as you pulled in, Lori. I'm scared. I think it was Derrick." Lori felt her sister's fear immediately. She was a believer that your gut never lied.

"Let's lock everything up and you go upstairs to sit with Ben. I'll turn off the light and keep a lookout for a while. If you hear anything strange, we'll call the police, okay?" Lori said. Maggie agreed as she headed upstairs. Lori turned off the kitchen lights and headed around the house, rechecking the locks on the windows and doors. Suddenly she heard her sister scream and Lori ran toward the stairs. She could hear a man's voice, muffled behind a closed door.

Lori slowly climbed the staircase then stopped and went back down the stairs. She heard Derrick hit Maggie and Maggie screamed again. Lori grabbed the phone in the living room and dialed the police. The dispatcher asked what was going on and Lori quickly explained who Derrick was and what he was doing. She hung up the phone as she heard Ben crying and screaming, "Stop!"

Just as Lori approached the final step she could see Derrick by the opened bedroom door. Ben was on the green rug crying and Maggie's lips were bleeding and her eyes were swollen. Derrick was going to kill them both.

"Where's that little bitch sister of yours? I'm going to kill her, too. The two of you are going to die together and I'm going to take my son with me!" he yelled as he kicked Maggie in the stomach. Lori gasped as she watched her sister fall to the floor.

He changed his voice to a softer tone as he spoke to Ben.

"Don't be scared, son, I'm your daddy. I've come to get you. We're going to go live together," he told Ben, who was hysterically crying as he held on to his mother. Derrick was irate at this as he forced Ben to release his grip on his mom. Ben was screaming. Maggie was barely conscious as she tried to hold on to Ben. Once again, Derrick kicked Maggie repeatedly then pulled out a gun. As soon as Lori saw the gun she made her move but Derrick felt the movement behind him as he turned around and shot once just missing Lori. She lunged at Derrick, tackling him to the bedroom floor, screaming at the top of her lungs.

"Run, Ben! Run!"

* * * *

Little Ben ran for the door and down the stairs as he ran across the living room he could see the colored blue and red lights shining outside. The police were there, heard the gun shot and were cautiously entering the house. Ben yelled.

"My daddy is gonna kill my mommy and Aunt Lori. He hit me and Mommy's bleeding. Help us!" he yelled and the police officer grabbed Ben bringing him to safety outside. The local police and state police were arriving on the scene. They had the house surrounded. They were aware that a fugitive was inside the house and a possible hostage situation was underway.

* * * *

Lori was wrestling with Derrick who was now hitting her with his fist and the gun. She was relentless, unwilling to give up fighting for her sister's life and Ben's. Derrick would not win. He wouldn't get Ben.

Lori's hand was over the gun and Derrick had it pointing straight at Maggie.

Lori gathered all her might and head butted Derrick causing him to release his grip on Lori and fall to the other side away from Maggie. Lori was telling her sister to get up and run just as multiple police officers were ascending the stairs.

"Stop. Police. Put down your weapon!" the officer yelled, but Derrick didn't budge as Lori fought him for power of the weapon. Her wrist was twisting the wrong way and the pain excruciating as she held the gun unsure of its direction.

"It's over, Derrick, you've lost. Give up!"

He screamed in anger like some crazed lunatic. The gun fell to the side of her as Derrick grabbed Lori's throat with both hands, choking the breath, the life out of her. The police were still yelling stop. They didn't see him release the gun, and Lori was losing strength as she reached for the gun, grabbing it, pointing at Derrick's side and firing. He released her throat and sat up on top of her as the police stormed the room. Derrick kept fighting, hitting officer after officer as they responded with mace, which just enraged him even more. One officer pulled Lori out of the way and as he pulled her toward him she dropped the gun onto the floor.

She was in the hallway and could hear the officers yelling, "No! Stop right there!" Then there was a gunshot followed by two more.

The police emerged unharmed, calling for an ambulance, as Derrick lay on the bedroom floor already dead. He had lunged for the gun and turned it on the officers, who responded by shooting him.

The officer helped Lori down the stairs and outside the house where Maggie and Ben held one another waiting for Lori to appear.

As Lori emerged from the doorway, she ran toward her sister and Ben. They were crying, holding one another, relieved that they were all alive.

Chapter 1

Charlie sat on the back porch with his feet up on the wood, drinking a beer. It was a quiet, peaceful night, but he couldn't sleep. He felt restless and even his jaw hurt. Instantly he thought of his mother Terry's words from last week.

"It takes more muscles in your face to frown than it does to smile. Don't you remember how to smile, son?"

What a loaded question that was. He wanted to respond to her. *I forgot, Mom. There's nothing in my life, in my memories, to make me smile.*

As the sour thoughts went through his mind, he took a slug of beer, thinking it tasted just as badly.

He felt restless, tired, pissed off, grumpy, and downright ornery. He knew it. He could tell, by the way people avoided him constantly, that he showed it, and he really didn't give a shit. He was fine with being alone but that wasn't a possibility with his two brothers Dante and Trevor living with him. They built this house from the foundation up. At least his brothers Andrew and Matt were on their own, married or getting married. That was never going to happen for him.

He heard the floors inside the house creak. He had great hearing. Being in the service, working in Special Forces, he could sense an enemy, or even a friend approaching from quite a distance. The back door opened.

"Can't sleep?" Dante asked as he walked outside, shook a little from the chilly evening air, then sat down.

Charlie reached down to the small refrigerator, pulled out a cold beer, and passed it to his brother.

"Thanks." Dante took a slug then stared out toward the darkness.

"It sure is dark out there at night."

"Hm." Charlie hardly responded. He wasn't one for chitchatting about bullshit. If someone had to tell him something, then he wanted them to just spit it out.

"Did you take anything to help you?" Dante asked.

"Don't work," Charlie replied.

"I've been using some over-the-counter stuff, you know, to take off the edge. I might not fall completely asleep, but at least my body is at rest. I wonder when we'll finally get past these sleepless nights and move on in peace."

"Beats the crap out of me."

Dante was quiet a minute and then turned toward the same sound Charlie just heard. Their brother Trevor must be coming from his room, too. Sure enough Trevor arrived and Charlie glanced at Dante. They shared a nonverbal understanding that they detected Trevor's approach early.

Charlie's brothers were also part of Special Forces. They did shit they could never talk about or would want to. The nightmares they had were enough to last a lifetime. However, Trevor and Dante seemed able to ease back into civilian life better than Charlie. That pissed him off, too. Then again, there wasn't much that didn't piss Charlie off.

"What are you two doing out here this late?" Trevor asked. He had to duck under the doorway to come outside. He was six feet three just like Dante. Charlie was an inch taller than both of them.

This time Dante reached into the refrigerator and pulled out a beer. He passed it to Trevor who shrugged his shoulders before taking a sip.

"Couldn't sleep either?" Dante asked.

"Nope." Trevor sat down on the swinging bench and stared out into the darkness.

He appeared on alert a moment. Charlie understood how he felt. It had taken the last three years to get used to the fact that he was safe here. The enemy wasn't lurking in the darkness of the woods surrounding their home or their neighbors' homes. The shimmering glow in the distance was fireflies, not the reflection of moonlight off the scope of a sniper rifle.

He sighed in annoyance.

"I'm glad we're out here together. I've been meaning to discuss something with you guys. Something we've talked about before," Trevor stated.

Charlie sighed again. Trevor wanted to be in a relationship so badly, but his nightmares and PTSS plagued him as well as Dante and Charlie. They visited their friends, Gunner, Garret, and Wes last week and saw how happy they were. A lot of their military buddies were finding happiness in ménage relationships and Dante and Trevor were pushing to give it a try.

"I think we should really start looking," Trevor stated.

"I think if we're going to meet someone to share, then it will happen. I can't see trying something as intense as this with just some random woman, Trevor. You heard what Garret and the guys said. It hit them all at once. They knew immediately that Gia was meant for them. They were each attracted to her and she was to them," Dante said.

"What do you think, Charlie?" Trevor asked.

Charlie stared out at the darkness. If he could take a picture of what he felt was inside his heart and his soul, this would be it. Pure black, darkness.

"I told you before, Trevor, and I'll tell you again. I'm not interested. I wouldn't do my part and it wouldn't be fair to the unsuspecting woman. You two have love to give. I don't." Charlie stood up, tossed his empty beer bottle into the recycling bin, then walked inside.

* * * *

"Aunt Lori, what's Grandma like? Is she really old?" Ben asked as Lori drove the car and Maggie looked at the map.

Lori began to laugh. "No, she's not old. Actually she's rather young to be a grandma. She's a great cook and baker and I'm sure she has lots and lots of plans for you. She told your mom and I that she has a surprise waiting for you when we arrive."

"What kind of surprise?" Ben asked excitedly as he held a red Power Ranger figure in his hand. It was one of his favorite toys to play with besides dinosaurs.

"If I tell you it won't be a surprise. Besides your mom and I have no idea either."

"That's right, Ben, we don't know what the surprise could be," added Maggie as she turned to smile at Ben.

"How long until we get there?" he asked impatiently.

"Not too long, maybe thirty minutes or so." Maggie told Lori which turn to take next.

Ben continued to play with his toys as Maggie and Lori spoke.

"How's your wrist?" Maggie asked.

"It's a little sore and itchy actually. I can't wait until I can get this cast off. Eight weeks seems forever," Lori said as she held the steering wheel with her good hand.

Maggie noticed Lori hadn't been the same since the night Derrick broke into their home. She kind of closed up and wasn't so willing to give her opinion. Maggie thought that perhaps Lori felt guilty for shooting Derrick. Even though it was the police officers who fired the two fatal shots, Derrick's family placed the responsibility solely on Lori. They could care less that their son was a murderer, a batterer, a fugitive, and a drunk. Derrick's father John even tried to get custody of Ben but he didn't have a chance once he and his wife were charged with aiding and abetting a fugitive. They were finally free of Derrick Lawson and his family. Now Lori, Maggie, and Ben were headed to Texas, to live on a large private piece of property next to an enormous ranch. No more running scared and their new lives could begin.

"You can probably find a job teaching, Lori, and maybe I could find an office job somewhere in town. Mom said there are plenty of businesses around and a need for good school teachers," Maggie told her sister as Lori made another turn.

"This looks like the street up ahead. There's no sign though," Lori added.

"Mom did say a long dirt road and that you could see the horse ranch," stated Maggie as Lori continued to drive a little too fast up the road. She came to the top of the hill and suddenly had to slam on the breaks. A man on a large brown-and-white stallion came out of nowhere along with two other men on brown horses.

The first man looked angry as hell as he threw up his hands yelling at Lori.

"Sorry, guy. You came out of nowhere!" Lori yelled back at him out the window.

"This isn't the goddamn highway, lady. Slow the hell down." He continued to yell at Lori as he and the other men rode the horses to the side of the road.

"Screw you, you jerk!" Lori yelled back out the window then stepped on the gas speeding down the dirt road.

Ben and Maggie were laughing as Lori turned bright red and carried on about the man on the horse, as she looked in the rearview mirror.

* * * *

"Hot damn, Charlie, why did you carry on like that? It's obvious they're not from around here," Jasper said out loud.

"No shit she wasn't from around here, driving like some kind of lunatic. Probably from the city or something," Charlie said in a huff as he continued to ride his horse.

"Not with a beat-up car like that. That thing sounded like the muffler was about to fall off," Freddie added to the conversation.

"Well whoever the hell she was, she's gonna kill somebody if she keeps driving like that," Charlie carried on with thoughts of the crazy driver filling his mind. They headed back to the ranch where Charlie's brothers, Andrew and Matt Henley, were talking by the horse stables with their father Phil.

* * * *

Terry watched from the front porch as all her men gathered by the horse stables. It was a beautiful day for riding and as she watched her sons and husband talking she couldn't help but smile. There was no mistaking which men were the Henley men. They each resembled their father and his strong, masculine, fit physique.

Andrew was the oldest at thirty-eight, married, and the local town physician. He was as handsome as some movie star or top male model but with a more masculine, sporty attitude. He wore his dark brown hair wavy and a little too long for his mother's taste, but it enhanced his matching dark brown eyes. He had always been the local heartthrob.

His brother Matt was thirty-six and engaged to get married to Janie, a local nursery school teacher. Matt had short dirty-blonde hair and light green eyes and he worked for the local newspaper as a journalist part-time, and the rest of the time he helped his brother Charlie take care of the ranch along with her other two sons, Dante and Trevor.

Dante was thirty-two and quiet as a mouse since returning from serving in the military. Trevor was restless and almost identical in appearance to Dante with matching hazel eyes and dimples. Their cousins Jasper and Freddie helped run the ranch, too.

Charlie was thirty-four years old and very attractive with his dark reddish-brown hair, hazel eyes, and tough rugged appearance that went along with his attitude. He was a hard-ass and proud of it as he ran the ranch along with his father Phil who was soft-spoken and old fashioned.

"Do you boys want to come inside now for lunch? I've only been waiting a half hour you know?" yelled their mother Terry from the front porch. She was a thin woman in her late fifties with salt-and-pepper hair she wore short and behind her ears. She had the same brown eyes as her oldest son Andrew. She was tough and full of energy even though the arthritis was kicking in more lately than ever causing her to slow down a bit. She still kept holding her own around the ranch. Today's lunch of cold cut hero sandwiches was a hit with all the men as they gathered around the large kitchen table. There was room for twenty if needed and when family got together, every chair in the house was taken.

"How was your ride?" Terry asked as she passed around the basket of hero rolls.

"Don't even get him started, Aunt Terry," Jasper answered as Terry looked toward Charlie.

Everyone listened as Charlie spoke about the rude, reckless driver from the city.

"Oh my. I wonder if that was Diana and Lou's girls. She said they were coming to live with them along with their grandson. They haven't seen one another in years. Excuse me while I go call her and see." Terry rather excitedly rose from the table and headed into the other room.

"What is she talking about?" Andrew asked.

"It's a long story, son, but from what Lou has told me, his two daughters and his grandson Ben have been through a lot in the past five years. They'll be home safe where they belong. So did you get to fix that fence out by the Riley's place?" Phil asked, obviously changing the subject. The men got the message as they continued to talk about the ranch and the jobs that needed to be done.

* * * *

Lori drove the car up the long dirt driveway and instantly saw their mother and father sitting on the front porch. The house was beautiful and appeared well maintained and country-like. Her hand was shaking as she felt the tears reach her eyes. They hadn't seen their parents in years.

She placed the car in park and turned off the engine. Their parents were running toward them with smiles wide. Lori, Maggie, and Ben got out of the car, rushing to see them. In an instant they all embraced, tears flowing, and Diana cried hysterically as she held her daughters and her grandson Ben.

"Praise the lord. Oh God, praise the lord," Diana cried out as her husband Lou joined the embrace.

Lori watched as her father picked Ben up and held him in his arms.

"Hello, son, I'm your grandpa."

"I know you are and you don't look old at all." Ben hugged his grandfather as they all chuckled.

"This is your grandma," their father told him.

"You have the cutest smile, Ben. You look just like your mama," Diana said as a tear rolled down her cheek.

Lori gave her mom a hug as they headed toward the front porch.

* * * *

Diana turned to look at her two gorgeous daughters and grandson. She needed to touch them, embrace them, kiss them every chance she got. They had missed out on more than five years of parental love and guidance. They were forced to leave their homes because of the power and obsession of another human being. Diana was a believer in destiny. She felt that love conquered everything and anything thrown its way. She didn't like violence, was turned off by television and watching the nightly news. It broke her heart to think of all the victims out there who didn't have help or who couldn't escape the violence. She was glad that Derrick was no longer walking this earth. She prayed to God to bring her daughters home safely, and here they were a bit worn out from the whole ordeal but alive and well.

"What's a matter, Mom? You're daydreaming and about to burn the bacon," Lori said as she took the fork from her mother's hand and took over the cooking task.

"I'm sorry, baby, it's just that I'm so happy you and Maggie are finally home, safe and sound. Never mind my handsome grandson. How did you like your surprise, Ben?" Diana asked as she sat down in the chair next to him.

"I love it, Grandma. It's the greatest swing set I ever had. We had a small, really old one at our last house but my daddy showed up and tried to hurt us."

Maggie rubbed his hair with her hand. "No need to worry about that anymore."

Diana's eyes filled with tears just knowing what her poor little grandson and daughters had seen and survived.

Ben took his grandma's hand and squeezed it.

"Don't worry, Grandma. We're alive because Aunt Lori saved Mommy and me. She was so strong because she loves Mommy and me so much that all her love kept us safe."

"That's right, big guy, and I do love you a whole bunch," Lori added as she took the last piece of bacon out of the pan.

"You bet ya I do, and Mommy loves me and Grandma loves me and Grandpa, too."

"You're right about that. Now let's make you something for lunch. You'll have to tell me what all of your favorite things to eat are, so I can make them for you." Diana rose from the chair then leaned down and gave Ben a kiss on the cheek.

"How about a grilled cheese sandwich? I could sure go for one of those with some bacon and tomato," Lou added as he took a seat at the kitchen table.

"Sounds yummy, Grandpa, I'll have one, too."

"Make it three."

"Four."

"I guess we'll all have grilled cheese sandwiches with bacon and tomato," Diana said as she went to the refrigerator to retrieve the ingredients.

Chapter 2

Maggie and her parents sat on the front porch while Ben lay sleeping in his new bedroom. Diana and Lou brought him a new twin-size bed and a Power Ranger comforter set. Lori had told her parents that the Power Rangers were his favorite toys and dinosaurs were his second favorite. They had picked up a few dinosaur toss pillows and some dinosaur toys at a store in town.

Lori was upstairs taking a shower, annoyed at how much of an inconvenience a broken wrist was, especially trying to keep the plaster cast dry. She was having some sharp pains protruding up her forearm and into her elbow. The doctor she saw told her to check in with a local physician as soon as she was settled in her new home. Maggie was concerned.

"How's Lori doing with that cast?" Lou asked Maggie.

"She's pissed off as anything about it."

"What did the doctor say at the hospital she went to?" Diana asked.

"That she had to keep it on for at least eight weeks but she needed to see someone locally to check it. She's been having some pain in her arm and elbow," Maggie told her parents and Diana showed concern immediately.

"I'll call Dr. Henley. He's a local physician in town and your father and I know his parents and family. They're our neighbors actually. Well your neighbors, too, now," Diana added with a smile.

"I'd talk to Lori about that first. You know she's pretty stubborn and sometimes overly self-sufficient. She likes to handle things on her own and believe me she's great at it. She should be the older sister, not me." Maggie smiled at her parents.

"We're so glad you're here now and she'll have to push that self-sufficient stuff aside for me and your father. We have five years to make up and we're gonna."

"I don't doubt that, Mom, and thank you for the toys and Ben's bedroom. He loves it all. Especially that swing set, he'll live on that thing."

"I hope he loves it and I hope he'll like fishing with his grandpa because I plan on taking him real soon," Lou said and Maggie smiled.

* * * *

Diana couldn't help but worry about Lori, too. She was awfully quiet and really took care of Ben and Maggie.

Just then Lori entered the porch wearing a light T-shirt and a pair of cotton shorts. Her parents watched her as she sat on the rocking chair, crossed her legs and sat up perfectly straight. She was gorgeous with her long blonde hair, green eyes, and perfect body. It was obvious she kept in shape and enjoyed her daily jog. She was already twenty-one years old, young, and vibrant looking yet mature, a true respectable lady.

Diana had so many questions for her daughters but knew to take her time asking. They were forced to grow up so quickly she didn't want to rush anything. She just wanted everything to go nice and slow.

"So what are you building above the barn house over there, Dad?" Lori asked as she slowly rocked the chair.

"Well, I'm turning it into a loft, kind of like an apartment separate from the house."

"Really? That's too cool. Who's going to stay there?" Lori asked excitedly.

"Don't look at me, Lori, I'm fine living in this house with Mom and Dad and Ben. I'd be too nervous living way over there alone,"

Maggie said with a smile.

"Well there you go, honey. It's yours if you want it when we're done," Lou added and Lori was excited.

"Can I check it out tomorrow? Who's building it with you?" Lori asked.

"Yes, you can check it out tomorrow, and Phil Henley, our neighbor along with his sons are helping me."

"Maggie said your wrist and arm were bothering you. I'm going to call Dr. Henley tomorrow and see if I can get you an appointment with him. He's our neighbor's son as well," stated Diana.

"It doesn't hurt that badly, Mom. I'll get around to making an appointment." Lori tried to argue with her mother but there was no use. By the time she woke up in the morning an appointment would be set.

They all sat on the porch a little longer talking about the town and some of their parents' friends. They were invited to a barbeque this upcoming weekend and the girls and Ben were invited as well. Diana hoped that she could bring some normalcy into their lives and get to know her daughters quickly and with ease. But something told her that it wouldn't be so easy.

* * * *

Business District, Houston, Texas

"I'm telling you right now, Don, that land up there in Valley Stream is calling to me," Jerry Connor stated as he paced back and forth in his office. "I want it and I don't care who owns it. That location someday will be worth millions. We've already seen the prices rise."

"Well I don't know what to tell you, Jerry, but Old Man Cantrell doesn't want to sell to you. He'd rather sell off that land bit by bit if necessary and he's already started."

"Well he doesn't know who he's messing with. I have a plan and he won't know who he's selling the land to. If all goes well, I'll own all that land and within the next ten years or less, we'll be sitting pretty, partner. I don't care if I have to buy it up piece by piece. I'm going to own that land."

Jerry was determined, and Don knew when his partner got like this, there was no stopping him. He worried about just how far Jerry would go and to what measures to get what he wanted.

Chapter 3

Sure enough when Lori walked downstairs after her jog and shower this morning, her mom had made an appointment with Dr. Henley in town.

"Your appointment's in a half hour. He had a cancellation and was happy to oblige. Did you bring your file from the hospital with you along with the X-rays?" Diana asked as she cleaned up the dishes from breakfast.

"No, I don't have them. The doctor from the hospital said I could have whomever I see here in town send for them. That won't be a problem." Lori sighed and poured herself a cup of coffee. She hadn't gotten a good night's sleep, and hoped the nightmares she kept having would disappear as soon as possible. She figured being in a strange place was the culprit and that things should improve.

Her mom left the room to switch the load of wash in the laundry room and Maggie entered the kitchen from the back porch.

"How was your jog?"

"Pretty good. I'll have to figure out a better route tomorrow because the terrain and dirt roads are going to do a number on my shin splints."

"Mom said from here to town is four miles and paved roadways."

"That's good to know. I'll probably try that tomorrow."

"How did you sleep last night?" Maggie asked her sister. She hoped that Maggie hadn't heard Lori jump up out of bed and pace back and forth in her room.

"Fine. How about you and Ben?"

"Ben was snoring away until he heard you and Dad get up this morning. After you left, he got up, dressed himself, and went downstairs to help Dad with the morning chores. He's been on the swing set in between."

"That's great. I'm glad he's easing right into things," Lori said as she looked at her sister. "Why are you looking at me like that?"

"The squeaky hardwood floors never lie, sis. Are you still having those nightmares?"

Lori knew there was no use in denying it her sister. They knew each other way too well.

"I'm sure once things settle down and I get into a routine I'll be fine, so don't worry and don't say anything to Mom or Dad, okay?"

"Don't tell me what?" their dad asked as he walked in on the conversation.

"Lori's been having nightmares since the incident. She had one again last night and couldn't sleep," Maggie blurted out and Lori punched her sister lightly in the arm.

"Well, I suppose that's understandable, honey, everything considered. Maybe you need to talk to someone about it. A professional I mean," her father said rather nervously.

Lori and Maggie looked at one another and then back at their father and simultaneously they laughed. The subject wouldn't be brought up again.

"Are you ready, honey?" Diana asked as she entered the kitchen carrying her purse and fixing her lipstick.

"What are you getting all dolled up for?" Lou asked, as Ben ran inside the house and jumped into his Aunt Lori's arms.

She kissed him and they hugged one another saying good morning.

"She's dragging me into town to see some doctor," Lori said, sounding annoyed.

"Oh…Dr. Henley, huh. You better keep an eye on your mother. I think she has the hots for that young man." Lou gave his wife a tap with his hand on her backside. She scolded him for making such a move in front of the children and they all laughed.

"He's married and has two children, Lou, so cut it out. As a matter of fact his mother Terry, and his wife Michelle, are going to stop by with the kids today for lunch. I thought Ben might like to make some new friends. Plus they're dying to meet you two."

"Sounds like women stuff to me. I'll be working on the apartment. You stop by, Lori, when you get back, all right?" Lou said as Lori nodded yes. Lou headed outside.

* * * *

The town was really nice and all the small stores took up about a half block. The main supermarket was another mile past the small town, which was surrounded by farmland.

Lori's mom pulled into the parking space in front of the hardware store, which was next to Dr. Henley's office. An attractive man stood outside talking to three other men whom her mom recognized immediately.

So did Lori, as she stepped out of the car and saw the man she had words with yesterday on the dirt road. He was tall and muscular and instantly recognized her as well.

* * * *

"Well lookey there," he blurted out, ready to start a fight with her as the others listened. "It's the crazy driver," he added.

"It's the loudmouthed jerk!" Lori retorted.

"Hey, Charlie, this is Diana's daughter Lori. Have you two met or something?" Dr. Andrew Henley asked as Jasper and Matt laughed.

Lori removed her sunglasses and introduced herself to the doctor. She gave Charlie a dirty look as the other men absorbed Lori's good looks and stunning green eyes.

"You'll have to excuse my brother, Miss. He failed the course our mamma gave on good manners and the proper way to speak to a lovely young lady like yourself. My name's Matt Henley." He reached out his hand to shake Lori's. Charlie appeared annoyed at his brother and even more so at Lori. Her mom laughed and smiled as if she were finding this conversation interesting.

"I'm going go over to the pharmacy. We'll meet up when you're done here, okay?" Diana said as she walked away.

Charlie and the others looked directly at Lori's hand and the cast as Andrew opened the office door for Lori and they headed inside.

* * * *

"Wow. She's a knockout. Did you see those green eyes?" Matt asked as he gave his brother Charlie a light backhand to his stomach.

"No, he was too busy pissing her off. I don't know how many times I have to tell you that's no way to get a woman to like you," stated Jasper as Matt started laughing.

"Let's get back to work. Lou is probably wondering what's taking us so long," Charlie said as he walked toward the truck.

"Maybe you'll get another chance to make a better impression at her house," Matt added. Charlie wasn't looking forward to seeing her again. Her reckless driving could have hurt someone. As annoyed as he was, he wondered what happened to her hand.

* * * *

Lori was hesitant to tell Dr. Henley about how she sustained her broken wrist.

"Does it really matter how I broke it? All want to know is why the pain is extending through my forearm and elbow?"

Andrew looked at her, obviously shocked by her abrupt response. She really didn't care. It was none of his business or anyone else's for that matter. He seemed to have gotten the message. Lori had a shell around her that he picked up on immediately. She was cautious and he didn't push the issue. Good, or she was outta here.

They spoke about the town a little and about his wife Michelle and two children. Lori was polite and felt that Andrew was sincere. He couldn't find anything wrong with her arm and felt maybe the tendons and muscles were still bruised. Lori gave her permission for Andrew to order the X-rays and her file from the other doctor. His secretary was already on the telephone with them as they exited the examination room. Dr. Henley then walked her to the front door. As Andrew opened the door, Sheriff J.R. Morgan was entering.

"Hey, Sheriff Morgan, how are you?" Andrew asked, and Lori was stuck between the two men. The sheriff tipped his hat toward her as Andrew introduced them to one another.

"Pleasure to meet you, Miss Shay. Your parents said you were due in town soon. Glad everything went all right for you and your sister."

She was caught off guard at the intimidating sheriff and then his comment. Had her mother told the sheriff about Maggie and her being on the run? She wasn't pleased to say the least. But if there was one thing she learned fast, law enforcement couldn't be trusted, but it also wasn't wise to piss them off. She played shy in hopes of getting out of there quicker.

"Thank you, sir, if you'll excuse me please, my mom's waiting for me over at the pharmacy. It was nice meeting you and thank you again, Doc," Lori said as she squeezed by the two men.

* * * *

"She's a real beauty, huh?" the sheriff asked as they watched Lori cross the street and head toward the pharmacy.

"She sure is but a bit on edge," Andrew added.

"You'd be on edge, too, if you'd gone through what she and her sister did. It's a miracle they're alive."

Andrew asked what he was talking about.

"I figured you and your family knew about it because your mom and Diana are such good friends. Your brothers and cousin are helping Lou out as well, aren't they?"

"They are but no one has said anything about what happened to Lori or Maggie."

"Well, it's not my place to say but you take good care of her and that wrist. She's a hero, that girl. I can tell you that much and tough as nails." The Sheriff headed out the door.

* * * *

Andrew's curiosity had the best of him as he went back to his office and called his mother. She was out already and the questioning would have to wait until later.

His secretary already had the hospital doctor on the phone from New York so he took the call to discuss Lori's X-rays.

By the end of the conversation he knew exactly how Lori had sustained her injury and he just sat there astonished. No wonder why she was so cautious and careful. She had every right to be and he would make a point of being more understanding at their next meeting.

* * * *

Lori was walking down the street and looking for the pharmacy. There were a lot of people around and everyone greeted her as if she were a local. Were they for real? What kind of a town was this Valley Stream? It also appeared that there weren't many places to work. She would have to head a little further out of town to get a job bartending or waitressing. She'd ask around when she met some people. She could have asked that guy Matt Henley or his brother the doctor. They seemed nice. Immediately she thought about the tall cowboy with the brown hair and thick accent. Man, was that guy mean looking. She turned around to glance back in that direction, now seeing the pharmacy across the way. When she turned back, she bumped into someone. Or they bumped into her.

"Whoa, sweetheart, are you okay?" She looked up, her head nearly reaching her shoulders, before she locked gazes with the man. He was a tall, handsome cowboy and he stared down at her. The glare of the sun cast a shadow over his face but she could tell he was good looking. She cupped her hand over her eyes as she apologized.

"I'm sorry. I was looking for the pharmacy."

"Oh, that's down this way and across the street. I'm headed that way." He gave her sleeve a tug as two nonstop-talking older women walked by them, nearly bumping Lori out of the way.

"Good day, ladies." He tipped his hat at them. They glared at the cowboy and he chuckled then looked at Lori and winked at her.

"I don't know who the hell those two old biddies think they are. They walk around town like they own the streets." He turned and gave her a nod to follow him.

She hesitated.

"Oh, how rude of me. I'm sorry, the name's Trevor Henley. You must be Diana and Lou's daughter."

Another Henley? How many of them are there?

"And you figured that out how?" she asked as she placed her hands on her hips.

"I saw you before with your mom, then talking to my brother and cousins. Everyone else around here right now I recognize, darling." He stared at her as if he were surprised by her attitude. Well, she wasn't some country bumpkin. She was used to being on guard and on the defensive. He gave her another wink and looked her over. She felt her body hum with awareness and it shocked her.

"I can find the pharmacy on my own. Thanks." She began to walk between the people on the crowded sidewalk when she felt the hand on her elbow. Instinctually she pulled and turned on him.

Glaring at the man, he glared right back at her then placed his hands on his hips.

"People are real friendly around these parts, darling."

"I'm good. Have a nice day. That friendly enough for ya?" she said, but turned and headed toward the pharmacy. As she crossed the road, the urge to turn and look back at the handsome cowboy who totally made her body come to life became too hard to resist. When she did, there he stood, Trevor Henley and that intense facial expression turned into a smile. She quickly turned around then covered her heart with her hand.

What in God's name just happened?

* * * *

Lori wanted to go see how the apartment was coming along but she didn't want to deal with another confrontation. Charlie was full of attitude as he was giving out orders and taking charge. She noticed that the other brother Trevor was there, too. So why was she heading over there right now instead of after the men left?

Maggie and Ben were talking to Jasper, and Lori could tell her sister was flirting. It was obvious that Jasper was interested as well and Ben was oblivious.

"Hey, Lori, are you going to come over here and check out the place?" her father asked as he carried some wood toward the barn.

Well here was her excuse to come take a look.

As soon as she started walking toward the barn, Ben came running toward her, bouncing a small blue ball as he walked.

"Aunt Lori, can I come with you?" he asked.

"Sure can, big guy."

They headed inside the barn where some other guy and Charlie were framing out the bedroom. Ben ran from Lori to get the ball he dropped just as the other guy was grabbing another piece of wood.

Lori and Charlie saw the wood falling at the same time, and Lori pulled Ben out of the way and took the hit instead. The wood scratched her elbow causing her to fall to the ground holding Ben. Charlie was at her side immediately then the other guy.

"Are you all right?" Charlie and the other guy, who looked a lot like Charlie, asked as they tried to help Lori to her feet. She pulled away instinctively and brushed off her pants. She didn't pay attention to the blood that was dripping off her elbow until the other guy was placing a cloth over it.

Charlie eyed her funny, as if wondering what her problem was. All he was doing was helping her up. But when the two men touched her, she felt a bolt of sexual interest shock her system.

"I'm so sorry, Lori, it was all my fault. The wood slipped," the man she didn't know, but who obviously knew her, said as he held her arm with one hand and the other held the bandage in place.

"I'm fine really. No one got hurt. Come on, Ben, let's go back outside. I'll push you on the swing set." Lori took the cloth from the cowboy with the amazing hazel eyes and walked out with Ben.

* * * *

Dante and Charlie watched Lori walk away then looked at one another.

"That was a pretty bad cut, I didn't see that other piece of wood, and do you think she's all right?" Dante asked, all concerned.

"By her attitude I'd say hell yeah. Let's get back to work. Women and kids shouldn't be around construction anyway." Charlie gave his brother a light punch then walked away. Dante still felt bad despite Charlie's words. Plus, it was his first glimpse at the woman who'd snagged Trevor's attention in town. He had immediately told Dante all about meeting Lori and her abrupt attitude.

Chapter 4

Lynn Cantrell headed outside to the front porch to have her morning coffee. She wrapped the white sweater around her preparing for the cool morning air. As she opened the front door the sight in front of her overcame her as she dropped the blue ceramic coffee mug onto the front porch causing a large bang as it shattered.

Old Man Cantrell came running from the kitchen as his wife stood out front crying.

"What's wrong?" he asked, but before she could respond, he saw it for himself.

One of their roosters was beheaded and hung from the front porch where all could see.

Tom Cantrell pulled his wife into his arms and back into the house to call Sheriff Morgan.

Within fifteen minutes the sheriff arrived annoyed as ever.

"This is the second time something like this has happened, Sheriff. Who would want to do something like this? That was my damn rooster." Tom carried on until the sheriff calmed him down.

They spoke about possible suspects, but Tom didn't have a clue.

"Well I'll go by the Henleys' and the Shays' ask the boys if they've seen anything and to keep a lookout. I'm real sorry about this, Lynn and Tom."

The Sheriff got into his patrol car and headed toward the Henley's place. It was 5:45 a.m. but he knew they'd be up. He headed down the dirt road and saw a young woman jogging. Immediately he knew it was Lori Shay as he stopped the patrol car in front of the Henleys' place.

"Good morning, Lori."

* * * *

Lori regrettably stopped to be polite to the sheriff.

"Good morning, Sheriff. How are you?" she asked politely.

"Good…good. How about yourself? You're running a little late this morning. Don't you usually leave your house around 5:15?"

"I guess I was a little tired this morning. I suppose you know everything that goes on in this town, huh?"

"Pretty much, well, I'll let you get back to your run. Are your parents home?"

"Yes, sir, Sheriff."

"Lori, please call me J.R. For some reason when you say 'Sheriff' it makes me feel older and unattractive." He winked. It was obvious he was flirting and she smiled back at him. He seemed pretty nice and she waved good-bye then went back to jogging. But she was still cautious and didn't want to come across as being overly friendly. The past proved that people aren't always as they seem.

* * * *

Charlie stood by the front porch and watched the sheriff talking to Lori. He noted the time and the fact that she was running a little late this morning. It was town knowledge that Lori jogged every morning and had the most stunning green eyes. For some strange reason it annoyed him how the other men in town talked about her, wanting to get to know her. A few of them made comments about asking her out at the barbeque today. Why should he care though? Lori was stuck up and unfriendly and acted like he had some kind of disease the way she pulled away from him the other day. It annoyed him even more that his mother thought she was wonderful after lunch yesterday and that his sister-in-law Michelle and brother Andrew thought the same thing.

In his eyes she was probably just like most women, on the prowl, playing hard to get and nothing but heartache.

He took another sip of his coffee as J.R. drove up in the patrol car and headed toward the front porch.

"Morning, Sheriff. Get ya some coffee?"

"No thanks, Charlie, I just came from Old Man Cantrell's place. He had some trouble out there this morning. The missus woke up to a bloody, headless rooster hanging from the front porch."

"What? This is the second time something like this has happened. Who could be doing this?"

"That's what I'm trying to find out. Could be some stupid game some kids are playing. I wanted to see if any of you heard anything last night."

"No, not a sound." Just then Dante and Trevor came outside and they hadn't heard anything either.

"Well keep a lookout for me and let me know if you see anything suspicious. I'll see you all later at the barbeque."

Chapter 5

The sun was bright and a gentle breeze kept the temperature at seventy-five degrees. Maggie was by the Hanson's porch talking to Jasper along with Phil and Diana. The party had begun and guests were arriving. Everyone brought some kind of food, appetizers, side dishes, or desserts to go along with the main meal. The aroma of barbeque chicken and baby back ribs traveled through the air and outshined the typical hot dogs and hamburgers the children were beginning to eat.

Ben was playing with Michelle and Andrew's son, Andy, and a bunch of other kids from town. He was having so much fun, laughing and enjoying the appropriate life for a five-year-old kid.

Charlie, Lou, Phil, and Matt were manning the barbeque, hand turning the ribs and chicken with such precision and master technique.

Lori was on her way across the yard to join the party. She arrived late due to the pains she was having in her arm and elbow. Everyone watched her cross the lawn as her long blonde hair danced in the breeze. The knee-length beige, floral skirt tapped against her long legs. The matching beige V-neck T-shirt accentuated her curves, and it was obvious that she was reserved but well endowed. She carried a light blue-jean jacket in her arms in preparation for the cool evening. Diana glanced at her husband who simultaneously looked from Lori to her. She smiled. Their daughter was gorgeous.

* * * *

Lori smiled politely and said hello to all the people who

introduced themselves or simply smiled. She hoped by coming late she would have missed all the nerve-racking introductions and stares. Her thoughts were wrong as a group of young men stopped her before she made it to the safety of the back porch.

They were introducing themselves and looking her over. It was overwhelming, and then she heard the firm voice.

"Give the lady some room, fellas. She just arrived and she's very shy. Believe me, I tried having a conversation with her in town the other day."

She turned to see Trevor Henley. He was decked out in a nice blue button-down shirt and tight blue jeans. He wore cowboy boots and smiled at her in a wicked, flirtatious way. She immediately noticed the tattoos on his upper arm and one that extended up his collared shirt.

As to not skip a beat or be intimidated by Trevor and his obvious self-confidence, she gave him the once-over.

"We met before? I don't recall. Excuse me."

He appeared shocked as the other cowboys chuckled then continued to vie for her attention. She needed an escape route and she needed one quickly.

* * * *

Charlie watched Lori as she arrived at the party fashionably late. He couldn't believe how fast the single men flocked around her, challenging each other for her attention. He didn't know why he felt kind of relieved that his brother Trevor moved in to impede the other cowboys' efforts, but he'd analyze that later. Right now he was getting an eyeful.

"There's Lori now. She was feeling a bit under the weather before. That's why she's late. I'd better go save her from those young men. She hates a lot of attention," Lou said as he excused himself and headed to his daughter's rescue.

"She shouldn't have come late then, huh?" Charlie said sarcastically as he turned the juicy chicken.

"What's your problem with her, son? You hardly know the woman and you're holding a grudge still from weeks ago?" Phil asked as Matt smiled wide.

"I think he's stupid. Look at her, she's gorgeous and sweet as anything just a little shy," Matt added.

"Stuck up is more like it," Charlie barked.

Both Phil and Matt looked at Charlie like he had two heads.

"Son, you're losing your mind. Be nice to her, you hear me. You don't know as much as you think."

Charlie looked back toward Lori where Lou was politely taking her away from the mob of eligible bachelors. Was she some kind of princess or something? She needed her daddy to get her away from all those cowboys flocking her because of her beauty. Shit, that woman was probably playing everyone, even her old man. As the thoughts entered his mind, he felt his stomach clench with guilt. *Why should I feel guilty for saying what it looks like? That woman is trouble.*

* * * *

"How are you, honey? Is that arm any better? I was afraid you might not come," Lou said as he held his daughter's hand.

"It still hurts a little and I was debating about being a no-show. I'm not up for all this socializing, Dad."

"Even with all these single cowboys around taking notice of you?"

"Although there are a lot of handsome men around, I am surely not interested. Thank you," she said jokingly, and her father gave her hand a squeeze.

They headed toward the porch where the ladies were sitting.

* * * *

"It smells fantastic around here. Is there anything that I can help with?" Lori asked as Maggie grabbed her hand.

"I'm getting ready to help peel the corn along with Michelle. Come help us."

They walked off the porch and onto the patio. There was a table covered with unpeeled corn and another table with corn ready to be dropped into the pots of boiling water.

"Wow. Now that's a lot of corn," Maggie said and the ladies started laughing.

Lori took a seat next to her sister and Michelle.

"You got a nice welcome before, Lori. Any of them your type?" Michelle asked.

"Yeah there were some real lookers there, sis."

"I don't know really. I'm not interested in dating right now. I have to find a job before the summer is out," Lori said as she began peeling a second ear of corn.

"What kind of job are you looking for?" Michelle asked.

"Lori wants to be a teacher," Maggie said before Lori could answer herself.

"That's great, Lori. Do you have your degree already?" Michelle asked.

"No, unfortunately my sister and I have been traveling a lot and I plan on registering for school soon. I took some college courses at a local community college in New Orleans. I need to transfer them to someplace that will accept them here. I want to start right away but I need a job to pay the bills."

"Where have you worked the past few years?" Maggie asked.

"She worked at a lot of different places. But I know she'll get her degree and be a great teacher." Maggie smiled at Lori.

"Well listen, Lori, I work on the education committee at the local town school. It's a great place to work and there are a few positions coming available. I could probably get you started in a smaller position as a teacher's assistant. It could be your foot in the door," Michelle told Lori very seriously and Lori thanked her for the offer.

"Don't worry I'll get certified and finally get my teaching degree." She felt her spirits lift.

Suddenly Andrew and Jasper appeared and interrupted the conversation.

"Hello, ladies, don't you think we have enough corn yet?" Andrew asked as he squeezed his wife Michelle's shoulders and joined the conversation.

"Ask your mom, Andrew. She's planning to feed an army."

Lori and Maggie laughed. Lori immediately picked up on the way Jasper and Maggie looked at one another then smiled.

"How's your arm feeling, Lori?" Andrew asked and Lori immediately felt uncomfortable. She knew the question would lead up to how did it happen?

"Fine, Doc. No worries," she said with a smile then rose from her chair.

"How did you break your wrist anyway?" Jasper asked, and Maggie immediately saw Lori's reaction.

"She was playing a friendly game of soccer then fell right on her wrist and broke it. She's beautiful but sometimes klutzy," Maggie lied for Lori and Andrew locked gazes with her. Andrew already knew the truth. He watched as Lori made up an excuse to leave and Maggie changed the subject.

"I'm starving. When are we going to eat?" Maggie asked as Jasper responded to her and she watched Lori head toward the side of the house.

"Excuse me a minute will you, honey, guys," Andrew said as he headed after Lori.

* * * *

Lori sat on an empty bench by the side of the house, only a

handful of children were playing tag nearby and she was grateful to be alone. She hated having to talk about herself and her life. She didn't want anyone else to know what she had done. That she helped send a man to his grave. That she broke her wrist as she fought to save her life and her sister's and nephew's lives. Here she was twenty-one years old, no college degree, just an education of the street life, staying safe on the run, just trying to survive. She didn't want to just survive anymore. She wanted to live, be free of fear and complication.

She felt someone come around the house and wasn't surprised to see Dr. Henley.

"Can I join you or do you want to be alone?" he asked cautiously.

"You can join me. This is your mother's house, and I'm probably sitting on one of the benches that you used to sit on when you lived here."

Andrew smiled as he took the seat next to her. "You might be right. I think I did use to sit on this bench. During large barbeques to get away from the noise and conversations."

"What can I do for you, Doc? You didn't come over here just to be friendly."

He chuckled low as he looked down at the ground then back at her. She knew he was a sincerely nice man, so why was she still giving him shit?

"That's not true, I wanted to see how your arm really felt. Your dad said you were feeling a bit under the weather and I assumed your arm hurt."

"My dad tends to talk too much. I'm fine really. Your wife Michelle is very nice and your children are adorable."

"Thank you. Michelle said she enjoyed having lunch with you the other day and I wanted to tell you that I received your X-rays from Dr. Marcus in New York. I spoke to him on the phone as well."

Lori swung her head toward Andrew, knowing that Dr. Marcus probably told him everything. She was silent then looked away as she nervously rubbed her hand against the cast. Andrew moved closer, looked around, and then whispered, "He told me how you really broke your wrist, Lori. It was very brave of you…"

"No, Doc. Please don't say anything else about it. I don't want to talk about it or about being heroic. All I want is this damn cast off my wrist and the attention from it to disappear."

"I think you're receiving so much attention because you're such an attractive woman. You're new in town, in your twenties, single, everything a single man is looking for. It has nothing to do with your cast. I also think that your arm and elbow are hurting because it's your body's way of dealing with the stress you've encountered."

"You're not talking about post-traumatic stress are you?"

"Actually, yes, I am and I was wondering if perhaps you are experiencing any other symptoms. Maybe nightmares, anxiety?"

Lori wasn't sure how to read him. Was he being nosy or did he really care? She didn't want to take the chance so she dismissed it.

"So this is a party right, when do we eat?"

Andrew reached out and touched Lori's hand. She didn't pull away but she wanted to as her whole body tensed up and she froze.

"I want to help you, Lori, and I want you to feel that you can trust me. There are ways of dealing with this if you would like to know. Sometimes all it takes are some relaxation techniques, breathing or stretching and other exercises you could do to release the stress and pressure. Just let me know if you're interested, okay?"

All Lori did was smile and nod her head yes as Charlie came around the house.

* * * *

Charlie saw his brother sitting on the bench next to Lori and she looked a little upset.

"Hey, Andrew, the food's ready and Michelle is looking for you."

"No problem, Lori and I were just talking about the stream that borders our property. I was telling her how we all used to go swimming down there when we were kids. You still go there sometimes, too, don't you?" Andrew asked his brother then winked at Lori.

"Yeah sometimes but it can be dangerous for someone who's not familiar with the area."

"Maybe you could show her after we eat. Tomorrow's supposed to be eighty-six degrees and no breeze. The perfect temperature for a swim, Lori."

"That's all right. He doesn't have to show me. I think I jogged near it the first couple of days I was here. I can find it on my own. If you'll excuse me, thanks again, Doc, I enjoyed the conversation," Lori said as she smiled and walked away. Charlie looked at her as she passed him by.

* * * *

"I like her a lot," Andrew said, and Charlie stopped watching Lori and looked at his brother.

"You're married for Christ's sake. What the hell's wrong with you sitting here alone with her holding her hand? What if someone else came around and found you two instead of me."

"Charlie, get real. I love Michelle and I wasn't sneaking around with Lori. Cut your crap out, brother. You think I don't know what's going on here. You're attracted to her and I don't think I've ever seen you look at another woman that way."

"Let's go eat before you say something else stupid."

Charlie turned around to walk toward the front of the house and Andrew followed.

"Keep lying to yourself, Charlie. She's a good-looking woman. The first woman I've seen get a reaction out of you even if it is filled with piss and vinegar."

Charlie shot him a dirty look and Andrew laughed as he walked away from him.

* * * *

He just arrived in Houston. Another town, another job, he knew he had to stay steps ahead of the police and small-town law enforcement agencies were the easiest to fool and evade. This job was a simple one and he enjoyed scaring people for a living. Maybe if he was lucky when his job was over, he could take a small treasure with him. Small towns usually had naive, attractive young women, and there was sure to be one he'd like.

He passed through the business district and headed toward Valley Stream. He would check out the small town and then decide the best location to lie low while he did the job he was hired to do. He saw a place, right off the highway en route to the town. He could rent a hotel room and stay unnoticed. He planned on taking a ride through the town first thing in the morning. He pulled into the parking lot of the Days Inn prepared to make it his home for the next few weeks at least.

He requested a room on the far end of the building where he could park his car right in front of his hotel room door. He accepted the key from some wiseass punk clerk who was too busy flirting with the little bimbo instead of doing his job professionally. That was fine with the stranger as he politely left the office and headed toward his room. He didn't have to worry about being identified by the punk kid if the cops got too close. Plus, he was wearing a disguise to ensure that he didn't get caught. That way, if the urge got to be too much, he could sneak a little delicacy in through the back exit door late at night and no one would notice a thing. He sure did like the pretty little Texas accents women had. He'd find one. Maybe sooner rather than later to feed his hunger.

The stranger entered the room and began to settle in a little as he put each item in a specific location and left his clothes in his suitcase.

He needed to stay organized and be able to leave in a hurry if necessary. Now all he had to do was wait for his new boss to call and plan his first attack. He looked forward to it and hoped the boss would change his mind about "nobody gets hurt." What fun was that?

Chapter 6

"I saw you talking to Andrew and Charlie before. I guess he's starting to act a little more friendly?" Michelle asked Lori.

"I wouldn't say that considering he was rather rude and barked at me. I don't know what his problem is," Lori said as she looked toward Charlie. He was sitting at a table with her father and his father eating the delicious food.

"Don't mind him, Lori, his bark is bigger than his bite. Charlie, Trevor, and Dante changed after serving in the military. They can be kind of abrupt and snappy. But they're good men," Michelle told them.

"They're single?" Maggie asked, and Lori gave her a shocked expression.

"What? I can't ask for you?" Maggie stated.

"For me? No, I'm not interested in dating at all. I've got too much going on. Too many plans. Maybe it's you that's interested?" Lori teased her sister back and Michelle laughed.

"Not for nothing, but I don't think they're interested in Maggie. Jasper on the other hand, maybe." Michelle joined right in the teasing, and Lori laughed as her sister blushed and shyly lowered her head.

Michelle gave Lori a little nudge with her elbow. Lori looked at her.

"The three of them don't date. They never bring any woman home and I mean ever."

"Why don't they?" Lori asked as she turned to look toward Charlie. Now Dante and Trevor were standing next to him and all three turned to look toward her. She nearly gasped at the power of their stare. One of them could send her heart pumping, just from their stare, but three at once? *God help me.*

"They've been more into the one-night stands, quick flings, and no strings attached. I guess it makes them feel in control. A lot of women want to date them but they don't seem interested. It's like they're waiting for someone or they have such guards up over their emotions that they won't risk letting go a little. I don't know really. It's just my observation over the last year or so. You know, those three do everything together. And I mean everything." Michelle raised her eyebrows.

Lori didn't get it.

"You know, while I was in town with Ben and Mom, I saw some couples walking around, but there were like two and three men with one woman. What's that all about?" Maggie asked.

Lori swallowed hard. A quick glance around the yard and it didn't take a genius to see that some rather unique relationships were publically accepted.

"Oh, you mean the ménage relationships? Yeah, that's like a totally normal thing around these parts. Andrew's best friend from medical school shares his wife Elizabeth with his two brothers. They're so totally in love with her, too. We visited them last year. It was amazing to see," Michelle told them.

"That's just crazy," Lori whispered then glanced back toward Charlie, Dante, and Trevor. They were big men. Strong and muscular and filled with so much attitude and testosterone it would take a saint of a woman to even deal with conversing with them. She shook her head and turned away. *What the hell am I even thinking about?*

"You see that pretty little brunette over there in the white dress talking to the handsome fellow in the tight blue jeans? Her name is Missy and she was infatuated with Charlie. He showed no interest and now she's engaged to the fellow she's talking with."

"Sometimes uncontrollable circumstances happen in life and they change a person. Other people around them might think it's no big deal but for the person dealing with it it's huge. Hopefully he'll see someday that life only gets better if you make it happen," Lori stated as she peeled another ear of corn.

"I never looked at it that way before, Lori. You're such a nice person. I can tell you have a big heart. I guess that's why we've gotten along so well so far."

Lori smiled as she looked back at the table where Charlie was before. He was no longer there and suddenly Ben was pulling on her leg.

"Aunt Lori, that lady over there has been singing some songs to the kids. I told them you have a great voice and about the song you sing to me all the time about the spider and the boy. Can you come sing it to them? Please," Ben asked as the children and a woman playing the guitar called her and Ben over.

Lori reluctantly followed Ben to the crowd of children.

Matt quickly pulled over another bucket, turning it upside down for her to use as a seat. He winked at her and she smiled. It appeared that Matt Henley was a flirt and then some.

Lori introduced herself to the woman playing the guitar who was glad that someone else was taking over. Lori borrowed her guitar and started fooling around playing some quick funny notes, talking to the children. It was a bit awkward with her cast on but she had plenty of practice, thanks to Ben.

"So who wants to hear about the spider and the boy?"

The kids quietly answered and Lori repeated her question telling them to answer more loudly. The cheering caused some of the other adults to turn around in their seats and watch the show.

Lori began to play the guitar and sing the words to the silly song, getting the kids to cheer and clap and laugh and scream at the appropriate times. Even the adults were joining in and having a good time. When the song ended, everyone cheered and the kids asked for more.

* * * *

Dante was surprised by Lori's natural ability with the kids. She seemed to be enjoying herself just as much as they were. She was only twenty-one, but she acted older, more mature, and he wondered about her. He noticed immediately how his brothers Trevor and Charlie noticed her, too. Charlie hadn't taken his eyes off of her and he looked downright pissed off. That was a sure sign that he was feeling something, but what? Charlie was tough and had a shell made of Teflon. There wasn't anyone or anything that could break through that wall he built up. Dante released an uneasy sigh. *Who am I to analyze? I'm just as happy being left alone in misery. So why can't I stop staring at Lori? What is it about her that has my heart racing and my dick harder than I remember ever having?*

Lori sang another five songs and on the final note Andrew saved her from further entertaining by announcing, "Who wants ice cream?"

The children went running toward a large, long wooden table set with everything a kid could want to make a sundae with. Dante wished he could go back in time and truly savor in his childhood. What he would give to feel that excitement over music, over ice cream, and swinging on a swing somewhere again?

* * * *

"You were great, Lori. That spider song was funny, I never heard it before," Matt said.

"That's because she made it up. She has a bunch of them," Maggie added as she headed toward the table to help Ben and the other kids.

"You're full of surprises, Lori. That was nice of you to do that," Andrew added.

"Yeah it was really great. You have a nice voice, too," Charlie said from behind her, and Lori turned, caught off guard by his closeness.

Matt and Andrew walked away leaving Charlie and Lori at an

awkward moment.

"It was nothing really. I like kids. That's all," she said with her head down, catching herself feeling shy, almost blushing in front of Charlie. He caught onto her uneasiness and took the opportunity to apologize to her.

"Listen, I think we started off on the wrong foot and I'm sorry if I've been kind of rude. There's no excuse for it."

"Don't worry about it. You don't owe me an apology really." She looked up at him directly into his eyes. They were a beautiful brown color, which matched his hair. He was tall, standing at about six feet two or so with broad shoulders, large biceps, and long, muscular legs. He had shaven today and he looked handsome. But she also liked the way he looked unshaven as well.

She locked gazes with his eyes. His facial expression grew darker. She felt it to her core immediately. She was so transfixed in his eyes and the anger, the pain and sadness she saw in them that she jumped as Michelle interrupted.

Michelle came over to introduce Lori to Carl Monroe. He owned a bar in town where different bands came to play on the weekends and during the week. In the summertime the place was packed. It was located right on a large lake with a boat dock and Tiki bar all set up for its patrons.

"I heard you were looking for a job and that you know how to bartend?" Carl asked Lori.

"Yes, I am and I do." Carl looked her over as he released her hand after shaking it. He smiled.

"Well, why don't you come down to my restaurant tomorrow around noontime. I'll show you the place and see what you can do," Carl told her, and Charlie looked really annoyed. He was giving Michelle a dirty look.

"That sounds great, Mr. Monroe. I'll come by tomorrow." Lori held out her hand to shake Carl's.

He pulled it to his lips instead, kissing it and telling her to call him

Carl. Then he walked away.

"Thanks so much, Michelle, you didn't have to do that."

"No, she didn't." Charlie sounded kind of sarcastic.

"Actually I didn't. Mr. Monroe came up to me and asked a few questions about Lori. I mentioned her looking for a job and he asked me to introduce him to you."

"Well thanks anyway, Michelle. I think I'll check out the place. It sounds cool and I sure can use the money."

Lori excused herself and headed toward her sister to tell her about the potential job.

* * * *

Charlie watched her walk away. It wasn't his business where she worked so why was he so aggravated? Charlie and Michelle headed toward Matt and Andrew who were helping to clean up the tables. Charlie couldn't help but think about Carl's place.

Carl's place was a local hangout during the summer months. It had an open view of the large lake and a small boat dock around it. Many boaters went tubing and sometimes during the summer there were water skiing events, too. Anyone who had a boat could just pull up to Carl's for lunch, dinner, or just a drink then head back out to the lake. It was always crowded, filled with plenty of partying people, and was a great place to pick someone up. Charlie and his brothers would go there sometimes and Carl always lined up some cool and talented entertainment. Everything from reggae to rock and roll.

Carl would hire Lori. One look at the way the man eyed her body over and she already had the job. She smiled so sweetly toward Carl, too. Maybe he was right and maybe Lori was full of shit, just like most women and most people. With an ulcer beginning to start in his stomach, Charlie headed out of the party and back to his place to be alone. It was safer than dealing with emotions brought on by strangers.

Chapter 7

Sunday morning rolled around and it was Lori's day off from jogging. Maggie and Ben were going to have lunch with Jasper in town at the local diner. They invited Lori but she had plans of her own. Their parents were invited for lunch to a friend's house and they would all meet back home later for dinner.

Lori packed her lunch and a few bottles of water into a red insulated bag. She added the ice packs and finally a container of fresh, plump strawberries. She took along a towel and a blanket to lie on along with a book and some college reading materials.

The sun was beating down hard and Lori was glad she brought some extra suntan lotion. She was determined to work on her tan especially if her interview at Carl's later today went well. Michelle told her the workers wore very short black skirts and tight-fitted T-shirts. Lori was used to those types of revealing outfits. She didn't mind as long as no one touched her or asked her to remove her clothing. She remembered the first time some guy, an owner of a bar she worked off the books for, approached her after work. He was older, kind of attractive but a complete pervert. He started off flirting with her and then hinting about fooling around. When she declined, he offered to pay her. What a creep he turned out to be. From there on out he harassed her and then she, Maggie, and Ben needed to take off because Derrick was on their trail.

She swallowed hard. There wasn't a day that passed by where she didn't think about that night he attacked. She swallowed hard then shook her head. *Don't think about him. Focus on the future and on going to college.*

She found the stream Andrew mentioned and she set up her little spot by the water. There was no one in sight. It was quiet and peaceful, exactly what she wanted.

She lay down on her back a while and could feel her stomach burning as she rolled over to change tanning positions.

Lori opened the college course book and began reading the information below each class she needed to achieve her teaching degree. She would finally be able to start college and pay for it herself if she got a good job. She had saved a lot already but still needed more. She also wanted to make her own money to decorate her loft in the barn house. Next week she would take a quick trip into town to one of the local boutiques or perhaps head into Houston.

Lori was engrossed in the descriptions of the courses as her stomach churned and she felt a pain in her wrist and arm. She was getting nervous about finally attending school and all the hard work and time it would take to achieve her dream.

"You found the place all right, huh?" Trevor interrupted her thoughts, startling her as she quickly sat up. She stared at him, sitting atop a huge horse that blocked the sun and cast a shadow over her body. He wore his Stetson low and had on dark sunglasses. She couldn't help but feel uncomfortable about him finding her here and nearly naked.

* * * *

Trevor was delighted that Charlie had been right about seeing Lori heading toward the water hole. He didn't know why his brother hadn't come down here, too. In fact, he seemed kind of pissed off at Lori. Well this was Trevor's chance to get to know her better. Since the barbeque, he couldn't seem to stop thinking about her.

Lori quickly grabbed her towel and covered the black bikini she was wearing. Damn did she have a great body.

"You scared me!" she scolded him as he got down off his horse.

"I'm sorry, I didn't mean to. You were so into what you were reading. What's this?" he asked as he picked up the folder Lori dropped, and looked at its contents.

"College courses, huh? That's great. What are you taking?" he asked nicely, but Lori appeared ready to bolt. He cleared his throat as he took off his sunglasses.

Lori pulled the folder from his hand. "I'm interested in becoming a teacher. I was just reading about the courses I need to take, that's all," she told him as she started to tuck the folder back into her bag as if preparing to leave. Then she pulled the towel tighter around her. Trevor immediately picked up on her uneasiness.

"You don't have to leave. I was just coming down here for a swim. I promise not to disturb you." He tipped his hat toward her and began walking his horse over to a nearby tree.

Trevor found it interesting that Lori was sitting in his and his brothers' favorite spot. Out of all the different places she could have picked, she had chosen theirs. Now he would have to sit somewhere else.

He glanced back toward her and she was still holding the towel against her body. That perfect body he had the opportunity to see, even from a distance. Her long blonde hair was French braided and hung down to the center of her back. Most women who had a figure like Lori's would flaunt it, or try to tempt him with it. Not Lori, she was shy, refined, and the way those green eyes looked up at him full of fear and embarrassment as she blushed, instantly attracted him to her. It was so odd for him. Trevor was a hard man, just like his brothers Charlie and Dante. Life had thrown him, them, some heavy shit and it weighed its toll on each of them. He was shocked at how nervous he felt. *Me, nervous around a woman no less? Being out of the service must be turning me into a pansy.*

His stomach grew sour and he felt the annoyed expression take over. Now he was just plain old pissed off.

* * * *

Lori glanced toward Trevor who was presently removing his jeans. Her heart dropped at the sight. She nearly gasped for air then glanced back and saw a pair of navy blue swim trunks that were hidden beneath.

Trevor couldn't help but tease her. "Sorry to disappoint you, no skinny-dipping today. I didn't wear my sunscreen," he said in his sexy thick Texas accent. Then he jumped into the water.

Lori was even more embarrassed and annoyed at him. The nerve of him. The man obviously knew he had a great body. Those damn muscles and tattoos covering his arm and shoulder were a sight. She was intrigued by them and by his perfect physique.

Stop drooling, you idiot. This man is experienced and playing you.

She was getting herself all riled up as she removed the towel, rolled back onto her stomach, and grabbed her bag to find the folder. Turning her back toward him should have given her the reprieve her heart and her libido needed to get a grip. But instead she hoped that her ass didn't look too big as she tightened it then tried to refocus on the brochure in front of her.

It was getting hotter and she wanted to take a swim but not with Trevor in there. She stayed put as the sweat pooled at the center of her back and dripped down her forehead to her cheeks. When it started dripping onto the brochure, she grew impatient for some cold water.

Suddenly she sensed too late, Trevor behind her and she wasn't quick enough as he shook his hair over her body and the cold-water drips made contact, instantly causing her to jump up.

"Hey! Why did you do that?" she reprimanded as she stood up.

"You looked hot," he teased her again as he walked toward his horse to grab a towel.

Did he mean I looked hot, or that I looked hot as in sweaty, smelly and ready for a bath? Yikes!

Lori took the opportunity to cool off and take a swim as Trevor made himself comfortable by her blanket.

The water was cold and refreshing and she couldn't help but want revenge on Trevor for sneaking up on her and dripping cold water. She reached down to the dirt and rock bottom as she attempted to grab something in the water. She avoided his stare as she tried to nonchalantly walk out of the water with her gift.

* * * *

Trevor watched Lori walk out of the stream. Her nearly tan skin glistening in the sunlight as she made her way toward him. He was shocked as the handful of worms landed on his stomach and he jumped up from the towel.

"What the hell!"

"Now we're even!" Lori told him as she took her towel and wrapped it around herself. Trevor went back down toward the water to clean himself off.

He was laughing at her tough attitude and the simple fact that she picked up a handful of worms like nothing and stuck them on him. He never knew a woman who would do such a thing.

As he emerged from the water, he grabbed a small violet flower from the bush and carried it to Lori.

"Truce?" he asked as he held the flower out to her.

"I guess so." She sighed as she took the flower and placed it behind her ear in between some strands of hair.

She was beautiful and the droplets of water that covered her lashes accentuated her jade-colored eyes.

He wanted a closer look. He wanted to kiss her and touch her perfect skin he was sure would be soft and feminine. Instead he rolled onto his back and the two of them stayed silent for a long time.

"So how do you like living around here?" he asked her.

"It's quiet and everyone seems nice."

"Have you gotten to go out at all, for fun I mean?" he asked, surprised by his nervousness. He was acting like a high school teenager instead of a thirty-year-old man.

"No. I really don't have time for that. I'm trying to find work, prepare for these college courses and help my family."

"That's a full plate ya got there, darling." He rolled to his side to look at her. The towel that was wrapped around her now lay open. He had a full, close-up view of her body and the urge to touch her, explore her curves was making his fingers inch across the blanket.

* * * *

Lori sat up and looked at her watch.

Trevor sat up, too, shocked at her abrupt movement next to him.

"Where are you going, kid?"

"Back home, I have to go on an interview."

"At Carl's?"

"Actually, yes. How did you know?"

"Charlie told me. Are you sure you want to work there?"

"What's it to you?"

"Just watch yourself, sweetheart. I'm just warning you."

"Warning me?" She stood up and so did he.

"It can get rowdy there. Guys come in, drinking too much and doing stupid shit. I just want you to know that it may not be safe for a young woman like you."

He could have sworn her jade green eyes turned red at his comment.

"Thanks for the warning, but I'll be fine," she told him with an attitude as she pulled her bag onto her shoulder.

"Some bad characters hang out there. You may not be used to that. Plus, you're on display like some piece of meat in those uniforms," he added, sounding as if he disapproved.

"It's really none of your business."

"Your problem." He wondered how the hell their nice, quiet, get-to-know-one-another time turned into an argument. *Is this what having her as a girlfriend or lover would be like? Fuck!* His dick instantly hardened as he watched her sashay her ass across the fields.

* * * *

Lori ignored him then turned toward the field, walking off in a huff. She thought he was a conceited, bossy jerk as she cursed him part of the way home. *The nerve of him calling me kid and treating me like some naive child. Charlie called me kid, too. What the hell? I'm not a kid. I'm a Goddamn woman and I've been taking care of myself for a long time. Men!*

Once she got past her tirade about Trevor's, Dante's, and Charlie's personalities thus far toward her, she then thought about Trevor's body. The rest of the way she thought about his great body, muscular physique, and bad-boy attitude. He thought he was hot stuff and for some strange reason she liked it. She liked the way his muscles rippled and covered every part of him. His arms were so big, his chest so wide, she knew he would give an incredible hug. He was so much larger than her he could crush her, but what a way to get crushed. She pushed the thought aside as she ran into the house to shower and change in preparation for her interview.

* * * *

Lori wore a short beige skirt with a light beige cotton embroidered shirt that fell off her shoulders. She wanted to look nice for the job interview. She wore her hair down and only a little lip-gloss as usual. As she walked from the parking lot toward the front entrance she could hear what sounded like island music from the band that was playing. A large crowd formed a long line by the front door, waiting to have their IDs checked before being allowed to enter. She immediately noticed the security bouncers and they noticed her.

The sun was still hot and dry and everyone waiting dressed accordingly, wearing light shorts, tank tops, or casual tank dresses. There was a mixed crowd, which usually meant a place was doing well. In Lori's eyes it meant that the owner, Carl, probably provided entertainment and services suitable and likable for all people from all walks of life. Lori noted the yuppie types that gathered at tables nearer to the docks so they could probably keep an eye on their boats. She noticed what she assumed to be the regulars who sat around the bar itself. She knew who they were immediately by the way they set up shop. Two men sat at the bar, a seat apart, with a drink in front of them and a pack of cigarettes along with their money. That was a sure sign to let the bartender know they were staying put for a while. Serve them well and you got tipped well. The regulars were sometimes the ones who kept the bar going.

Lori made her way through the crowd and bouncers letting them know she was expected as they each gave her the once-over. She flirted a little which brought her immediate courtesy. She was told that Carl was waiting outside by the Tiki bar, and as she entered through the dining room and passed the large set of double glass doors she heard the band begin another song. She smiled wide as she made her entrance to the sounds of "Hot Legs" by Rod Stewart.

* * * *

Carl watched as Lori entered through the doors. She was absolutely stunning and he noticed all heads turned as she came into view. She was a definite knockout which would draw in a lot of guys to the bar. The better-looking the bartender the more drinks were sold, and a good bartender knew how to keep those orders coming. He hoped Lori was capable and he had to admit, he was actually very attracted to her.

"Lori, you look lovely," he told her as he took her hand and lightly kissed it.

"Thank you, Carl, I love your place. It's great. Is it always this crowded?"

"Sometimes even more so, that's why I wanted you to come down today. I'll show you around. Then I would like to test you a little. Is that all right?"

"Sounds good to me," she said with a smile as Carl started to introduce her to a few people. After the tour Carl asked her to go behind the bar so that he could have a few of the regulars order some drinks from her as well as some other people.

"Give me five minutes to check out where everything is?" she asked as she began to look through the bar locating the ice, the alcohol setup, the mixes, and everything she would need to make any drink they asked her for.

"Only five minutes, huh?" one of the other bartenders asked. Her name was Shelly and she seemed a little annoyed that Lori was invading her space. Lori knew how to handle Shelly as she made a joke then complimented her.

* * * *

"Okay, I'm ready," Lori stated before her five minutes were up and the drink orders began. They started off simple. Then they tried to confuse her with complicated orders or asking how certain drinks were made, changing the ingredients. It was no problem and as Lori made the drinks she spoke to the men, making jokes, drawing their attention away from tricking her. Plus it gave her the extra few seconds she needed working with the wrist cast. It would come off in a few more weeks. Shelly watched as Lori took over and the bar became more crowded.

"Okay, Lori, I think I've seen enough. What do you think, guys?" Carl asked the men at the bar.

They all began to holler "yes" and whistle as Lori said good-bye to them and Shelly.

"What do you think about the uniform?" Carl asked her as Lori looked at Shelly and the other waitress staff. The skirt was pretty short and the shirt was very tight but the place was busy and she was sure she'd make good money.

"How do you work it with the tips, do I share what I make with whomever I'm working with at the bar? Do the waitresses share their tips with the bar since we're making the drinks?" Lori asked.

Carl smiled, seemingly impressed that Lori knew the bar business and he felt hiring her would only be positive.

"You get your own tips at the bar, your own container to put them in or a drawer under the counter, whichever you prefer. Also the waitresses contribute ten percent of their nightly earnings to you. I also pay you a small salary on the books for tax purposes. Does that sound good to you?"

"Sounds fine, Carl, I appreciate the job. You won't be sorry."

"I know I won't be. Now how about having a drink with me?" he asked.

Lori debated about the drink but she didn't want to give him the wrong impression.

"Actually, Carl, don't you think that may look a little unprofessional of us? I wouldn't want the others to think you're showing me favoritism. It will only lead to problems for me at the bar and working here. You understand, right?" Lori asked as she gently touched Carl's arm.

She was in complete control and he fell for it as he agreed with her. Lori had dealt with men like Carl before, even worse than him, and she knew exactly how to handle them.

They said good-bye and she left for home knowing that she would start her new job Monday night at 5:00 p.m.

* * * *

It was a Wednesday evening, cooler than the past few nights. It was only fifty degrees. The town was quiet and the moon was dull with a light veil of clouds moving softly with the gentle breeze. He moved swiftly and carefully so as not to be noticed. Quietly and with precision he began placing the flammable substance around the shed. The animals were restless. Their instincts told them something was wrong as the horses whined, stomped their hoofs, and paced in the stable next door.

The boss said not to hurt anyone, just scare the Cantrells. He wanted to do more. He needed to inflict pain to satisfy his own desires. He watched the town for a week and had already planned out the next few moves.

He flicked on his trusty brass lighter, staring at the flame a moment, absorbing the power he held in his hand. He savored the moment, the feelings of adrenaline that radiated through his body. He laughed a little then placed the flame against the liquid. In an instant the flames made their way around the shed and close enough to the stables to inflict the fear it was meant to cause. The stables and animals would be safe, there was only a slight breeze tonight, he was sure of what he was doing. Quickly he disappeared into the darkness, escaping once again unnoticed, uncaught, and free to destroy again.

* * * *

Tom and Lynn Cantrell awoke to the sounds of horses whining and then a large explosion. They jumped from their beds and headed downstairs to the front porch. They were in shock at the sight and intensity of the flames.

"The horses, Tom, we have to release the horses!" yelled Lynn. Tom was already tying the laces of his boots. He had thrown on his jeans upstairs and now ran across the field to the stable with no shirt on. Lynn stayed in her nightgown, called the sheriff and fire department, then headed outside to help her husband. "Who would do something like this?" was all she said as she raced across the field.

* * * *

The sounds of sirens and fire trucks woke the Henleys and the Shays as everyone headed toward the Cantrells' to help.

Lori ran over with her parents while Maggie stayed home with Ben.

Lori could see Matt, Charlie, Dante, Trevor, Jasper, Freddie, and the Cantrells trying to release the animals while the fire department was putting out the fire.

Lori grabbed the jet-black stallion following Jasper with another brown stallion over toward the holding corral.

Once the animals were all safe, everyone gathered around the front porch watching the firemen reduce the flames to smothered smoke and ash. The whole shed was destroyed.

Mrs. Cantrell was shivering and Lori ran inside to retrieve a jacket from the Cantrells' front closet.

She emerged holding two jackets then placed a beige one around Mrs. Cantrell and a black one around Mr. Cantrell.

"Who would do something like this?" was all Mrs. Cantrell kept saying.

"I'm gonna find that out, Lynn, don't you worry," Sheriff Morgan said as he gave Lynn Cantrell a hug.

Charlie, Lou, Phil, and the others stood talking a few feet away from everyone.

* * * *

"I smell a rat. I can tell you that much," Charlie stated and Phil told him to quiet down.

"Now we don't know for sure, son," Phil stated as he stuck his hands in his pockets trying to keep warm.

"Bullshit, Dad. You know as damn well as I do that men like

Connor don't care who they hurt to get what they want. He's part of this I just know it," Charlie stated, and Dante, Trevor and Matt agreed.

Phil walked toward Lou and Tom leaving Charlie, Matt, Jasper, Dante, Trevor, and Freddie.

Dante stared at the mess as smoke vanished into the darkness of the night.

"I was wondering what that woman wore to bed," Matt whispered as he nodded his head toward Lori who stood shivering by the front porch.

The men looked toward Lori noting the light hip hugger boxer shorts and short, tight-fitting raspberry T-shirt. Her tan, toned belly was showing and her long blonde hair was pulled back into two long braids.

She had a voluptuous figure, an amazing smile, and a mature, unselfish personality. Yet she wore her hair in a childish style. She was shy and refined.

Dante watched as she retrieved the two jackets for the Cantrells and helped gather the horses. Now she stood there shivering and he wished he had grabbed his sweatshirt before running from his house.

Some firemen were handing out blankets and immediately a few of them offered one to Lori.

"Fucking guys. They're drooling," Dante whispered then glanced at Charlie and Trevor who were in a dead stare at the firemen and Lori.

Dante was annoyed as he watched the way other men flirted with her. He didn't want to admit it but he was jealous. By the expressions on Charlie's and Trevor's faces, they were, too.

It was as if his brother Matt was reading his mind as Matt whispered to his brothers, "If you're gonna make a move, you'd better make it soon. She's not going to be single long."

Dante, Trevor, and Charlie didn't say a word. Dante knew there was no use in denying the obvious. His brother Matt knew them well but he feared taking a chance on such an intense relationship. He didn't trust women and Lori was too young. Plus Charlie wasn't willing to admit his attraction to Lori just yet. They needed to tread carefully.

* * * *

The deputies returned with no leads or strangers in the area and the sheriff promised a full investigation.

The fire was completely out and the firemen continued their cleanup. Diana and Lynn made their way into the house planning on making some coffee.

"I'm gonna head home to grab a sweatshirt and let Maggie know what's going on. I'll get one for you, too, Mom," Lori said, and Lynn stopped by the door.

"You'd better not walk through the dark alone. Boys, go with Lori, please. We don't know who might be out there," Lynn stated and the thought suddenly made everyone nervous.

"We'll go with her, Mrs. Cantrell," Trevor said as Charlie grabbed a flashlight and they headed toward the Shay house.

"You really don't have to come with me, it's not that far," Lori told the three men. She wasn't used to having escorts.

"We don't know who may be out there, Lori. This is a serious situation," Trevor told her as the four of them walked closely together across the field. They were trying to keep warm. It didn't take much. The three Henley brothers were extra large and towered over her as they took a flanking position around her. She swallowed hard and all she kept thinking about was them as soldiers escorting her, protecting her through enemy lines. But that wasn't the case here. They were older, thought she needed babysitting, and she wasn't in any danger except maybe of having a heart attack. *God, they're so good looking and sexy.*

"Yeah, kid, whoever is responsible for this isn't dealing with a full deck," Charlie stated, and once again Lori was annoyed at the way he called her *kid*.

"Who would want to do something like this to the Cantrells?"

"We're not sure, Lori, but hopefully Sheriff Morgan will find out. In the meantime I don't think there is anything wrong with taking extra precautions," Dante said before Charlie made his opinion known. Lori's impression of Charlie thus far was that he seemed hotheaded and didn't care who he pissed off.

"So, Lori, how do you like working at Carl's?" Trevor asked, and Charlie made a noise as if annoyed at the thought of her working there.

"It's going well. I like it but I'll be even happier once this cast is off, it kind of gets in the way. What do you think are the chances that your brother Andrew will remove it sooner?"

"Pretty slim. He's a by-the-book kind of guy. You can't mess around with broken bones and casts," Trevor added.

Lori thought that Trevor and Dante were nice yet authoritative in a way and that Charlie continually came across as angry and impolite. They seemed on edge and abrupt and as if being nice to her was difficult. It was just a feeling she had, but it did bother her. She thought of herself as a well-rounded person who was always nice to people even if they weren't so nice to her. For some reason she felt the lack of patience with these three men that she had with others. It was crazy.

They arrived at the house and Maggie was waiting downstairs in the kitchen.

"What happened? Is everyone all right?"

"There was a fire but no one got hurt," Lori told her sister as she grabbed some sweatshirts. Charlie, Dante, and Trevor told Maggie what was going on and about keeping the Cantrells company.

"Well as soon as Ben gets up, we'll head over. This is terrible. I wonder who would do something like this?" Maggie asked.

"J.R.'s involved now, so hopefully he'll figure out who's behind this," Lori said.

She told the men she was ready to head back.

* * * *

Charlie noted that Lori was on a first-name basis with the sheriff already. J.R. was too old for Lori but some women found the whole lawman quality very attractive despite the age difference. The more he thought about her with another man the angrier he became. He had no right to have these feelings and he wanted to avoid them. He would refuse to give in to temptation no matter what happened.

He felt like hitting something. He was pissed that someone was trying to hurt or scare the Cantrells. He was annoyed at the talk around town about the hot new bartender at Carl's place knowing it was Lori, and he hated the fact that he was turned on walking across the field with her and his brothers. He liked the idea of her flanked between the three of them. Trevor behind her, him on the right and Dante on the left. It brought some wild images to his mind and sexual ideas he hadn't thought about since before the war. He knew a lot about sex and satisfying a woman as well as his own sexual needs. But when he walked with Lori, watched her converse with others, he felt something tug at his heart. The fucking organ was dead until she showed up. How the fuck could something like this happen? Who was she really? What did she want in a man, in life, and would she even consider a ménage relationship? She seemed so innocent and sweet, yet her body told a different story. Maybe that was his hope. A no-strings-attached sexual encounter with her and then be done. He shook his head. *That wouldn't work. There's something about her that makes me feel. How can she do that? Who is she? I'm going to find out, no matter what it takes. Dante and Trevor need me to protect them. They've had enough heartache and pain in their lives. They don't need any more and neither do I.*

Chapter 8

Andrew showed up at his parents' house with loads of questions and concerns. His brothers were there and they were talking about Jerry Connor.

"Is the sheriff going to question him?" Andrew asked.

"How can he accuse him without any evidence? There's no legitimate reason for questioning Connor," Dante stated as he took a seat on the back porch railing.

"It's damn obvious he's responsible. He's been after that land for two years now and he's threatened the Cantrells," Charlie said as he sat in a rocking chair next to Jasper.

"Power and money, brother, that's what this is all about. The best we can do is try and keep an ear opened around here and a lookout for anyone suspicious in the area," Matt said as he rose from his chair.

"I'm worried about all the neighbors and our place," Trevor said.

"Yeah, and what about the Henleys? We're building that loft and apartment for Lori. There's opportunity for this asshole to do something there on site," Dante said.

"Shit. I didn't think about that. Maybe we should ask the sheriff to patrol a bit more?" Andrew suggested.

The men talked for a while then had some lunch. Charlie was sitting outside on the porch again preparing to start the day's work.

"You headed back to the office?" Charlie asked.

"Yeah I have a patient coming in at 3:00 p.m. Then I'm busy for the rest of the day.

"That's cool."

* * * *

Trevor and Dante stood next to Andrew.

"The patient is Lori and I'm not looking forward to arguing with her. She's one stubborn woman, let me tell you. She's insisting that I take her cast off. I think it has to stay on another week." Andrew leaned against the porch post. He knew his brother Charlie was attracted to Lori and he wondered why he hadn't made a move. Then Matt mentioned that Trevor and Dante liked her, too. He was concerned, knowing Lori's past and all the fears of everyone involved here. Not that Lori would say yes to dating Charlie, considering how rude he'd been to her. Perhaps the four people could help one another heal?

"Well you're the doctor, you should know," Charlie said dismissing the conversation.

"I don't know how she's bartending with that cast. So far I've heard she's doing great. Carl was in the other day and said he swears the place has been busier because of her. You know Carl though, he'd love to get his hands on a fine woman like Lori," Andrew said, testing his brother's denial of caring about Lori.

Charlie swung around toward his brother, angry as hell with his fists clenched at his sides. Dante and Trevor did the same, cornering Andrew.

"Don't talk about her like that. She not some damn piece of meat." Charlie caught himself and settled down.

"She's too young for him, she's only twenty-one," Trevor added.

"If he touches her, I'll fucking rip Carl's head off," Dante stated.

"Twenty-one and gorgeous, a great personality…the list goes on. Why are you guys getting so mad?"

"I'm not mad, just drop it." Charlie walked off the porch and stomped away.

Dante and Trevor gave Andrew a dirty look.

"Don't fuck with us, Andrew. This is a volatile situation. We'll take care of this so butt out," Dante said, He and Trevor walked off the porch following Charlie.

Andrew crossed his arms in front of his chest and smiled.

Son of a bitch. The three of them are attracted to her. God, I hope this works for them. They all need to feel again.

* * * *

"Don, things are going as planned and there's no need to worry. This guy is good, he's one of the best I'm telling you," Jerry Connor said as he poured himself a glass of brandy then offered one to Don.

"He set the whole shed on fire, what if the stables went, too?" Don asked all annoyed.

"Shhhh…Be quiet! Someone might hear you! No one was hurt, no animals were hurt, and no evidence was left behind," Connor said with confidence.

"This time no evidence was left behind! This guy better be as good as you say he is or the police are going to be making a visit real soon."

"Don't worry," Jerry said as Don left his office.

Jerry walked around the large mahogany desk to sit down in the black leather chair. He picked up the phone as he took another sip of brandy then smelled his Cuban cigar. He was feeling good about his plan and everything was going along schedule. He called his new employee who insisted upon being called the "stranger" and he suggested something else the stranger could do for an additional fee then hung up the phone.

"This is more fun than I expected." Jerry leaned back in his chair with a huge smile on his face.

* * * *

The week had passed slowly and Lori couldn't take the damn cast any longer. She didn't want to wait until Monday. It was three days away and she'd had it. The damn thing was making her so itchy that it was driving her insane. She sat up in bed. It was a warm night, nearly eighty degrees as she slipped on her flip-flops and tiptoed down the hallway.

Even with her blue tank top and cotton shorts she was hot as she pulled her hair up into a ponytail then walked through the kitchen. She searched the kitchen drawers and cabinets looking for something sharp. She figured if she could make a hole in the cast then use a sharp knife to file through it she would be home-free. "What's three days early?" she whispered as she searched.

She was unsuccessful but her mind was set. The cast would come off tonight. Then she had an idea. She remembered seeing the small handsaw in the barn along with some other tools. There was bound to be something in there she could use. She was so determined, she would use the electric saw if she had to get this damn thing off.

So she headed out the door and across the grass. The moon illuminated the sky and there was a plethora of stars. She moved slowly, holding her flashlight and ignoring the sudden uneasy feeling she had walking through the darkness. She told herself the barn wasn't so far from the house as she heard crickets chirping and the leaves rustle together from the very light breeze. It was comforting considering the evening temperature and the added ten degrees inside the house. The thought of sleeping outside on the porch for the remainder of the night entered her mind but first there was the task at hand. She looked at the cast as she unhitched the latch on the barn door.

* * * *

Charlie was awoken by some noise outside near the truck. He jumped out of bed and headed downstairs. As he walked out the front door he could see his parents' house in the distance. His father and brother Matt were out by the deck. Then he saw the sheriff patrol car and he knew something was wrong.

He grabbed his T-shirt and tossed it on him quickly. He wore his boxers and threw on a pair of blue jeans, socks, then his boots.

"What's going on?" Dante asked.

"I don't know. I'm headed over now. I don't like the feeling I have."

"Let me grab Trevor," Dante said.

"No need. I'm right here." Trevor was putting on his boots.

They ran over toward the house where Jasper and Freddie just arrived.

"What's going on?" Charlie asked.

"Looks like our criminal strikes again. He left a headless rooster on the front porch, broke the stable door and now the horses are off in the fields," Jasper told his cousin Charlie.

"Did you see anyone or hear anything?" Charlie asked as his father Phil saddled his horse along with Matt.

"Yeah, I heard the horses then some noise. I thought I saw someone headed toward Lou's place, that's why we called the Sheriff," Matt added as he headed along with his father.

"You three go with the sheriff and Jasper to make sure Lou and the women are all right," Phil told them. Charlie, Trevor, and Dante headed toward that direction as Matt and his father went after the loose horses.

By the time Charlie, Dante, Trevor, Jasper, and the sheriff arrived at the house, Lou and Diana were up and standing by the front door.

"Is everything all right? What's the matter?" Lou asked.

The sheriff filled them in as Maggie came down the stairs all worried.

"Lori's not in her bed," she exclaimed and the look of panic filled everyone's faces.

"What do you mean she's not there? Where could she be?" Charlie asked with concern.

"Let's start looking for her. I'm sure she's fine, Diana. My guys haven't found anyone roaming out there or nearby," J.R. said as he turned on his flashlight.

They all scattered out looking for Lori or any sign of the guy responsible for the night's events.

"Where the hell could she be?" Trevor asked.

"Fuck if I know. Damn woman thinks she can walk around wherever she wants. We told her the other night about being safe," Charlie barked.

"I swear she'd better be in one piece when we find her," Dante added.

* * * *

Lori didn't hear a thing as she moved the saw back and forth across the cast, in the dim glow of her flashlight. The large hammer and chisel lay across the wooden worktable. She was planning on using them next.

Suddenly she heard the barn door open and a light appear.

"Lori, are you in here?" she heard Charlie yell and she wondered what he was doing there.

"Charlie, is that you?" she asked all surprised as he came running toward her.

"What the hell are you doing in here? Everyone's looking for you!" He was yelling at her and the look on his face scared her.

"What are you talking about? I just came out here like twenty minutes ago."

"Come with me!" he demanded as he grabbed her arm. He looked wild and she had no idea why he was there in the barn.

Angrily, Lori pulled away from him.

"Get off of me. What's wrong with you?"

Trevor and Dante approached.

"You found her. Thank God," Trevor said.

Instantly Charlie backed her up, pinning her against the table.

"Everyone is looking for you, someone let the horses out of the stable, left a message on my parents' porch, and was seen headed this way. You weren't in your bed, damn it! What the hell are you doing out here in the middle of the night? Are you really this naive, this oblivious to the dangers around here, what were you thinking!" He carried on and Lori couldn't take it anymore. He was yelling at her like she was a child. That was exactly how he saw her as she raised her hand to slap him.

Charlie was too fast as he grabbed her wrist then the other one, placing her arms behind her back. His body was against hers as she struggled unsuccessfully against his strength.

Then out of nowhere his lips were over hers. His tongue invaded her mouth shocking the hell out of her. At first she fought it then participated by returning the kisses. She felt just as wild as he was acting. His rage, the way he yelled at her and pissed her off, disappeared and was replaced with hunger. He released her wrists letting his hands grab her hips, her back, then her neck as he cradled her head and the kisses slowed down, were softer, gentler. She placed her hands against his chest and felt her whole body shake. His leg was wedged in between hers. He towered over her, so powerful, so in control.

She felt another hand wrap around her wrist as Charlie released her lips and stared at her. They were both breathing heavily. She looked to the right and there was Trevor. He looked just as wild as Charlie and appeared to be breathing heavy as well. She glanced to the left and there was Dante. He took her other wrist. Charlie remained holding her around her waist and she felt his thumb brush against her skin between the elastic of her shorts and her raised tank top.

The four of them were silent. No one said a word and she couldn't move, but only feel. Trevor caressed her inner wrist with his thumb as he reached up with his free hand and touched her cheek and chin.

Dante caressed her other arm slowly up and down, avoiding the cast. The fact that three men touched her in such a way brought her body to life. Her nipples pebbled, her pussy leaked as she tried to tighten her thighs together, but Charlie's thigh remained wedged between hers.

They could hear the yelling from outside the barn door. It interrupted the moment and she felt both relieved and disappointed.

Charlie called out to them.

"Lori's fine. She's in here!" He was out of breath still.

"Thank God! Listen, I'm going with the sheriff. He said his men found some tire tracks down the road a ways. Is everything all right in there?" Jasper asked.

"Everything's fine!" Charlie said as he stared into Lori's eyes.

She swallowed hard.

"You scared the hell out of us, do you know that?" he asked her as he squeezed her hips and Dante caressed a loose strand of hair behind her ear. Trevor gently squeezed her wrist. She suddenly felt bad for something that seemed not to be her fault. She didn't give it a second thought as Charlie released her. So did his brothers as they stepped back.

She rubbed her wrist and then licked her lower lip. The three men watched her. As she looked down at her torn cast, she quickly put it behind her back.

"What are you doing out here?" Dante asked in a deep voice that made her jump as he picked up the flashlight he'd dropped and looked at the table.

"You're not doing what I think you're doing, are you?" Trevor started laughing and Lori was once again annoyed at them.

"I'm fine. Why don't you go tell everyone." She tried to act unaffected and tough but he didn't fall for it.

"I don't think so, kid. You're coming with me and that cast of yours is staying on until Monday, you got it!" Charlie told her as he grabbed her hand with the cast and her flashlight pulling her toward the door.

"Excuse me, but what do you think you're doing?" she demanded as she pulled her hand away, placing her hands on her hips.

Instantly Trevor wrapped his arms around her waist from behind and used his free hand to push her braid away from her neck then whispered. "You better listen to Charlie, baby. He's letting you off easy."

She didn't dare turn to glare at Trevor. His mouth was against the skin on her neck. And the way he called her *baby* and the meaning behind his words aroused her.

"Letting me off easy? What the hell?" she began to say when Dante stood in front of her. He stared at her breasts and they came alive again. The nipples hardened to tiny buds and once again her pussy leaked with arousal.

Dante cupped her chin.

"He let you off easy. The next time you place yourself in danger, he'll throw you over his knee and we'll each spank that ass of yours. Got it?" Dante said.

"Oh God." She practically moaned then closed her eyes and leaned back against Trevor. Trevor chuckled, and his warm breath tickled her ear.

"Lori?"

They heard her father's voice and Trevor released her but not before he gave her ass a small spank.

She jumped as her father entered the barn.

"Is everything all right in here?" Lou asked as he entered.

"Everything is fine, Lou. Your daughter was trying to remove her cast with a handsaw," Charlie said, laughing at the thought.

"Lori! You only have three more days until Dr. Henley removes it. We were worried about you. Did the men tell you what happened at their parents' place?"

"No, they didn't get around to that, Dad." She headed toward the door.

Charlie stopped her by grabbing her cast. He looked at the torn material.

"My brother's not going to be happy when he sees this, kid."

"He'll get over it." She snapped back at him, and then tossed her braided hair back over her shoulder hitting him with it before she exited the barn.

* * * *

Lori was thrilled to finally have the cast removed from her hand. She was wiggling her fingers, cracking her knuckles, and the smile on her face made Andrew smile as well.

"How does it feel?" he asked her.

"It feels awesome! This is so great, Doc, you have no idea. There's nothing weighing my hand down, I feel everything against my fingers and palm. This is fantastic!" Lori exclaimed as she sat on the examination table.

Andrew looked over her hand and her new X-rays looked perfect.

"So I heard you had some kind of scare the other night? Apparently while you were attempting to remove the cast?" Andrew asked sarcastically.

Lori looked away from him. "Let's not talk about that. My wrist is fine, I'm fine."

"I heard Charlie, Dante, and Trevor found you and were very upset."

"When are your brothers not upset, or angry, or trying to boss everyone around?"

"Jasper told me that they were pretty worried about you, Lori. They're good men, you know, just a little hotheaded sometimes. They'd do anything for any of us. Whoever is responsible for these incidents means business. Roaming around in the middle of the night is not such a good idea."

"I wasn't roaming around. Besides I didn't hear anything or see anyone. I was perfectly safe in the barn. I can take care of myself,

Doc. Maybe you should give that message to your brothers."

Lori was annoyed as she jumped down off of the examination table and straightened out her skirt.

"It's hard to take care of yourself when you don't know what you're up against. Besides, Lori, all I'm saying is that there's no need to feel that you have to take care of things on your own. Our families and the Cantrells have become pretty close and we're all willing to help one another out."

"Is this conversation once again leading to me and my past, Doc? Haven't I made it perfectly clear that I'm fine? All I want to do is leave it all behind me, move on, experience life. Do you have any idea how much this means to me to have this cast off my wrist? The constant reminder of what I did, what could have happened to Maggie and Ben?" Lori looked down at her wrist and rubbed her hand, relieved to be physically free of the symbol, the evidence left behind from her part in killing a man.

Andrew took her hand into his, shocking her.

"I would never ever try to say I understand, Lori. I've never gone through anything like you have, and from what I understand took place you have nothing to be ashamed of. You saved your sister and your nephew's lives. You've applied for college, you're working now. I'd say you're moving on with your life."

"I appreciate the vote of confidence, Doc. I'm in a great mood today, nothing's going to change that," she told him and he smiled.

* * * *

Lori went to work Friday night looking forward to not having the cast in her way. She was glad to be working with Shelly who was now becoming more of a friend. They got together yesterday and went to the mall. It was the first time she had done anything so "normal."

Carl's was extra crowded and the regulars were getting annoyed, as they were being bumped left and right by the enormous crowds of people. One regular named Gary was headed toward his routine Friday night drunken stupor. A group of young guys were starting with Gary and Lori stepped in.

"Hey, guys, leave him alone. He's not bothering anyone."

"We're just having some fun, sweetheart. Don't worry about it. Just keep the beers coming," one guy, Stan, said as he tossed some twenties on the bar. He and a few of his friends arrived on a boat a couple of hours ago and had been pounding down beers like water.

Shelly was staying until closing and Lori was preparing to leave around eleven. She packed up her stuff as Stan and the guys continued to flirt with her. Lori didn't like the way one of the guys, Tanner, was staring at her. He was drunk. His eyes took on a glaring, cold stare she had seen before and knew he was up to something.

She said good night to the regulars at the bar and headed in to see Carl. On her way out she saw Matt Henley.

"Hey, gorgeous, how are you?" Matt asked as he kissed Lori's cheek.

"I'm good. What are you doing here?"

"Just having a couple of beers after some dinner with Charlie, Dante, Trevor, Jasper, and some friends. Do you want to join us?" Matt asked.

"I don't think so. My wrist is a little sore and I'm kind of tired. Maybe another time though." She tried to get out of it. She didn't want to see Charlie, Dante, or Trevor. Not after what happened the other night. Apparently they didn't want to acknowledge the other night either. They had acted like the kiss never happened and she figured Michelle was right about the Henley brothers being into one-night stands.

"Come on and have a drink with me. It would make my night." He winked. She rolled her eyes at him and shook her head.

He took her hand. Matt insisted that she stop by the table to have a beer as he led her toward a table near the back. She fixed her skirt, trying to pull it down further but it was no use. The damn thing was short and there was nothing she could do about it. She was glad she had fixed her lip gloss and her hair.

As they approached the table, two women were standing by Charlie's chair obviously flirting and he didn't seem to mind.

"Hey, look who I found getting ready to leave," Matt said as the other men at the table got up to give Lori their chairs.

Charlie, Dante, and Trevor looked surprised as they instantly ignored the two women and gave Lori the once-over.

Lori said hello to everyone then took a seat next to Jasper.

The two women said their good-byes then wiggled away.

"You've got the touch, Charlie!" yelled Jimmy as he took another sip of his beer. He worked at the hardware store in town and was feeling pretty good from the six beers he'd already consumed. The bottles were lined up in front of him.

Charlie ignored the comment and immediately Matt drew attention away from Jimmy.

"You said your wrist is a little sore? What did my brother say about that?" Matt asked Lori.

"I haven't told him. I'm sure it's normal, and since I haven't used it in a while, the muscles need to get used to things again."

The waitress Linda came over with another round of beers and Matt handed Lori his. "We need another one, Linda, and keep them coming," Matt told her as he put the mug of beer in front of Lori.

She said thank you and took a sip. The conversation continued with the guys telling some childhood stories and the crazy things they did. Lori sat and listened, rather amused at the crazy outcomes.

"So do you guys normally hang out here?" Lori asked. "I don't think I've seen you here before."

Trevor moved his chair closer to hers.

"No, we don't usually come here. There's a nice place we like to go to about thirty minutes from here. Some friends of ours own it."

"Really? Is it like Carl's?" she asked Trevor, absorbing the scent of his cologne and the way his hazel eyes seemed to darken to chocolate as he spoke to her.

Suddenly someone bumped into her chair and was hugging her from behind.

"Hey, baby, I thought you went home," Tanner slurred as he nearly knocked the chair over. Charlie, Trevor, and Dante rose from their chairs as Lori pried Tanner's hands off of her.

"Hey, fella, it looks like you've had a few too many. Where are your friends?" Lori asked, trying to stay calm and keep the guys out of this and at a safe distance. Once again Charlie, Dante, and Trevor took on similar angry expressions she was sure would not bring a good outcome as she stood up. She looked around and saw one of the guys who acted kind of like a bouncer and waved him over.

"Don't walk away from me, sweetheart. You're mine tonight, baby," Tanner repeated as he grabbed Lori's hand.

Gus the bouncer was on his way over but Trevor and Dante already intervened.

The three of them helped Tanner back to his friends and Gus asked for them to leave. Charlie stared at her and the uniform she wore. It was as if he was blaming her for what just occurred. *How dare he judge me? Like I enjoy wearing this? It's not my fault that Tanner is drunk.*

As soon as Trevor and Dante returned, Lori decided it was time to leave.

"I really should get going. It's late, thanks for the beer and conversation. I'll see you around."

The guys acted disappointed and she walked away.

"Hey where are you guys going?" Matt asked his brothers.

"We're going to make sure Lori gets off okay. That guy was pretty drunk," Dante said as he followed Trevor and Charlie.

"Yeah that's really nice of you!" Jimmy blurted out and the others made their comments.

* * * *

Charlie came around the corner with Trevor and Dante and saw Lori leaving with Gus. They headed toward them just as Carl came outside looking for Gus.

"Gus, I need you in the back. Where are you going?" Carl asked.

"I'm just walking Lori out to her car."

"All right, hurry up then. I need you."

"You can go, Gus. We'll walk her out," Charlie said and Lori swung her head around toward them.

"Is that all right with you, Lori?" Carl asked, sounding a little annoyed.

"Yes, that's fine," she said as she started to walk away.

"I don't need bodyguards you know." It was more of a statement than a question. Charlie and his brothers took position around her.

"I didn't say I was your bodyguard," Charlie stated.

"My car is way over there, you don't have to…"

"I'm already walking with you, kid, let's just leave it at that."

"Fine!"

"Fine!" Charlie responded as they made their way across the parking lot.

Charlie could see the beat-up vehicle that Lori called her car.

"Are you still having problems with that muffler?" Dante asked.

"It's just loud that's all."

"Maybe to you but to everyone else in the neighborhood it lets us know when you're coming and going," Charlie added with an attitude back at her.

Lori turned toward Charlie, surprised that no one mentioned this before.

"I'm so sorry! I had no idea. I'll bring it somewhere tomorrow," she blurted out and Charlie realized he made her feel bad.

He took her hand to stop her from opening up the driver side door.

"Lori, I didn't mean to upset you. It's all right, really."

Lori pulled away from him with her head down mumbling about

how she would pay to get the car fixed. The money she made from tips tonight would have to pay for it.

"I guess I'll have to rearrange a little. I could probably work something out with Calvin. I just met him the other night at the bar. I think he said he was a mechanic...where the heck did he say he worked?" She was talking to herself when Charlie turned her toward him by her shoulders.

"Lori, it's all right. That's what I was going to tell you. I can fix it for you. I know a lot about cars and trucks. It's a hobby of mine. I'll take care of it."

"You don't have to do that, Charlie. I'll come up with the money."

"Let him do it. He likes working on cars," Dante added as he leaned against her car.

"It relaxes him," Trevor said.

Charlie gently touched her face with his hand and Lori froze.

He smiled then laughed a little under his breath. She hoped that she looked attractive when she was worried. She felt so self-conscious around these men. He put his hand around her waist, pulling her toward him.

She didn't say a word. She just waited for Charlie's next move as his other hand softly touched her hair giving it a gentle yank.

"I'll take care of it."

"I'll pay you."

"No, I'll take care of it. Now don't argue with me. There is one thing I want from you right now."

Her heart was pounding, her hands sweaty. "What would that be?" she asked, trying not to sound as scared as she was. She had never been this close to a man before, had never been intimate with anyone before, and she didn't want him to know that.

"A ride home."

Her fear and anticipation of being kissed by him again turned to anger, but before she could lash out at him he smiled then kissed her softly.

She thought he was crazy or maybe she was as he released her and she allowed herself to be taken control by this man, giving in to his orders, his demands, his way as she prepared to drive him home. But as he opened the door, Trevor pulled her into his arms and smiled at her right before he kissed her. It was crazy, but she was totally turned on by this. She just let Charlie kiss her, now Trevor was and all she could do was hope that Dante kissed her next.

When Trevor released her he whistled.

"Damn, woman, you taste real good."

She shyly lowered her eyes and Dante took her wrist and pulled her to him next. He leaned back against the car and kissed her deeply. Pulling her against his chest.

When he finally released her lips, she was shocked. She pressed her forehead against Dante's chest.

"I think I've lost my mind."

"So should I drive?" Trevor asked and they chuckled.

She pulled back and took a deep breath. The three big men stared at her with hunger in their eyes and appeared less angry than usual.

"We'll follow you guys," Dante said as he and Trevor headed toward their truck. Charlie got into Lori's car on the passenger side.

* * * *

"I'm surprised it's this neat inside. From the looks of the exterior I was expecting—"

"A strange smell, a sticky seat, garbage everywhere?" she asked sarcastically as she started the engine and the loud noise replaced the uneasiness.

He turned in the seat to watch her as she drove.

"I have to stop at the convenience store on the way."

"No problem. What do you have to get?"

"Ice cream and some M&M's. I'm celebrating tonight." She smiled and continued to drive down the road.

"What are you celebrating to be indulging in such pleasure as ice cream and M&M's?"

"Getting my cast off actually and some other stuff," she added with a smile as she turned the car around the corner and pulled into the parking lot.

She asked Charlie if he wanted anything then headed into the store. Her long, tan legs looked fantastic in the short, black uniform skirt. Charlie was tempted to make a move but his gut told him not to, so he denied himself the pleasure. He thought about Dante and Trevor. They were just as attracted to Lori as he was despite his lame denial. He was pretty much making a public statement anyway. By following her out of Carl's and driving home with her with his brothers following, their point would be made.

Stay clear of Lori. She's ours.

As he said the words and watched her make her purchase in the store, he felt his chest tighten. He gripped his knees and released an uneasy sigh. This was insane.

He watched her walk back to the car. He noticed the guys hanging out by the front staring at her. One guy said something but Lori ignored him. She just stared straight ahead. She acted tough, but he worried about her. She opened the car door but not before looking at his brothers who sat in the black pickup truck in the spot right next to her car. She got in, tried to adjust her skirt but it wasn't budging and that was fine by him.

They talked about Carl's place and some of the regulars.

"You should have someone walk you out at night. It's not safe, especially wearing a uniform like that." He couldn't resist. If he wasn't able to touch it, at least he could mention it.

"A short skirt doesn't give a man a right to put his hands on me," Lori told him all annoyed.

"You try and use that rationale with some drunk and see if he takes no for an answer, kid."

"First of all, this isn't the first bar I've ever had to work in and secondly, I can take care of myself. Look…there's your house!" Lori said sarcastically before Charlie could respond to her.

She pulled the car in front and put it in park.

"You're going to eat that ice cream all alone?"

* * * *

The nerve of him talking to her like some child, telling her what to do, insulting her maturity and now asking to share her celebration with him? Lori didn't say a word as Charlie reached over and turned off the ignition. Trevor and Dante were out of their truck and approaching the car. As Charlie pulled the keys from the ignition, his arm caressed her knee and thigh. She gasped from the instant effect he had on her as she looked toward him.

"I'm sorry if I hurt your feelings. Let's get out and enjoy the night sky."

"You know, Charlie, you have some nerve. Do you realize how bossy and arrogant you are? What makes you think that you can tell me what to do, treat me like some child, and just take control?" She was raising her voice to him as he got out of the car with the brown bag.

Lori got out, barely looked at Dante and Trevor as she slammed her door shut, and walked around the front of the car toward Charlie who hopped up onto the hood of the car.

"I'm talking to you, Charlie!"

He was making her so angry, and when he looked at her, he had a smirk on his face.

"Look at that sky, baby. Tell me you want to miss that?" he asked her as he pointed up.

She had no choice but to look and of course once again he was right.

"It is beautiful, now let go of my bag," she demanded as she moved closer toward the hood of the car.

She should have seen it coming as Charlie grabbed her hand, turned her around, placing her back in between his legs and against the car.

He held her from behind as he spoke to her and she could feel every breath against her hair.

"Relax will you!" He moved her hair away from her neck, clearing a path to make his next move.

"What seems to be the problem?" Trevor asked with a smile as he leaned against the car on her left. Dante took position on the right. She felt panicked, unnerved being surrounded by all this testosterone.

Charlie kissed her neck softly and then her shoulder.

"We'd better have the ice cream before it melts," Lori said as she quickly moved away from him and began taking the ice cream out of the bag.

* * * *

Charlie found her shyness appealing. He intimidated her, made her nervous. He was starting to realize that her sexy, tough attitude was mostly an act.

Lori placed some M&M's on top of the already melting vanilla ice cream.

She took the spoon and dipped it into the container.

"Wait, shouldn't you make a toast or something?" Charlie teased.

Lori raised the spoonful of ice cream with the two pieces of colored candy on it.

"No more cast, good-bye to the past!" she said as she took a bite with her eyes closed. Charlie watched her and the seriousness in her voice as she made the toast. He glanced at his brothers and they seemed just as intrigued. He couldn't help but wonder what could have possibly occurred in her past that she needed to leave behind. She was only twenty-one. His father and brother did mention her going through a rough time and no one, including Lori, had explained exactly how she broke her wrist.

"Don't I get some?" he asked.

She took the spoon and handed it to him as she looked up once again into the starlit sky.

* * * *

Despite the fact that Charlie, Dante, and Trevor made her extremely nervous and that she was uncontrollably attracted to them, she felt an excitement for the future.

She felt Trevor wrap his hand around her wrist and tug her gently toward him. "I want a taste, too." He took her into his arms then kissed her softly. It was so unexpected. But he was smooth and suave in his move and it excited her. She had wondered what his kiss would feel like and if it would be as powerful as when Charlie kissed her. She immediately felt the chills run through her body as he deepened the kiss and knew she was in serious trouble. The man had large hands. She felt the palm of one move over her lower back to her rear as he squeezed her closer against his chest. This was too much. She shouldn't allow them to kiss her like this.

Slowly Trevor released her lips and smiled down at her. He looked kind of happy. That was a different expression for Trevor. He and his brothers always looked so sad and angry.

"Hmmm, tasty," he whispered. She felt her cheeks blush as she shyly pulled away from him. Instead of getting a reprieve from the sexual tension in the air between them she got another dose of lovin' from Dante.

"Damn, woman, I've got to know, too." He pulled her toward him, wrapped his arms around her waist, and kissed her fully on the lips. He held her hands behind her back, as if she would resist his move. What a fool, she was, because she didn't resist. Instead she wished he would let go of her wrists so she could run her hands up his chiseled chest and feel what it was like to be held in such large, strong arms.

She felt the second set of hands on her waist. Charlie was gently rubbing his hands up and down her hips and thighs. Since she was wearing the short skirt, he reached her bare skin and she felt the skirt moving upward. In a panic she pulled forward and Dante released her lips.

"Whoa, baby, it's okay. Don't be scared of us," Dante said.

But she was scared. She was scared at how easily she accepted kisses and touches from three men, brothers she hardly knew at all. She knew nothing about relationships, dating, and sex. She sure as shit didn't have a clue about a ménage relationship and being shared by three men at once.

Lori felt the panic attack coming on. She covered her chest with her hand and tried to calm her breathing. She felt the hand caressing her back.

"Relax, honey. Don't panic. We'd never hurt you." *Trevor.*

As she stood up straighter and pulled her skirt down out of self-consciousness and need to not portray herself as easy, she locked gazes with Charlie. Holy shit the man looked primal.

"How did you break that pretty little wrist of yours?" he asked her, and instantly Lori's mood changed. She felt that nauseous feeling in the pit of her stomach and her head began to ache. She didn't answer. She refused to, no matter how much he demanded. The control Charlie had was limited to what she would allow and this was crossing the line. This whole damn ménage thing was crossing the line.

Charlie appeared as if he analyzed her facial expressions and so did Trevor and Dante. She suddenly thought about who these men were and their experiences as Special Forces. They knew how to interrogate and infiltrate the most difficult of locations. They could surely interrogate her and she didn't want that. This was why she avoided getting friendly or close with anyone. People wanted to ask questions and she wanted to forget her past and start all over.

One look at the three men before her and their very stern expressions in their eyes and she knew she was busted. She knew her expression changed, her body tensed up, and they would know that she was hiding the circumstances of her broken wrist. But would they push for answers?

"I guess it's a secret, huh? Well however you broke it at least it's healed now, right?" Dante said as if he were taking over the conversation. Now Charlie looked pissed off at Dante. He probably wanted his brother to push for answers. These men got answers to anything they asked. They were that intimidating and that sexy and lethal. A woman would be putty in their hands, but not her. No way was she falling for it. She took a deep breath and regained the attitude she worked so hard to acquire as a front.

"Right. It's healed, but I'm pretty tired. The night was long," she replied, and deep down inside she knew it was a lie. She wondered if she would ever heal as she took another bite full of dessert.

They stared at her. They surrounded her and every part of her body was completely aware and aroused. She needed sleep and she needed to get her head screwed back on tight.

"Well I'd better get home, it's getting late," Lori said as she gathered up the bag.

"You have off on Sunday right?" Trevor asked.

"Yes, I do, why?"

"If you don't have any plans, there's going to be a street fair near our friend's restaurant. I thought you might like to go, a date?" he added but then looked surprised by his own words. It was so weird to watch. One minute these guys were so confident and dominant and the next they seemed unsure of themselves. It made her belly tighten and a feeling of empathy fill her. She was feeling stupid and giddy over it.

"Maybe, can I let you know?"

"Why a maybe, what is there to think about?"

"Well I guess it's whether your brother Charlie fixes my muffler tomorrow or not?" she teased him as she walked around toward the driver side. Charlie hopped down off the hood of the car.

"Do you need it in the morning?"

"No, I won't need it until 4:00 p.m. when I have to leave for work."

"In that case we'll drive you home and you can leave your car here. I'll get it to you by late morning or I'll drive you to work myself." He told her. Dante placed his hands on her shoulders and whispered into her ear.

"He knows what he's doing. He's pretty damn good at it."

She agreed as Dante took her hand and led her to their truck.

She stared at the passenger side door and the height to get up into the truck.

"Um, there's no way I can get up there. Not in this stupid uniform." But before she could turn, Dante lifted her into the air and placed her onto the seat. He then covered her knee with his hand.

"Scoot on over, darling, Trevor is coming, too." Charlie jumped into the driver side. She was pressed against him as his two brothers moved into the cab, too.

As they drove the short distance to her parents' house, she noticed the large shotgun up on the rack, the Marine Corps sign, and a rather clean truck.

"I'm impressed. I thought it would be a mess in here. Don't you guys take this truck to work?"

Charlie kept looking straight ahead.

"We like it neat. You never know who we might offer a ride to," Trevor whispered then placed his hand on her knee. She knew his words had hidden meaning. They sure did make her heart react.

Finally they were at her parents' house and once again Dante helped her down. As he lowered her to her feet, he remained holding her.

"We'll take things slow, Lori. Just give it a chance." He kissed her softly before releasing her.

As she wondered what he meant and began to move, Trevor

stopped her. He leaned down from the seat above, placed his fingers under her chin and looked into her eyes.

"You're very beautiful." Then he kissed her ever so softly.

She kissed him back and then he released her and smiled. "See you tomorrow."

"Good night," she replied, and as she headed toward her front porch, she caught a glimpse of Charlie's facial expression before the beaming headlights blocked her view. Her chest tightened.

Why does he always look so heated?

Chapter 9

"Now listen to me, old man, things are going to get worse around here if you don't ease your hold on this land. You better keep this between you and I or your old lady is gonna get hurt next. Do you understand?" the stranger told Tom Cantrell over the telephone. It was the middle of the night and he looked toward Lynn knowing that nothing was worth her getting hurt over.

"I understand that. Now tell me what you want."

"When someone comes along interested in buying some land, you better be more willing to negotiate. If not then things could get worse."

The stranger hung up the phone.

Tom heard the click, feeling sick and angry. He had somewhat of an idea who was responsible for the fire and other events, but he couldn't be one hundred percent sure because two other building companies had approached him in the past two weeks. One of them he was actually considering working with because they were going to build nice, affordable homes that would build up the community. The other one wanted the land to build some kind of condominiums and factory of something. That wasn't even an option. Tom figured he would wait and see what took place next. He wanted to keep Lynn and his neighbors out of harm's way. This land was too beautiful to destroy with condos and business buildings. Tom needed to think things through, but ultimately his wife was his top priority and nothing was worth her getting hurt over.

* * * *

Lori got up earlier than usual to go for her jog. She couldn't sleep at all last night as she kept thinking about Dante, Trevor, and Charlie. They were so handsome and strong. She hated to admit it but she actually liked it when Charlie grabbed her, pulling her into a hug to look up at the stars. She loved how sexy Trevor appeared as he asked for a taste, too, then pulled her into his arms to kiss her. And of course there was Dante. Damn, that man was big and quiet, but when he wanted something, he just took it. She liked all three of them and it just felt so crazy. She didn't need this kind of thing right now. She wanted to stay focused on going to school, establishing a life and career. This whole ménage thing could be a mistake. She didn't know them really and they seemed so angry all the time and untrusting. She didn't need that. What if they were violent like Derrick? They did like grabbing her and sort of restraining her when they kissed her.

Lori felt her pussy clench and a bit of arousal fill her. She liked that, so who was she kidding? But then again, what did she know? Maybe her sister had that kind of relationship with Derrick. He was a big man and very strong. He could have easily broken her or Maggie in two like a toothpick. So could Dante, Trevor, and Charlie. Plus they were Special Forces. *Goddamn, I can't do this. I can't take that kind of chance times three. Three huge-ass men, older men who would dominate, control, and perhaps hit me.*

She recalled the conversation she had with Michelle at the barbeque a few weeks back and how Charlie, Dante, and Trevor were into one-night stands. Noncommittal ways seemed to be their thing. They didn't act like that last night. In fact, the way things ended with Trevor and Dante made it sound like there was more to come. Lori wondered if she really needed the hassle, and every time she asked herself that question the word *yes* came to mind. As much as she wanted her first time to be meaningful, romantic, and involving someone she loved who also loved her, a part of her couldn't wait to just get it over with.

For Christ's sake, I'm twenty-one years old! Sex for the first time would definitely be considered memorable. But they're so much older and experienced. It wouldn't mean as much to them as it would to me. I can't do it.

She thought about Charlie. He was an older man, attractive, sexy, kind of nice when he wasn't bossing everyone around and never mind the effect his kisses had on her. Maybe he was just playing some kind of game that she just wasn't experienced enough to know about? Maybe that was all he wanted from her? A one-night stand, sex, a roll in the hay, all the different ways to describe meaningless sex she'd ever heard in any movie she'd ever seen. Add in his two brothers and perhaps it was their version of a fantasy come true. Once they had their fill of her, they'd get rid of her and move on to the next stupid, naive woman to screw around with. *God, that gets my blood boiling.*

She wanted more, so much more than that when it came down to something so personal, so intimate. She wouldn't just throw it away, toss it off as something minor, a nuisance. She had waited this long and there was no need to screw it all up now. She didn't need heartache on top of all the other emotions she held deep inside. As attracted as she was to Dante, Charlie, and Trevor, she would need to be one hundred percent sure that she was at least in love with them before sharing such an intimate part of herself.

As she returned from her morning run, she saw the lights on in the detached garage near Charlie's house. He and his brothers lived in their own little place across the way from their parents' house. Lori figured he had started working on her car already so she ran inside her house to make some coffee and an egg sandwich to drop off to him. It was the least she could do.

She ran the sandwich and coffee to Charlie real quick, which he appreciated, then headed back home. As Lori walked into the kitchen, Maggie was sitting there waiting for her.

"Where's your car?"

"Charlie has it, he's fixing the muffler. He said it was so loud that everyone knew when I was coming and going." Lori poured herself a cup of coffee.

"Honey, if you think the muffler is what's keeping him up, then you're more naive than you look."

"What the hell is that supposed to mean?"

"Come on, Lori, he's a good-looking man and is very attracted to you. So are his brothers Trevor and Dante. You can't see that?"

"So what if they are? I don't know them. I don't even know anything about relationships with one man, never mind three."

"Bullshit you don't like them. You just made him a damn egg sandwich and coffee and ran it over to him. You gave him a ride home last night and are letting him work on your car. You were with all three of them last night. Come on!"

"He won't let me give him any money. Last night they were together and they live together so when I drove Charlie home, Trevor and Dante were there, too."

"He doesn't want your money, sis. He wants your body and so do Trevor and Dante."

"Maggie Marie Shay, I won't have that kind of talk in my house. Your father and your son might hear you…lower your voice," Diana added as she joined the conversation. Maggie laughed and Lori was embarrassed.

"So are you gonna go on a date with Charlie?" Diana asked her daughter.

"I don't know, Mom. It's not what you think."

"You mean the ménage thing? Honey, please, that's been going on around these parts for years. Sure, when your father and I arrived from New York we were a bit taken aback by it. But we've learned through observation how intense and committed those people are to one another. There are nearly just as many traditional relationships around here as there are ménages."

"Oh God, I don't believe you've accepted this thing so easily. We just arrived and I'm not sure I can digest the idea fully of its existence, never mind contemplate trying it."

"Honey, it isn't something to take lightly. Falling in love takes a little time and you need to be sure that Charlie, Dante, and Trevor are the ones for you."

"I cannot believe this conversation. It's not even normal. Three men, Mom? Come on, you can honestly sit there and condone a relationship like this for me? I don't know if I'm ready for any kind of intimate relationship, never mind one like this," Lori said as she leaned against the kitchen counter.

"Ready for this? You're more than ready, Lori, you're gonna burst!"

"Damn it, Maggie, stop it. This is serious. You know what, I don't want to talk about this anymore." Lori turned her back toward her sister.

Diana walked over to Lori and placed her hand on her shoulder to turn her around.

"Honey, I know I haven't really been physically there for you girls for the past five years, but I've always hoped and prayed you'd stay safe and continue to be good girls. I know there are a lot of temptations out there. You're young, attractive, and you should be proud that you've saved yourself for this long," Diana was saying.

"Way too long," Maggie added, laughing.

"Maggie!" Diana warned her daughter to quit it.

"I'm not going to lie, Lori. I'm actually glad you waited, and as scared as you might be and as much as your sister teases you about it, when the right time comes, you'll know it. You'll be so much in love that you're going to want to give every single inch of you to that person to show them how much you love them. If he's the right person, he's going to love you and respect you even more for waiting. Now if it turns out that Dante, Charlie, and Trevor are the ones, then it will be even more special because you'll have three men to love you and care for you." Diana hugged her daughter.

Lori never felt more confused in her life.

* * * *

By lunchtime Charlie had Lori's car all fixed and parked it by the barn.

"Hey, where have you been? We start at 7:00 a.m. remember?" his cousin Freddie teased him as he walked toward the door. Then Matt, Dante, Trevor, and Jasper came over as well.

"I had something I needed to take care of," Charlie told them as he started putting on his tool belt.

"What are you doing driving Lori's car? She the one who gave you a ride home last night?" Matt asked as he winked at his brother.

"Leave it alone, Matt. I told her I'd fix that loud muffler of hers, and I didn't think it was a good idea for her to go home alone after that guy at the bar harassed her last night."

"Oh how neighborly of you, cousin," Jasper teased as he picked up some more wood and headed toward the inside of the barn.

"Hey, brother, I think it's great you finally made a move. She's a rare find let me tell ya, and not going to stay single for long. You should have heard the guys talking about her last night. I know you, you would have been pissed," Matt told his brother as they began hammering away at the plywood. Jasper was using the nail gun and working quickly.

"Who was talking about her?" Charlie asked, not worried about how jealous he sounded.

"Too many to tell ya, man. So when are you two going out on a date?" Matt asked and Charlie didn't answer him.

"You do know that Lori is definitely the kind of woman you have to date, and take her nice places, restaurants, romantic picnics?" Matt teased.

"No shit, Matt, what the hell do you think I am, stupid? I'm older than you and a lot more experienced, so don't start your shit with me. Besides, I'm not the only one involved here." Charlie looked at

Trevor and Dante. They stared at Matt. Matt's eyes widened.

"The three of you? Holy shit," he said. Then they went back to work.

Charlie thought about the conversation he'd had with his brothers last night. They made a decision together. Lori would belong to them. They would start working on a relationship sooner rather than later and hopefully without a fight from Lori.

They continued to work through the afternoon finishing up the exterior of the house and began working on the interior. It was nearly 4:00 p.m. and Lori was just emerging from her parents' house. Matt and Charlie were outside the barn carrying some long pieces of Sheetrock.

Charlie watched Lori as she kissed Ben good-bye and he pulled Lori back toward him for a hug as well. The scene brought a smile to Charlie's face, which Matt saw immediately.

"Why don't we lean this piece against the wall here. Then I'll get Jasper to start measuring and cutting?" Matt asked as they placed the Sheetrock against the outside of the barn.

Lori looked over and saw Charlie and Matt as they grabbed some bottles of water. Charlie was perspiring, wearing no shirt and some loose-fitting blue jeans.

Lori looked right at him then lowered her eyes. She seemed embarrassed to stare at his body and he wondered why. Most women tried to get his shirt off of him. Charlie turned toward her and caught her staring at him.

"Hey, kid, your car is all fixed." He walked over toward the car meeting Lori by the driver side.

"I know, I saw you pull up earlier and was surprised how quiet she was. Thanks a lot, Charlie, I mean it."

"No problem, I told you don't worry about it. You heading to work?"

"Doesn't the uniform give it away?" she asked and he bit the inside of his cheek. He hated the fucking uniform except when she was with him and his brothers.

"So, how about going out with Dante, Trevor, and I tomorrow? We know a great place about thirty minutes out of town. Our friends own it."

She seemed hesitant and then looked toward her front porch where her mom stood and waved. Charlie waved back.

"Come on, it will be fun."

"Okay. I have to go. Maybe I'll see you later."

"Be safe," he said.

"I don't know about any of you guys but I was thinking that happy hour and some barbeque wings at Carl's might be the place to go after work today," Matt teased.

"Oh yeah, some nice cold beers, a gorgeous blonde bartender to talk to. I'm there, man," Freddie added.

"Well good for you guys. I'm going home, taking a shower, and getting to bed early. I've been up since 4:00 a.m," Charlie yelled back then glanced at Lori who shook her head and chuckled as she got into the car.

The guys continued to try and get Dante, Trevor, and Charlie to join them but it was no use. They wanted to wait until tomorrow to see Lori and he wasn't sure how he'd handle the jealous feeling he already had about other men watching her and talking about her. He continued to ignore them, then went back to work, and after a while the others gave up.

Chapter 10

He watched her intently as she served the drinks and spoke respectfully to some drunken old-timer who continued to flirt with her. She was sweet and kind despite the disgusting way others around the bar looked at her, undressing her with their eyes. It angered him and that was how he knew she was the one for him. The job itself was never enough. He always craved more, desired more in order to complete him. It was like an addiction. The idea of a beautiful, naive young woman, barely used, refined, desirable and easy to capture made his life complete.

He'd done it so many times, she would be so easy to get to, to capture and take with him when his job here was done. She was the added bonus for staying in this Godforsaken county, the surprise pleasure he'd stumbled upon one very early morning only a few weeks ago. He would take enormous pleasure in having her, and knowing that so many others wanted her as well just made her even more desirable. His body ached for her as he continued to drink his beer and watch the way she worked and socialized. She had an amazing laugh, and an appealing smile. As if her eyes couldn't get even more mesmerizing, her now naturally tan skin caused them to appear even greener. She would be his. He promised this to himself as he finished the beer and left the bar.

* * * *

Charlie drove his classic 1939 hunter-green Ford pickup truck out of the garage and down the driveway. It was his prize possession and he only took it out for special occasions, car shows or summer Sunday drives. He slowly drove by the Cantrells' place where he saw Tom finishing up talking to some man in a business suit.

Tom didn't look too happy as the businessman entered the dark blue Lincoln town car.

Tom saw Charlie and waved him down.

"Hey, where are you going in this beauty? I love this truck of yours, Charlie," Tom told him as he stood by the passenger side window.

"I'm headed to Casper's."

"All alone?"

"Not exactly." Charlie looked away from Tom and toward the road.

"Oh…a date, huh? She must be someone special. Seeing how you're all spiffed up, clean shaven"—Tom sniffed the air as he leaned into the window a little—"nice cologne, your fancy truck. This is great, Charlie. How about Trevor and Dante? They going, too?"

Charlie couldn't help but smile at Old Man Cantrell. Others who didn't know him well thought he was a mean old bastard. Charlie and his family knew better. He was the best friend and neighbor anyone could ever ask for and he was always willing to help or give a hand.

"Yeah, they're coming along. She is very special. So who was that guy you were talking to? Someone else interested in your land?"

"Yeah, some business tycoon from Houston. He wants to build condominiums. If I'm going to sell this land, I want nice houses, developments for young people like you to start families, build up the community. Then maybe start some small businesses, a park, that kind of stuff."

"You have some great ideas, Tom. Why not just get together with an architect and builder and come up with something on your own. It could be your project, perhaps a hamlet of Valley Stream called Cantrell."

"You and your brothers have degrees in engineering and

architectural design. Why don't we all become partners and come up with something really great?"

"You don't want to do that, Tom. You said the whole point of selling was to not have to worry about making plans, working with architects, builders, and dealing with the bureaucracy and politics of the town. Even if we work together, we're going to have to do all that stuff. There's a lot to consider."

"I know, son, but it just seems that my land is grabbing the attention of the wrong types of buyers. You and your brothers, I would be willing to work with." Tom looked away from Charlie and stuck his hands into his pockets. Instantly Charlie knew something was wrong.

"What's wrong, Tom? Has someone been harassing you?"

"Nothing I can't handle, son. I just don't want anyone to get hurt and I feel that my hands are slowly being pulled behind my back. But no need for you to worry, you go have a good time with Lori," he told him with a smile.

Charlie laughed, knowing it was probably obvious to everyone that he and his brothers were interested in Lori.

"Listen I'm here for you, Tom, so how about when I get back later or tomorrow morning you tell me about things and maybe Dante, Trevor, you, and I can come up with some plans. I feel change is coming and just maybe I might be ready to do something different."

Charlie waved good-bye and Tom watched as he drove off in the classic truck.

* * * *

Lori was applying her lip gloss and looking at herself one more time in the mirror.

"You look beautiful, sis." Maggie sat on the edge of her sister's bed.

"Thanks, Maggie. What about my hair and this outfit?" Lori asked for the tenth time at least, and Maggie knew her sister really liked Dante, Trevor, and Charlie. They were perfect for her, and after Maggie interrogated Jasper about his cousins, Maggie felt they may be perfect for Lori. They were a lot more experienced than she was and Maggie hoped that the men would take things slow.

"I've told you a hundred times, Lori, you look great. The one-piece, sleeveless dress was the perfect outfit to wear. The black dress is so versatile. Plus it brings out your beautiful tan, and if the temperature drops, you have this nice light green sweater that brings out the green in your eyes. If they take you to a nice place for lunch, more than likely it will be air-conditioned. Just throw the sweater over your shoulders and tie it in the front like this." Maggie showed her the different styles she could get from the sweater alone.

"Thanks, Maggie, I appreciate your help. Am I all ready?"

"You sure are and you smell fantastic, too. That jasmine body cologne smells wonderful on you. It's not too much, just the slightest hint."

"As long as they're not allergic to jasmine. Oh man, maybe I should have just used some powder," Lori said rather nervously.

"Lori, stop it, everything is perfect, now you stay up here and I'll call you when Charlie comes. He should come to the door you know," Maggie teased as she left the room. Lori was just as nervous about her parents sitting on the porch right now like bodyguards. She had no idea that Jasper was out there as well.

Lori gave herself an approving smile in the mirror. Then she heard her sister call to her.

Charlie was already there.

* * * *

Lori walked out to the front porch where Charlie was talking to her father and Jasper about his truck. Dante and Trevor weren't in sight and her stomach clenched. Maybe they changed their minds.

Maybe they decided they didn't like her that much after all. She looked past him toward the truck parked up front. It was a gorgeous green color, a two-seater and Lori was surprised that it belonged to Charlie. She really didn't know that much about him but it was obvious that her heart and body didn't care. She was attracted to him and hoped things would only get better.

Jasper whistled as Lori walked onto the porch and everyone turned toward her. She was completely embarrassed as she felt her face turn red, her heart pound even faster, and a ball form in her throat. She could have killed Jasper for making the sound.

"You look beautiful, Aunt Lori," Ben told her as he gave her leg a hug. "And you smell great, too." Maggie called him over to her.

"Hi!" she said nervously as she stared at Charlie, who looked amazingly handsome. He was clean-shaven, wore a light blue button-down shirt and a pair of beige khakis. Instantly he was at the porch steps, gently taking her hand to escort her down the three steps. But his facial expression seemed strained. Maybe he didn't like the dress? Maybe it was too much for his friend's place they were going to?

"You looked gorgeous."

"So do you," she replied.

They said good-bye then headed toward the truck.

* * * *

"Now that was something else. I'm so glad I was here to witness that," Diana said as she smiled wide then sat back down in the rocker.

"You think she'll be all right?" Lou asked, and Diana smiled, nodding yes.

"That was incredible. Did you see the way they looked at one another? I've never seen anything like that before. If Trevor and Dante look at her in the same way, there's no way she won't be head over heels in love in no time," Maggie said as she spoke to Jasper.

"You've experienced it before though," he whispered to her, and she smiled, knowing exactly what he meant.

"You looked at me that way just the other day," he told her.

She was embarrassed at his directness. She had no right to get into a relationship with another man. She had Ben to worry about and he had gone through enough changes. Maggie getting involved with another man could be the worst thing for Ben right now.

Jasper took her hand into his and her parents watched, knowing that Maggie was hesitant.

"Go out with me, Maggie. Everything will be fine. Ben will be fine. I'm sure of it."

"Yeah, Mommy, you should go on a date with Jasper like Lori did with Charlie. You have a pretty dress you can wear." Ben stood between Maggie and Jasper. They both hugged Ben and Maggie had a feeling that just maybe things would be all right.

* * * *

Charlie still hadn't said a word. He didn't want her to feel uncomfortable as they pulled out of the long driveway and headed out of the neighborhood. He just couldn't seem to speak when all he wanted to do was pull her into his arms, inhale her heavenly perfume and kiss her deeply. He was shocked at the overwhelming need to touch her. But he needed to remain calm. He and his brothers decided that it may make Lori feel less overwhelmed if one of them picked her up at home. They wanted to ease her mind about getting involved in a ménage relationship and make her understand that it meant three men would share in taking care of her.

"You look incredible, Lori, absolutely amazing." He lightly squeezed her hand. When she looked up at him, her serious expression turned to a small smile. He had succeeded in breaking the ice. Good.

"Thank you, Charlie, and you look great as well. I love this truck. How long have you had it?"

"For a couple of years. It was a hunk of junk actually and sat in my garage for about a year. Then when I had some free time, I decided to fix her up." He left out the part about tearing it apart one night in a fit of anger over a series of terrible nightmares he had. He had met a woman, thought she was kind of special, but soon found out she wanted him for his money and good looks. He wasn't some stupid soldier who only knew about war and guns. Nor were Trevor and Dante. He got rid of her quickly, breaking things off and letting her know how spoiled and deceiving she was. It soured him even more.

He glanced at Lori. He prayed she wasn't pretending to be so innocent and sweet. It would send him over the edge.

"So is there anything original on it or did you completely restore it?" she asked him, and he wondered if she was really interested or just making nervous conversation.

"It has the original V-8 motor with a three-speed manual floor shifter in its original style and condition. I updated the interior with vinyl seats, a new headliner, and new rubber flooring. She's my prize possession."

"That's fantastic, Charlie, where did you learn about cars and trucks?"

"I started out working pumping gas when I was fourteen then watched the mechanics do oil changes, brake pads, and eventually full engine repairs. One of the guys, Johnny, Sheriff Morgan's cousin, worked on classic cars on the weekend for some big shot in the city. I used to hang out with the mechanic, and I guess I had a knack for it. By sixteen I was working as a mechanic and helping Johnny fix up these classic cars. I knew someday I'd have one." He headed onto the highway.

"My dad had a cousin they called 'Fast Freddie.' He was a nut, a real crazy guy," Lori told Charlie laughing. "He was always getting pulled over by the police, sustaining injuries from crazy stunts he did. I could tell you some stories about him. Anyway he owned a 1970 Plymouth 440 Barracuda."

"Wow. Those are nice, do you know if it was a 6-cylinder or what?"

"Originally it was but that wasn't good enough for 'Fast Freddie.' He did an extensive, full-body, rotisserie restoration and turned it into a 440 Big Block with a four-speed pistol grip. It was a gorgeous deep yellow color."

"It must have been a beauty. You sound like you actually like this kind of stuff."

"I do, I've always found it interesting. I was around it enough and I know from watching that it's not easy work to do. Plus the closer you keep the vehicle to its original condition the better it is. Restoring vehicles is an awesome hobby. You should be proud of yourself for having this truck."

"I am and I'm glad you like it and can appreciate my work." He smiled at her. She just kept amazing him the more they got to know one another. Conversing with her was getting easy, despite that little tug on his gut forewarning him to be careful.

Charlie was enjoying the ride to Casper's and Lori smelled wonderful. The fragrance was jasmine. He was sure of it, but it was light and clean smelling, not pungent.

"Ben was right. You do smell good."

"Thank you, I'm glad you like it," she told him then looked back out the window. Charlie was realizing more and more how wrong he was about Lori. She was shy, very ladylike, and proper as she sat in the passenger seat with her legs together, ankles crossed, and her hands atop one another on her lap.

"Ben's a great kid. My brother Andrew said all his son Andy does is talk about Ben. They get along well, and if Maggie sends him to the same school, they'll probably be in the same class."

"That's what Ben was telling Maggie and I. He likes your nephew Andy a lot, too. I'm glad to see him so happy."

"Your dad said the three of you were traveling a lot, where did you go?"

Charlie noticed Lori hesitate and start fiddling with her fingers. He had no idea why she was so secretive and now he was curious.

"We were all over the United States, but I'll tell you this much. I'm glad I'm back home with my parents and my mom's cooking. She's a great cook, you know? How about your mom? Does she cook all the time?" Lori asked. He got the hint that she wanted to change the subject. So he followed her lead.

"Yes, she cooks all the time. She taught me a lot about cooking. Maybe I'll make you dinner sometime," he offered with a smile as he searched the streets for a parking spot. The town was crowded and there were people everywhere. There were so many different tables and booths set up selling everything from homemade fudge to handmade jewelry. Dante mentioned there was a street fair going on as well.

"Trevor and Dante are meeting us here. I thought maybe you would feel more comfortable if just one of us showed up at your doorstep for our date."

"That was nice of you." She looked like she was going to say something but he saw Trevor waving him over toward an empty spot.

"There's Trevor over there!" Charlie stated as Lori looked toward an older man, Trevor, and Dante next to a row of classic cars. He moved two orange cones out of the way making room for Charlie's truck. People who were walking along the sidewalks stopped to check it out.

"Now that's service," Lori stated as Charlie gave her a proud smile.

"Every year the same spot and my good pal Al who owns the body shop right there. We've known one another for years," Charlie said as he got out of the truck and then went around toward Lori's side to open the door for her.

He held her hand, making it clear to her that he wasn't letting go of it as they stepped onto the sidewalk.

"Al, thanks a lot for the spot. This is Lori. Lori this is Al."

"It's a pleasure to meet you, miss." He nodded his head and Lori smiled in return. Charlie and Al exchanged pleasantries a few moments as people continued to walk by.

"You look beautiful, baby," Dante whispered, taking her into his arms and kissing her softly on the cheek. She shyly pulled back only for Trevor to approach. They looked so good. Trevor wore a dress shirt in black, dark jeans and cowboy boots with a matching black Stetson. Dante wore a black Stetson, too, but a royal blue button-down shirt and blue jeans. She glanced at Charlie and his dark green button-down shirt and jeans as he placed the black Stetson onto his head.

Three gorgeous, sexy cowboys stared at her.

"There's a band playing down by the water. You probably wouldn't have a chance of getting a seat near that place today for lunch," Al told them.

"Maybe we'll check it out anyway," Charlie said as they said good-bye and continued on their way.

The sidewalks were crowded as Charlie took Lori by the hand, moving closer to her and whispering about the stores they passed, which ones were new and which ones were old. He even told her a little bit about the building structures and the builders who created the expanding town. It was very interesting and obvious to her that he enjoyed talking about it.

"So how long have you liked architectural designing and building things?" she asked. Now it was Charlie who was caught off guard. He wasn't quite sure if he wanted to explain his life to Lori just yet.

"Well I have a degree in engineering and architectural design. I have my master's in business."

"Really? That's fantastic, Charlie, did you ever work in the field or what? Because I thought you and your brothers were in the service?"

"Trevor and Dante have their degrees in engineering and architectural design, too. When I got out of the service a few years back, I looked into working in the city for a bit, but things didn't work out well. I liked being around home more."

"And what about you, Dante?" Lori asked.

"The three of us like taking on smaller projects now. We built our house together," he said.

"That is amazing. Your parents must be very proud of all three of you."

Trevor took her hand and brought it up to his lips. He kissed her knuckles.

"I missed you," he whispered and she blushed as she shyly looked down.

They all continued to walk and look around. Charlie and his brothers paused a moment to observe a group of young soldiers in uniform enjoying the festivities. They were flirting with some girls and having a good time.

"They look like babies," Trevor said rather somberly.

"They sure do," Dante added.

"They won't look like that when they return home," Charlie added.

"No, they sure won't," Dante said.

"You sound like if you could tell them to not become soldiers you would," Lori stated.

"It's not all glory and excitement like the way it's portrayed on television or in the movies."

"It sure the hell isn't," Trevor whispered.

"You saw a lot of bad things while you guys were serving, huh?" Lori asked.

Dante took her hand and stared down into her eyes.

"Things we'd never talk about."

"Things you'd never understand," Charlie stated. She looked at him then continued to walk along. When she spoke, they all listened.

"Sometimes events happen in life that are out of our control. If a person can get over the shock of it all, believe that it was truly out of their control, then maybe, just maybe, they can move on, continue living again, and hopefully survive. It sounds like you guys did that," she told them softly as she continued to look straight ahead. Charlie stopped her by holding her arm and moving her next to a building they were passing. They were in a less crowded area of the fair and no one seemed to notice them by the building.

Lori looked up at Charlie who stood a good six inches above her. He still held her arm, then placed his free hand against her cheek.

"How do you know how we feel?" he asked her rather angrily.

"Maybe I get it. What's the big deal?"

He pressed her body snugly against the building. His brothers flanked her on either side.

Trevor touched her cheek and tilted her chin up toward him.

"You're too young, too innocent to get it."

She shook her head, making him release her chin.

"I'm not a kid like you keep calling me, Charlie. You don't know everything."

"I know that you get under my skin."

"And mine," Trevor added.

"Mine, too," Dante said, and then Charlie kissed her.

That kiss grew hot and heavy quickly.

She felt Charlie's hands move against her thigh and under her skirt. She knew they were in a little side alley and that Dante and Trevor blocked any onlooker's view, but it made her feel scared, yet entirely too turned on to analyze at the moment. Instead her complete attention was on Charlie's hands exploring her body as he made love to her mouth. She attempted to touch him back, letting her hands explore the ridges of hard muscle on his arms, his chest and then she felt his fingers against her panties. She pulled from his mouth. He pressed his body harder against hers. His breathing was just as rapid. She felt the thick finger press against her pussy despite the cotton panties she wore.

"Charlie."

"You're wet." He licked her neck and kissed her skin. She grabbed onto his shoulders, embarrassed by his observation. Surely they would know she was inexperienced and exactly what she was trying to prove she wasn't—a kid.

She pressed her hands against his chest.

"There are people around. Please stop."

She locked gazes with him. His eyes were dark and sexy. The vein by the side of his temple and eyes pulsated. She felt his thumb brush back and forth over her clit. She wanted to move, to squirm against his touch, to make him increase the pressure.

"Not here, not now, but later." He kissed her softly, slowly pulled his hands from under her skirt, and fixed the material.

She swallowed hard as all three men stared at her, appearing stunned and hungry.

"Take my hand. We'll walk the fair a little longer then head to Casper's. You'll like it there." Dante took her hand and led her out of the alley. She glanced over her shoulder at Trevor and Charlie. Charlie was running his fingers through his hair. She could see Trevor trying to calm him down and she wondered why he was so upset.

"I'm fine," he said, and Trevor turned back toward her and Dante. He smiled then nibbled his bottom lip as he stared at her backside. Dante pulled her over toward a group of vendors selling different items, but all she wanted to do was feel Charlie's hands on her. She wanted to feel the three of them touching her at once. That realization scared her as much as Charlie's show of aggression as he appeared angry and about to hit the building.

* * * *

Lori was having a good time at the fair. They walked past an older woman whose table contained handmade jewelry. That's where the most precious bracelet caught Lori's eye. It was gold with little tiny angel charms scattered between hanging half moons and stars. It was simple, elegant, and Lori wanted to buy it. She flipped the tag over and saw the price. Forty dollars. Her mouth dropped as the old lady helped others around them but kept an eye on Lori.

"I am the designer, my dear, and I believe that each piece I make is for someone special. That bracelet calls to you. It is dainty, ladylike, and beautiful as you are."

Lori said no thank you and began to walk away. Years on the run taught her to be wary of everyone. There was always some trick or a scam and it upset her to think that she liked the bracelet and the lady could see that and only cared about selling it. Lori felt that she really didn't need the bracelet. She just liked it and wanted it. She wasn't in any financial position to splurge like that. Saving would get her that college degree she wanted so badly.

* * * *

"Hey, Lori, you looked like you really wanted that bracelet. What's wrong?" Charlie asked her as he held her hand to stop her, but she pulled him along with her. She put a smile on her face pretending that it was no big deal. She didn't fool him, though. Something was on her mind.

"I didn't like it that much really. Plus there are so many other booths and tables around. Maybe I'll find something else. Look over there, snow cones. Do you like those?" she asked, instantly changing the subject. Charlie noted how good Lori was at that. He would make her see that she could trust him and didn't have to hide anything from him, especially her feelings.

"Are you kidding me? Who doesn't!" Dante said as they went over to the snow cone vendor and bought four.

An hour later the four of them headed over toward their friend Casper's place. It was a really nice bar and restaurant. Her mom mentioned that she and Dad knew the owners and had dined there every so often.

"This must be Lori," some tall man with a crew cut said as he reached out to shake her hand.

"I'm John Luke. I'm friends with your parents. They told my brothers and our wife that you and your sister were living with them. Welcome to Casper's."

She smiled, shook his hand, and hoped that her parents hadn't told them everything about her and Maggie.

Before long, the brothers came out along with their wife Eve. This was Lori's first real up-close observation of a ménage relationship until about thirty minutes later when a bunch of other rowdy cowboys came storming through the door. There was a loud "oorah" and then cheers and backslaps. Lori couldn't help but laugh at the way the men teased one another or how absolutely huge and macho they all were. She learned quickly that a few of the men were involved in ménage relationships and that Charlie, Trevor, and Dante hardly hung out here.

She felt the arm go around her waist. Then Dante was there smiling at her.

"Hey, take a look around at all the pictures. There are a bunch on the wall of John Luke and his brothers as well as their sons. You'll meet Gia and Marianna in a bit. Gia is engaged to Gunner, Garret, and Wes. You just met them and their fathers who own the place. Marianna is engaged to Jax and Jameson. Both of them are really nice."

"Okay. I'll look around." She headed toward the ladies' room first.

She absolutely loved the place. There were so many pictures of real-life soldiers, brothers, and friends posted everywhere. As she looked at some of the pictures of Charlie, Dante, and Trevor before they were in the service and out of high school, she noticed how young they were and how very handsome. She looked at more pictures and then one that looked like it was at Casper's. It didn't seem like it was from too long ago, and as she looked closer, she could see the difference in the men.

They looked drawn out, beyond exhausted and emotionless. Her emotions were caught in her throat as she realized this was a picture upon them returning from war. They almost appeared robotic or just hard, stiff, and angry. She glanced toward them now as they spoke with some friends.

They looked a bit better. But she could still see the blank stares Charlie, Trevor, and Dante had in their eyes when they watched her or when they first met.

A mix of emotions went through her mind. She feared that these men had experienced things that made them close up their hearts and remain distant. Those weren't the type of men she wanted to be with. They would be cold to her. They would never truly open up to her and would probably make excuses when she asked them to. *But haven't I been doing the same thing? I avoid any conversations about the past, about my broken wrist, and about how I killed another human being.*

She felt like crying and forced herself to move on to the other pictures. She wouldn't make them feel uncomfortable or ruin the date they were on. Perhaps staying away from them would be best after today.

"Lori?"

Lori turned around to see Eve, John Luke's wife, standing there. She smiled softly and appeared very motherly.

"Your mom and dad told me so much about you, Maggie, and Ben. I was so happy to hear that you got home safely."

Lori must have appeared surprised because Eve looked around then whispered to her. "Don't worry, my husbands and I wouldn't say a word. I just want you to know that you're welcome here any time you'd like to stop by. I've been trying to get your mom to come shopping with me in Houston but she's kind of adamant about it."

"I'm sure she would love that. I mean, now that my sister and I are around to help in the house."

Eve smiled.

"I will call her next week and set something up."

"Excuse me, Eve, could I steal Lori from you?" Dante asked, and Eve smiled.

"Of course, Dante. So nice to see you, Trevor, and Charlie here. You should come in more often. And bring Lori, too." Eve winked then walked away.

Lori looked up into Dante's hazel eyes. She absorbed the way his dress shirt sat snug against his chest. She knew from seeing him doing construction work that he had a great chest. It was filled with muscles, and he even had a series of tattoos. She wondered what meaning that had for him considering how much getting tattoos hurt. But then she reminded herself that after today, it may be best to keep her distance.

"Come on, Trevor grabbed a table in the back. We can have some privacy and enjoy one another's company," Dante said. That was when she noticed that Charlie wasn't there.

As they headed into the other room with Dante's hand against her lower back, she noticed the many people in the dining area and how some stared at them and smiled.

"Where's Charlie?" she asked.

"He got a phone call. He'll be back," Trevor said as she sat down next to him. Dante took the chair beside her, leaving room for Charlie.

They were looking over the menu when she felt Trevor's hand smooth over her knee. She jerked a moment then turned to look at him. She couldn't help but to remember the sunken look on his face in the picture and the lines of age or stress that now shown near his eyes. He didn't look as spent, but she could still see the sadness. She nibbled her bottom lip.

"See anything you like?" He squeezed her knee.

She tried not to be so affected by him, but it was hard.

"Let her look at the menu, Trevor," Dante whispered then nudged her arm.

"Do you know what you want, Dante?" she asked, trying to steer clear of Trevor's megaflirtatious techniques.

Dante leaned closer. "Yeah, sweetheart, but you're not on this menu."

Oh God.

She felt her pussy leak. Thank goodness the waitress returned with the drinks Garret had sent over from the bar.

Dante and Trevor raised the two beers and Garret waved back.

"Is a beer okay?" Trevor asked.

"Sure. I like beer."

"A woman after my own heart," Trevor stated, and then Charlie returned.

She felt that jolt of happiness at seeing him again. It was then that she realized she did care for these three men together as much as individually. The more her heart, her body, and mind reacted to them and to her emotions, the more confused she got.

* * * *

They waited for their food to arrive and talked about the apartment her father had them building.

"So, you're sure about moving out there alone?" Dante asked her.

"I wasn't expecting that when Maggie, Ben, and I arrived home. I'm kind of looking forward to having my own place."

"How come Maggie and Ben wouldn't take it? There's going to be two bedrooms in there?" Dante asked.

"She didn't want to. She likes being back home with my mom and dad nearby. I guess she feels safer."

Dante looked at Charlie, who now leaned back in his chair and played with the rim of his beer bottle.

"Being in your own place is quite the responsibility. You know with everything going on around the area lately, it might be better to hold off on moving in there."

"I can handle it, Charlie. I'll lock all the doors before I go to bed at night." Dante watched Charlie and Lori staring at one another and he didn't want them arguing again. Charlie was so stubborn and bossy. They were used to it, but Lori was tough and independent. He decided to change the subject.

"So did you register completely for college yet?" he asked her, knowing how determined she was to achieve her college degree.

"Yes I did, and I signed up for some online courses, too. Thanks to busy nights at the bar I pretty much have the first semester paid for. I've asked the other bartenders to call me first if they need a night covered. Even if they need a day covered, I'll do it. College is expensive." Lori took a sip from her mug of beer. The waitress brought it over when she brought over the round of beer bottles from the bar.

"It sure is but once you have a college degree, no one can ever take that away from you. So you think you'll stay working at Carl's for a while?" Charlie asked, and she knew he didn't like her working there. That had become obvious.

Lori folded her hands on her lap then locked gazes with Charlie.

"Charlie, I have no choice. Bartending brings in good money. I can't hold off going to college. I've waited so long for this."

"I realize that, I do, it's just that damn uniform, the guys talking about you. That night when the drunk guy came over to you at the table, what if we weren't there, or what if he followed you out to your car?" He reached across the table for her hand. She raised one up and placed her hand into his. He had such big hands and her hand felt so delicate and feminine in his. Trevor placed his hand on her knee under the table and Dante placed his arm over her chair and she felt his fingers on her shoulder.

"We don't like it," Trevor said.

"We could help you find something better. We know a lot of people," Dante replied.

She shook her head. "I've worked at worse places than Carl's, guys. I've always taken the extra precautions. Didn't you see me with Gus? I asked him to walk me to my car that night because of that guy.

I can take care of myself. I have no choice. Sure, my parents could probably help me out a little but why should they? You know I've been taking care of myself, Maggie, and Ben. They've been my responsibility. Everything I've earned has gone into keeping the three of us safe, fed, clothed, the basics. Now we're all back home where we belong and I can start to focus on myself a little. For me to achieve this on my own will be more than just a college degree. It will mean that all the sacrifices I've had to make over the years, all the steps backward, all the putting my family before me, will mean something even more."

"My God, Charlie, can you just imagine how I'll feel when I walk up to the dean of the college and receive my degree?" she asked, looking away from him as if imagining the moment. It was obvious she was determined to achieve that goal.

"You'll do it, Lori, I know you'll do it and if you need any help with your classes, you just let me know." He squeezed her hand. Trevor and Dante nodded their heads in agreement as the waitress brought over their food.

They ate and talked about the area and about Mr. Cantrell. Dinner was great and soon they were sitting back waiting for coffee and dessert.

"So Tom wants to talk to us about partnering up?" Dante asked.

"Yeah, he has some concerns. I think some business guy stopped by his place pushing for him to sell. He looked pissed off when I left this afternoon."

"I hope we're wrong about the dead animals being left behind," Dante said.

"What do you mean? You think someone is trying to get Mr. Cantrell to sell his property by threatening him?" Lori asked.

Charlie, Trevor, and Dante looked at one another.

Charlie spoke first.

"I have my suspicions and if Tom wants us to be partners, then I think it could keep him and his wife safe."

"Charlie, maybe you should talk to J.R. about this. He seems knowledgeable."

"We don't need his help," Charlie snapped at her and she looked away from him.

The waitress returned, bringing over four small cups of fresh espresso and four glasses of sambuca. Along with the coffees were a dish of plump, fresh red strawberries, a bowl of whipped cream, and a small dish containing a pink satin pouch, which Charlie removed immediately.

The waitress asked if they needed anything else then left.

Dante took a strawberry and brought it to Lori's lips. She blushed, making his cock instantly hard.

"Open, baby," he whispered, and she did, taking a small bite of berry into her mouth.

Dante knew that his brothers watched him feed Lori the strawberry. He was aroused and so very attracted to her, he didn't think he could slow things down the way she needed. It was insane, but he felt so much for her. This date was lasting long and he didn't want her out of his sight. He was trying not to be demanding or to come across as if he was ordering her to do what he wanted to do. He saw her response to Charlie's demands and bossy tone.

"Let's get out of here," Trevor stated and Dante, Charlie, and Lori agreed.

They paid the bill and said their good-byes as they exited Casper's. The evening was beautiful and Lori shivered as they made their way back to the truck.

Before they reached Charlie's truck, the men stopped her.

"Are you cold, baby?" Trevor asked then pulled her into his arms. She laid her face against his chest, feeling the muscles beneath her cheek. He smelled so good. His cologne was fresh like soap and outdoors. She inhaled, instantly feeling protected and warm. Trevor rubbed her arms and Dante rubbed her back.

"Better?" Trevor asked, and she nodded her head.

"Let's sit over here a minute," Charlie told them as they walked toward the truck. He pulled down the back lift gate and then Trevor lifted Lori up and placed her gently onto the back. Dante was tall enough to lean right back and so was Trevor as he took position on either side of her. She crossed her legs and Charlie moved closer. He stared at her eyes and she smiled softly, wondering why he was being so serious and also if he would say something to challenge her or to get angry with her about.

"If I haven't told you, you look stunning tonight, Lori, absolutely beautiful. I hope you're having a good time," Charlie said.

She was shocked by his sincerity. It looked like it took a lot for him to reveal his emotions. "I am, Charlie. Spending time with the three of you and visiting with your friends has been nice."

"We're enjoying spending time with you, too, Lori," Dante said.

"And showing you off to all our friends. You're going to get to know them and they'll be your friends soon, too."

"Dante, I'm not sure—"

"I wanted to get you something to remember today and tonight," Charlie told her.

"Charlie, you really didn't have to do that. I'll remember today and tonight, you can count on that." She touched his cheek with the palm of her hand. His skin felt rough with tiny whiskers like she imagined. She looked toward Dante and Trevor. They placed their hands on her leg.

* * * *

Charlie loved her sincerity, her gentleness. She wasn't fake, and she wasn't pretending. He was sure of it as he handed her the satin pouch. She opened it, saw the charm bracelet she had fallen in love with earlier, and a tear escaped her eye. Her lips quivered and her hands were shaking as she held her head down, not wanting to reveal her emotions to them. Instantly he took her hands into his, opening up the bracelet clasp and placing it around Lori's wrist.

"Do you like it?" he asked as he lifted her chin with his hand.

She had tears in her eyes as she pulled Charlie toward her, hugging him. "I love it," she whispered, and at that moment he knew he loved her.

She said thank you to Dante and Trevor, and Charlie chuckled to himself. They hadn't a clue what he left for a few minutes earlier. He just felt compelled to get Lori that bracelet she fell in love with. She was determined to take care of herself and provide for herself, but he wanted her to see that this relationship between the four of them would be different. They would rely on one another. They could lean on one another and share in any burdens or concerns. So badly he wanted to tell Lori to quit the bar, let him and his brothers pay for her college and take care of her. But Dante and Trevor agreed, that move would make Lori run from them.

They all had a lot to learn about opening up their hearts and sharing their emotions. He was the worst at doing that, but Lori seemed to have the ability to make him share his feelings. She was special, and he would do anything to protect her and take away the fear and uncertainty in her eyes. Anything.

* * * *

Charlie pulled the truck alongside the roadway as Dante and Trevor pulled their truck behind him. They met them by the dark wooded pathway and Dante placed a light jacket over her shoulders. It smelled like his cologne and she pulled it snugly against her.

"Where are we?" she asked them.

"We're not far from our place. There's this beautiful stream and waterfall we want to show you. On a night like tonight with the moon so bright, it's too perfect to not share with you," Dante told her and she took his hand.

As they led her through a winding path, the sounds of flowing water filled her ears. Just as she followed Trevor and Charlie into the clearing, the stream and cascading waterfall came into view. It wasn't a traditional-looking waterfall, but instead it was one set in multiple tiers of rocks, the highest at least twenty feet or more that descended into the water below.

"It's beautiful," she whispered in awe.

Dante wrapped his arms around her from behind and they stared at the flowing water and the way the moonlight cast its glow over it.

"You were right about the moonlight, Charlie, good call," Trevor said.

Dante began to kiss along her neck and shoulder, pushing the jacket away from her skin to gain better access.

She loved the way his strong arms felt wrapped around her and how soft and gentle his kisses were.

"You're so beautiful, Lori."

She felt the arm that was around her waist move higher and then he kissed the corner of her mouth. She turned into the kiss and in doing so gave him complete access to her breasts. Dante cupped one as he plunged his tongue between her lips.

She moaned into his mouth and held him tighter as he continued to explore her mouth.

When the second set of hands landed on her shoulders, she tightened up as Dante slowly released her lips.

"Easy, baby, it's just me," Trevor whispered then kissed her shoulder and then her neck as he maneuvered his hand under her hair.

Dante brushed his finger across her nipple and despite the fact that she was fully clothed, she felt it entirely too much.

"Dante, please."

But Trevor turned her head so he could kiss her now as Dante released his hold and allowed Trevor his chance at kissing her.

Trevor was a lot wilder and hungrier with his kisses. He stroked his tongue into her mouth, and they battled for control until his hand moved up her dress and gripped her hip bone.

She pressed her hands against his hard chest and he gripped her hip tighter, pulling her against his body. She felt his hard erection and knew that this was going too far too quickly. It was merely a first date.

He must have read her body as she tensed up because he slowly released her lips, and Charlie was there, pulling her into his arms and hugging her tight.

As she ran her hands up his chest to his collar, he stared down into her eyes and looked dangerous. She wasn't stupid. The man was a lethal weapon in all aspects of the words. He lifted her up and took three steps forward until she felt the boulder under her feet. Placing her feet on there, he squeezed her tighter as he began kissing along her neck and shoulder.

"I need a little more, sugar. Just a little something." She didn't know what he meant but she wanted to give it to him. He was sexy, hard, and turned her on to the point that her pussy actually ached for his touch. As if he read her mind, he kissed her on the mouth as she felt his hands move under her dress.

His kisses grew deeper as he made love to her mouth and she held on to his shoulders. When his hand moved between her thighs and against her wet panties, she jerked from his mouth.

"Oh God, Charlie, we have to stop."

He looked so intense and needy. She was in the woods, in the dark, with three well-trained military men. She should be running for the truck not ready to give them anything they wanted.

"It won't go too far. I promise, just a little something." He moved his fingers under her panties and pressed them to her pussy lips.

Lori tried to hide her gasp as she parted her lips, letting his tongue swirl deeper into her mouth, and squeezed his shoulders.

"Relax, baby. Let him in." Trevor moved his hand along her thigh and under her dress. He lifted it up against Charlie's waist as Charlie thrust two fingers into her.

"Charlie." She moaned his name and closed her eyes until she felt

Dante pressing his large palm under her dress, too. She felt her body shaking. She was so turned on right now, she wasn't sure what was right or wrong. Dante and Trevor were massaging her ass cheeks, kneading her flesh as their knuckles made contact with her cunt and her anus. Charlie continued to plunge his fingers in and out of her. She was overly aroused.

"Look at me," Charlie stated. When she opened her eyes and absorbed the feel of these three hard, sexy, big men fondling her with the intense expression in Charlie's face, she shook and came hard. Her legs felt like they were giving out but the men caught her, caressed her, then kissed her wherever they could. As Charlie's fingers left her body she felt a mix of emotions. She felt empty again and scared to not experience the feelings they gave her, loving her this way together. She worried that this type of relationship was a farce and might not truly last the test of time. And she felt relieved to finally be touched intimately by men she cared for instead of just doing it to get it over with.

Charlie hugged her then grabbed her face between his hands and stared down into her eyes.

"Going slow is going to be torture, woman. Pure fucking torture." He covered her mouth before she could respond and kissed her.

When he released her, it was to Trevor who kissed her with just as much passion as his hands explored under her dress and then to her breasts.

"You feel real nice, sugar. All the right curves in all the right places," he whispered flirtatiously then allowed Dante to take his place.

Dante kissed her then lifted her up into his arms and carried her all the way to the truck.

She held on to his shoulders and nuzzled her face against his neck, absorbing his cologne. She wondered, too, how she was going to make this go slow when all her body wanted right now was fast, fast, fast.

Chapter 11

The guys were all working on the house this morning, placing the Sheetrock against the walls in the area that would be the bedroom. Lou was talking to Charlie about finishing off the rest of the barn.

"I was thinking about turning the whole place into a small house for Lori. Maybe we can take this whole area here and create a large living space, then possibly a living room area over here and a fireplace over there, then a big kitchen. She loves to cook and bake when she has the time. What do you think, Charlie?" Lou asked. "Can we do it, the plumbing and electrical work and all? I'll pay you guys for your time, too."

Charlie was sure they could do it. "Yeah, it would take some time but I think it would work."

"Great, she'll love it. You know, Charlie, she's sacrificed a lot for her family. This is the least I could do considering she won't accept any financial help from her mother and I. I want it to be perfect." Charlie went back to working on the bedroom while Freddie and Jasper continued to work on the plumbing and electrical work.

"How was the date last night?" Matt asked Charlie, Dante, and Trevor as they worked.

"Went good, I think she had a good time," Charlie said.

"I think it went great, too," Trevor added.

"So tell me what happened? Did conversation flow comfortably? Did you take her to a nice place?" Matt was truly interested as Trevor told him a little about the date.

"I'm glad it went well, guys."

"To be honest with you, the more I get to know her the more she surprises me. I was so wrong about her. She's special, you know what I mean?" Dante asked as he looked at Matt.

"I know exactly what you mean. That's how I see Janie. I love her more than anything and I can't wait until we're married."

Charlie smiled at Matt knowing that Janie was a great woman and perfect for Matt.

* * * *

Lori headed out of the pharmacy in town and nearly knocked into Dr. Andrew Henley.

"Hey, Doc, how are you?" she asked him as they moved to the side of the walkway.

"I'm doing good, how are you, and how's your wrist?" She looked really cheerful today and he was glad.

"It's fine, no complaints."

"How did your date go with my brothers yesterday?"

She blushed a little at his bluntness then answered. "Very nice, I suppose a lot of people know we went out?"

"Hearts are breaking all around town."

"Well, your brothers are very attractive and have a lot to offer any woman."

"I meant over you."

"That's nice of you, Doc."

"I know that they're my brothers, but I'm just telling it the way it is. I hope it works out."

"How are Michelle and the kids? Maggie said she was getting together with them today, for the kids to play."

"They're doing great. Andy loves playing with Ben. Ben's a good kid. You and Maggie have done a great job."

Lori smiled wide. She was proud of Ben and the fact that he truly was such a well-behaved kid. There wasn't a mean streak in him and she hoped he stayed that way.

"So I hear my cousin Jasper has a date with your sister tonight."

"You heard right. Can I ask you honestly, Doc, what kind of a man is Jasper? He seems kind of quiet. I see him come into the bar on the weekends." She didn't want to sound like some overconcerned parent but she worried about her sister. Maggie didn't need anyone with baggage or the potential to hurt her.

Andrew seemed to have read her mind and immediately attempted to put Lori at ease.

"Your sister will be in good hands, Lori. Jasper is a nice guy, never been married, he's not a drunk if that's a concern. As a matter of fact I don't think I've ever seen him smashed," Andrew said with a smile as they sat down on the bench outside of his office.

Lori released a sigh of relief.

"You know I understand your concern and realize that not everyone knows what happened to you, Ben, and Maggie. I can honestly say don't worry about Jasper. He'd never hurt her, he likes her a lot and he's made that clear. You know Maggie already told him about Ben's father and the way things went down."

Lori was surprised and concerned that now Jasper would tell Charlie.

"Lori, you have nothing to be ashamed of. You haven't told my brothers yet, have you?"

"No, I…I guess…I guess I'm just scared to. You're gonna have a field day with this one, Doc, but if I talk about it, say what I'm feeling out loud, it hurts too much. All the fear, the secrecy, the pain reemerges."

"I can understand that, Lori. You've had to take care of Ben and Maggie for so long, and focus on only them, that you don't know how to think about yourself and what you might need. You can trust Charlie, Trevor, and Dante. They're in love with you."

Lori was shocked by Andrew's words. Was that what she was feeling? Love? She knew she had to tell Dante, Trevor, and Charlie everything that happened in order for their relationship to continue but she didn't want the drama. She didn't want them to feel sorry for her.

"Isn't love amazing? It can lift your spirits higher than anything in the whole world. Confide in them, Lori. You can trust my brothers. Believe me they won't hurt you. They know what it feels like. They can understand what you're going through and you may be able to help them as much as they can help you."

"I know they do. Michelle told me about how much they changed after returning from the service. I saw a picture of them before they left and then when they first returned. I could see the pain, the sadness, and the dullness in their eyes. I want to help them to feel happy."

Andrew smiled at her.

"They probably want to do the same for you, too."

"You know, Doc, besides offering your basic, general family physician stuff you should also offer some private counseling on the side. You're good at it, easy to talk to, and don't sound condescending, or like a know-it-all. You sincerely want to help and I appreciate that. Sometimes doctors get all caught up in being busy, showing little empathy for their patients and so on. You don't do that, and you need not change a single thing. Thanks."

Lori gave him a kiss on the cheek and rose from the bench. They said good-bye and Andrew watched as Lori walked away.

He took out his cell phone and called his wife Michelle. She was outside on the porch with Maggie having some iced teas as the kids played on the jungle gym.

"Oh hi, Andrew, how was lunch?" Michelle asked.

"Great, I just wanted to call you and tell you I love you."

"I love you, too, sweetheart. What brought this on?"

"Lori Shay, that's who. She's an amazing person, Michelle, and I hope things work out between her and my brothers." He then told her a little bit about their conversation.

"Here I was trying to encourage her, and she encouraged me,

lifted my spirits, made me see how lucky and how blessed I am. Tell Maggie her sister is amazing, will you?"

"I will, I love you, good-bye," Michelle said.

* * * *

"Hey, Charlie, Mr. Cantrell is down here looking for you." Freddie yelled up to them and Charlie headed down the stairs.

Charlie walked out of the barn and headed toward Tom and Lou who were talking by his pickup truck.

"Morning, Charlie. You guys are doing a great job on the place."

"Thanks, Tom, how's everything going?" Charlie asked as Lou excused himself and went back to working on the house.

"Pretty good, listen, about what we talked about yesterday. I ran everything by the wife and she thought it sounded like a great idea. If you were willing to become legal partners with me, invest your money in this land, maybe together we could build that community I was talking about. I'm serious, Charlie, what do you think?"

Charlie wasn't sure what to do. "I don't know, Tom, it's a big responsibility. Dante and Trevor are willing to assist because it's a lot to handle and I'm not sure. Can you give me a few days?" Charlie asked.

"Sure, son, take your time. I know it's asking a lot but I think we could do it. Let me know, all right?" Tom said then Lori pulled up in her car.

"How did the date go last night?" Tom whispered to Charlie.

"Good, I think," Charlie responded, laughing a little at how everyone was acting.

"Hi, Mr. Cantrell, Charlie," Lori said as she got out of the car. She had her long blonde hair pulled back in a low ponytail, and was wearing a short pumice skirt with a light blue, spaghetti strap top. Charlie thought she looked beautiful as usual. He couldn't stop thinking about her, nor could Dante and Trevor. Trevor stated this morning over breakfast how he couldn't wait to wake up with Lori in his arms. That comment got the three of them going onto a major discussion about pushing a little harder for this relationship to move along. Lori seemed resistant. Was there deeper meaning behind it? He wondered, remembering Trevor's concerns.

"She hasn't told us anything about her past, just that she worked at a lot of places," Trevor said.

"She said worse places than Carl's. I'm personally not liking that," Dante added.

"She's shy and more often than not I catch her deep in thought and she looks sad. What could a woman as young and lovely as Lori be sad about?" Charlie told his brothers.

"Her eyes light up when we're around her. My whole body ignites the moment she comes into view. I can feel it in my heart, and deep in my soul. She's special and I want her in our bed, and in our home. This isn't temporary for me," Trevor added.

"I agree. She belongs to us. We have to be honest and tell her what we want and how much we adore her already," Trevor said, very seriously.

Charlie had stared at his two brothers, worried that he couldn't love her the way she needed. *What do I know about love, or about providing for a woman as special as Lori?*

* * * *

Lori eyed Charlie and her spirits lifted at the sight of him. He looked rugged and macho with his unshaven face, blue T-shirt, and loose-fitting blue jeans even though they were covered with white Sheetrock dust. As if reading her mind, he dusted off his shirt and pants unaware of the smile they both received from Tom Cantrell.

Lori pulled out two large grocery bags along with her purse and Charlie walked over to help her.

"I'll talk to you soon, Charlie. I have to get going. Good seeing you, Lori." Tom got back into his truck.

"Let me help you with those." Charlie took one of the bags from Lori.

"Thank you. You guys are Sheetrocking the bedroom already?" she asked as he followed her to the house porch steps.

"Yeah, it's pretty dusty up there. What are you up to?" he asked her as he placed the grocery bag down on the porch floor. Diana Shay came to the door to retrieve the bags, saying hello to Charlie then walking back inside.

"I had to go to the store, I saw your brother Andrew in town. He's a really great guy."

"He's married you know?" Charlie said, joking around as he took Lori's hand.

"I know that, Charlie, I just meant that nice guys run in your family."

"That's safe to say."

"How about Jasper, is your cousin like you and your brothers?"

"Jasper's a good guy, why do you ask?"

"He's going on a date with Maggie tonight."

"Really, he didn't mention that? You sound concerned, baby."

She loved the way he called her baby. She smiled as he took a step closer to her.

"He's a good man. Your sister will be safe on a date with him. Speaking of dates, how about the four of us go on another one? If it's not too short of a notice, how about tonight?" he asked as he gently tugged on her ponytail. She giggled at the gesture and he smiled.

"I kind of said I would keep an eye on Ben with my parents."

"We could go for ice cream after dinner and take Ben with us."

"That sounds good, Charlie, then you can drop him back off to me and the four of you could go out alone," Diana said as she stood by the porch door. Both Charlie and Lori hadn't even heard her approach. They were so caught up in each other.

"Well there's your answer." Lori looked at him then back toward the empty porch doorway where her mother stood only moments ago. Now she was gone.

"I'll call you later." He kissed her on the cheek and went back toward the barn.

* * * *

Charlie, Dante, Trevor, and Matt headed home after work, and on their way past their parents' house they saw their father waving them down.

"Hey, Dad, what's going on?" Charlie asked from the passenger side of Matt's pickup truck.

"Your mom wants to know if you guys are coming to dinner or not. Andrew, Michelle, and the kids are coming, too."

"Yeah that sounds good," Matt said. "I don't know about these guys though. I think they have another date tonight."

Charlie shot him a look.

"Oh really?" Phil asked, sounding curious.

"Yeah but not until later. We'll be there," Charlie said and Matt headed over to Charlie's place to drop them off.

An hour later Charlie, Dante, and Trevor arrived at their parents' house where Andrew, Matt, and the others were sitting on the front porch enjoying some cold beers.

"There they are," Andrew said as Trevor, Dante, and Charlie walked onto the porch to join everyone.

"You guys are working hard at Lou's place. Can't wait to see it." Phil handed his sons a beer each.

"Yeah it's coming along nicely. Lou's daughter should be pleased with it," Charlie said as he leaned against the porch railing and peeked out toward the yard where his niece and nephew were playing.

"Lou's daughter? You mean Lori, don't you? There's no need to hide it, brother. Everyone here knows you three went out on a date with her last night," Matt said and the others started laughing.

"What do you mean everyone knows?" Charlie asked kind of on the defensive.

"The whole town basically. I told Lori earlier today that hearts were breaking," Andrew added.

"You're not kidding," Jasper said as he approached the entrance to the porch. Everyone started whistling and hollering at how good he looked all cleaned up for his date with Maggie.

"You look fantastic, Jasper," Michelle said as she held Andrew's arm.

"Thanks, what do you think about the flowers? Too much?" he asked very seriously.

"She'll love them, son," Phil told his nephew as he patted him on the shoulder. Jasper said good-bye and off he went to pick up Maggie.

Michelle and Terry started setting the table on the enclosed screened porch.

"So I guess it's safe to assume that things went well with Lori the other night?" Andrew asked as he stood next to Charlie, Dante, and Trevor.

"Yeah, things went well," Trevor said then took a slug of beer.

"Good, she's a great woman," Andrew stated.

"She's a knockout!" Matt added as he joined his brothers.

Phil just listened as he sat down on one of the large green cushioned chairs.

"You're engaged, Matt, remember?" Andrew teased and Matt laughed.

"A woman as perfect as that can make a man stray."

"Mathew David Henley, what would Janie think about that?" Phil asked his son and Charlie, Dante, Trevor, and Andrew laughed.

"Janie knows I tell it the way it is. I do it all the time at the newspaper," Matt stated as he took a sip of his beer.

"That's why they haven't let you write anything lately. You've caused so much trouble around there," Andrew said and they all laughed.

"Matt could be onto something. I haven't seen you three clean shaven and smiling in a long time," Phil added, and both Matt and Andrew agreed.

"Seriously, guys, she's special. I do like her a lot. Most people do the second she starts to talk to them. Carl swears business at his place has doubled since Lori started working there," Matt told them.

"She's a caring person that's why. I bumped into Jay Carton the other day and he said that when Lori works the late shift she gives his old man Patch, a ride home so he doesn't try to drive himself," Andrew told them.

"See what I mean. She's a good person," Matt added.

"I tell you just this afternoon I bumped into Lori in town and we sat down outside my office," Andrew began to say.

"Yeah, he had lunch with Lori and called me telling me how much he loves me and how blessed he is to have me and the kids in his life," Michelle interrupted as she started placing food on the table.

"What did you think, Michelle, that he cheated on you?" Matt teased.

"No, I've gotten to know Lori pretty well and she's a very unselfish person. She's a strong, independent, extremely intelligent person. To survive the ordeal she and Maggie and Ben went through, forget it, I would have never been able to." Michelle left the room to retrieve the remainder of the meal.

"What is she talking about?" Matt and Dante asked at the same time.

"Lori and Maggie were on the run for the past five years. They had to escape from Ben's father. He was abusive," Andrew stated. Charlie, Trevor, and Dante were in shock. Michelle and Terry entered the room.

"Lori worked day and night to support her sister and the baby. Diana said she worked in some real bad places and sometimes slept in that car of hers for months at a time," Terry added as she began to serve the meal.

"Oh my God. We had no idea," Trevor said.

Charlie was in shock. He, too, had no idea that Lori had experienced any of this. "Weren't the police involved?"

"Apparently from what Lou and Diana told us, Ben's father came from a well-known family in the community. It wasn't until he assaulted another young woman, then killed a man outside a bar that the police were after him," Phil told them.

"Diana told me she wanted her daughters to call the police since Ben's father was a fugitive, but the girls feared that his family would blame them for their son's mistakes and try to convince a court to give them custody of Ben. Lori and Maggie stayed in hiding until that dreadful night." Terry sighed and held her hand against her chest.

"What happened?" Dante asked.

"Andrew, you received her medical files and spoke to the doctor Lori saw. How exactly did it happen?" Terry asked her son.

"I don't think it's really my place to tell her story. When Lori's ready, I'm sure she'll share it with you." Andrew took a deep breath and released it as if the thought of what happened to her really bothered him.

"She saved Maggie's and Ben's lives," Michelle said. "Maggie's ex-boyfriend broke into the house they rented and attacked Maggie and Ben. He was going to kill Maggie and Lori intervened. He had a gun and planned on killing them both then taking Ben away. Lori got the gun away from the ex-boyfriend, yelled for Ben to run since she had called the police already, and saved him. During the struggle, Maggie escaped and Lori shot the ex-boyfriend. That's how she broke her wrist. Then apparently he resisted arrest, grabbed a weapon prepared to shoot at Lori and the police, and the police shot him, killing him."

"I can't believe this." Charlie leaned back in his chair.

"When Lori does tell you guys, which I'm sure she will, I wouldn't be surprised if she minimizes her actions. She doesn't really want anyone to know. She doesn't want to be seen as a hero," Andrew told them just as little Andy and his sister Kerry came running onto the porch.

"We washed our hands!" Andy yelled and Kelly repeated her big brother as they showed their parents their hands for approval then sat down at the table. Naturally the conversation ended.

"I can't believe what we just heard in there," Trevor said as he ran his hand through his hair.

"I'm in shock, too. They must have been scared out of their minds, and poor Ben had to experience that," Dante added.

"Andrew said that Lori struggled for the gun and shot Ben's father. She took care of her sister and Ben as if they were her children and she's younger, only twenty-one. That's fucking crazy." Trevor began to pace.

"Calm down. We need to think about what we're going to do. I want to see Lori right now. Not in an hour, but right now," Dante said.

"No," Charlie stated and both Dante and Trevor looked at him. He hadn't said a word and Trevor wondered if Charlie even felt as strongly for Lori as he and Dante did? Would that man ever open his heart to take a chance?

"What the hell do you mean, no?" Dante asked.

Charlie looked as if he were biting the inside of his cheek. His arms were crossed in front of his chest, making him appear tough and dead serious.

"We're not supposed to know what happened to Lori, Maggie, and Ben. We need to make her feel safe and comfortable enough to tell us," Charlie stated.

"God, I just want to hold her. I wish she hadn't experienced that type of violence and trauma," Trevor whispered.

"She's amazing. She's tough, independent, and gorgeous. She's everything and more than we ever talked about wanting in a woman. I mean, she's perfect for each of us," Dante replied and they nodded in agreement.

"So, we need to keep this information to ourselves and tread carefully. When Lori feels safe, she'll confide in us," Charlie said and they agreed.

* * * *

The evening was beautiful and Jasper showed up around five thirty to pick up Maggie for their date. He wore a nice pair of navy blue Dockers, a matching button-down shirt, and some dress shoes. He brought along a bright, colorful bouquet of assorted flowers.

Maggie emerged wearing a pale pink one-piece, snug-fitting sleeveless dress and carried a matching shawl with her.

Jasper's eyes widened at the sight of her and both Lori and her parents were happy to have witnessed the attraction between Maggie and Jasper. Lori wondered if that was what she'd looked like when Charlie came to get her the other night.

"You look stunning, Maggie. That color looks great on you." Jasper handed her the bouquet of flowers.

"Thank you, Jasper, you look great as well and thank you for the flowers. They're beautiful," she told him as she smelled them.

"Why don't I put those in some water and you two get going?" Lori said as Maggie passed her the colorful bouquet.

"You be a good boy for your aunt and your grandma and grandpa," Maggie told Ben as she kissed him and hugged him good-bye. Lori knew that Maggie felt a little bit of anxiety leaving him for the night to go on a date.

"He'll be good and besides we're going for ice cream with Charlie, Trevor, and Dante later."

"Oh great, ice cream. I'll be good, Mommy, have fun," Ben said as he hugged Lori. They watched as Maggie and Jasper left.

An hour later they finished up dinner and Lori touched up her makeup before the guys came over.

"Now be a good boy and after ice cream Lori and Dante, Trevor, and Charlie will bring you back home and we'll get you ready for bed. Maybe we can watch that movie you like so much," Diana told her grandson as she gave him a pat on the head. Ben was excited as he headed to the front door to greet the men, who had just arrived.

Lori straightened out her beige capri pants and put on her pink light sweater over a matching pink spandex, short-sleeve top. The shirt was a little short, stylishly revealing her tan, toned belly, which peeked out a little from the bottom of the sweater.

Charlie, Dante, and Trevor looked her over in approval before they each gave her a light kiss on the cheek hello.

They headed to town for ice cream and Ben entertained them with various questions the whole ride over.

They ordered their five ice cream cones and headed toward a bench near the parking lot.

"Two scoops, huh, buddy? You must have really been in the mood for ice cream?" Lori asked as she watched Ben begin to lick the ice cream as it melted off the cone.

"I was and Andy said that this place serves the best ice cream. It's better than the Carvel place down the road," Ben added and Trevor laughed.

"Andy is right about that. I used to eat ice cream at this place when I was a kid. It's the best," Dante told them as they enjoyed the dessert and the warm summer night.

"Aunt Lori, do you think Mommy is having a good time with Jasper?" Ben asked as he finished his cone.

"I'm sure she is," Lori said as Ben stood in front of her.

"Will she be safe?" Ben asked and Lori's heart immediately ached for Ben's concern. He was worried about her just as Lori was.

"I'm sure she's safe, Ben. Jasper is a nice man and you know that Charlie, Dante, and Trevor are his cousins. They grew up together. Even Matt and Andy's daddy."

"I know that, but is he anything like my daddy?" Ben asked and Lori had to swallow hard to stop the tears from filling her eyes.

"No, Ben, he's nothing like your daddy. You don't have to worry about Mommy. She's probably having a good time right now and missing you a bunch. I bet you she'll tell you all about it tomorrow morning." Lori gave him a hug.

She locked gazes with the three men behind Ben and could see their angry expressions. They knew about her past or at least about Derrick chasing them. They didn't appear surprised or shocked, and they didn't bombard her with questions. She felt sick to her stomach now.

"Your mom is perfectly safe with Jasper, Ben. Did you know he used to be a soldier? He's a Green Beret," Charlie told them. That seemed to interest Ben as Charlie told him a little more about Jasper. The story even put Lori at ease.

They were just getting ready to leave when some man wearing shorts and a funny-looking button-down tropical shirt stopped to talk to Charlie.

"Hey, I heard Old Man Cantrell is having some trouble by your way. I hope he's thinking about selling that land," Steve Henshaw said as Charlie took on a face of anger. So did Trevor and Dante. Lori could tell immediately that the badly dressed man was no friend of theirs.

"What do you know about it, Henshaw? Any idea who's behind it?" Charlie asked, accusing the man of being involved.

"Hey, I don't know anything, just that the old man better sell that land soon. A lot of companies have been calling the agency asking about it. Some of them willing to spend a lot of money," Henshaw told Charlie with a smirk.

"Well that's his business not yours," Trevor stated firmly. Then Dante took Lori's hand and Ben's hand and headed toward the truck. Lori was concerned that Charlie might physically fight with the man but she did as Dante told her.

Lori watched from the truck while Charlie, Trevor, and the man exchanged words. Then the man walked away.

"What was that all about?" Lori asked Dante as Trevor and Charlie approached the truck. Trevor and Charlie appeared angry but tried to conceal their emotions.

"Nothing to worry about. He's a nobody but we're worried about Tom a little. His land is definitely worth a lot of money and sometimes people in that business will do anything to convince a landowner to sell to them," Dante explained as she helped Ben get up into the truck. Then Dante lifted her up to assist her. He gave her a quick kiss on her cheek and she smiled.

Charlie and Trevor got into the truck next and neither man smiled.

"J.R. said he's conducting an investigation, maybe he should question that guy?" Lori suggested, and Charlie smiled.

"You're on a first-name basis with our local sheriff, huh?" he asked, jokingly trying to change the subject. Lori got the message and laughed.

They dropped Ben off to her parents at the house where he hugged Lori, Trevor, Dante, and Charlie good-night then went inside with Diana.

"How about a walk down by the water?" Trevor asked, and Lori agreed as they grabbed a blanket and some flashlights.

They headed across the field and down toward the stream where the moonlight shone across the sparkling water and along the bank.

"It's a great night, perfect," Charlie said as he spread out the blanket then took a seat. He opened his thighs and patted the spot between his legs. Dante and Trevor offered her a hand to sit. She placed one hand into Trevor's and one into Dante's and then she lowered to the blanket taking a seat between Charlie's legs.

Charlie undid the braid in her hair and ran his fingers through the strands.

"You should wear your hair down more often. You're beautiful," Trevor said then leaned over and placed a hand against her cheek, right before he kissed her.

They smiled at one another as he pulled back.

She stared out toward the night sky, amazed by the beautiful evening and how comfortable she felt sitting here with Dante, Trevor, and Charlie.

Charlie wrapped an arm around her waist and pulled her back against his chest.

"Lean on me and enjoy the sky."

They were silent a moment.

"I think Ben enjoyed the ice cream," Dante said then chuckled as he pulled a piece of grass from the ground and played with it.

"He definitely did," Lori replied.

"It was like he never got to go out for ice cream before," Dante added, and Lori swallowed hard.

"He didn't get to do a lot of things he should have. But he can now. Thank you for bringing him with us."

Dante covered her leg with his hand and began to rub back and forth across the material. It gave her the chills and made her feel really good. She loved it when they touched her.

"What was Ben's father like?" Charlie asked, and instantly Lori knew this was it. It was time to tell them everything as she took a deep breath and waited.

"You don't have to tell us. It's none of our business."

"It's okay, Charlie, I should probably tell you guys everything." She turned toward him and he looked at her attentively. She sat legs crossed in front of the three of them on the blanket.

Charlie, Dante, and Trevor listened as she explained about Ben's father and escaping from the town they lived in. She told them about how they made money, secretly kept in contact with her parents and about finally making the decision to settle down.

"I've never had much. That was the only way to save money for the future. We never knew when we would have to just pack up and leave in the middle of the night. Take a bus or a train to get away faster. Those things cost money so we saved for those emergencies. A small suitcase a piece is what we had. I worked and Maggie stayed with Ben. I felt that he needed his mother to constantly be there to protect him and I learned fast how to mix drinks and wait tables. I mostly worked at hole-in-the-wall places or anyplace I could work off the books and keep my clothes on. I'm not lying about that, Charlie. I would never take my clothes off for money or prostitute myself."

She lowered her eyes and fidgeted with her hands until Trevor covered them with his own.

"In all honesty I was asked, I was even tempted, but when times were tough suddenly out of nowhere we'd catch a break. I would find work or Maggie would babysit somebody else's kids," she told them and he believed her as they listened.

Lori told him about the night they received the prank calls after moving into a house they rented.

"You must have been very scared," Trevor whispered as he moved closer and began to caress her thigh.

"We heard Derrick was on the run now that he killed someone. We tried to take the extra precautions, but they weren't enough. We thought about calling the police but we feared that Derrick's family would try to say he acted this way because we had his child. His family had connections and we couldn't take the chance of losing Ben. I would have rather died than seen Derrick get a hold of him."

Lori wiped a tear from her eye and her heart was beating rapidly.

"It's all right, baby, you can trust us," Charlie whispered to her as he took her hand.

She knew she could trust them. She was just scared as she squeezed his hand tighter.

* * * *

Dante was trying to remain calm, but he just wanted to hold Lori in his arms and love her. That thought rocked his world.

She explained how she heard Maggie scream upstairs, how she called the police then headed up the staircase. She quickly ran through the part about the gun and breaking her wrist but Michelle told them the whole story as Maggie explained to her. Dante wondered why Lori tried to act like it was no big deal.

"So you saved their lives. You were willing to die for them?" Dante asked as he watched Lori struggle with the story. She didn't want to sound like a heroine, she tried to minimize what took place, and he could tell she felt horrible for pulling the trigger.

"You're so brave, baby." Charlie held her face in his hands. She tried to push him away, turning her head as the tears flowed from her eyes.

"No, Charlie, I helped kill a man. I took a life."

"No, baby, you saved lives, Ben's and Maggie's. They're here now and so are you because of your strength and love for them. He was going to kill the two of you and take Ben. You said it yourself that you would rather die than let Derrick get Ben. Thank God you didn't. You survived and now we're here together," Dante told her as Charlie pulled her against him.

He wiped the tears away from her eyes then gently laid her down on the blanket.

Charlie stared into her eyes as Trevor lay on the other side behind her.

* * * *

Charlie felt his chest tightening and his heart racing. He pressed a hand over her belly and against her skin as he stared into her tear-filled eyes.

"It's not easy to take a life, Lori. But in a situation where it's your life or the bad guy's life, there's only one choice. You had to do it to save Ben, Maggie, and yourself. I'm proud of you for being so strong." He lowered his mouth to kiss her.

She immediately reached up and touched his hair, running her fingers through the short strands, making his cock come to life. He caressed along her belly then under her shirt. Lori wiggled a little and he moved one thigh over and between her thighs as he deepened the kiss. He loved her taste, the feel of her underneath him and all he wanted to do now was make love to her under the stars.

She was shaking as she stopped his hand from unbuttoning her sweater.

"This is happening too fast," she whispered, out of breath and he traced her lips with his finger.

"I'm sorry, it's just that you drive me crazy. I want you, Lori. I want to be inside you." He began kissing her again.

She pulled her lips from his and looked to the left, right at Trevor.

"Charlie, stop. I need to tell you something." She pleaded with him as well as herself. She wanted more of him, every inch of him, but not here, not this soon. She hardly knew him.

"I need you to slow down, Charlie. I don't want to make a mistake."

"Do you want me as much as I want you?"

"Yes, I do but…"

Charlie could see she was fearful and shy. He assumed she probably wasn't as experienced as him and maybe it was too soon.

"You want the three of us right? Me, Trevor, and Dante?" He feared that she would say no and that this would all come to an abrupt end.

"I'm scared, but yes, I want all three of you. I want to make this work."

He smiled with his hand pressed over her belly and partially under her shirt.

Suddenly they heard something in the brush behind them.

"What was that?" Lori asked, and instantly she was scared.

"Shhh." Charlie eased himself off of her then put her behind him.

Dante and Jasper pulled out their flashlights. Charlie looked at them.

He whispered, "When I say 'now,' point your flashlight on the bushes."

"Now!" he said and they could hear someone running through the bushes then the field.

"Let's go, Charlie, I don't like this." Lori pulled the blanket up off of the ground.

"Whatever it was we scared it off." Charlie couldn't help but be concerned after the recent events around the area.

"Or whomever?" Dante added as they brushed off their clothes then headed back toward Lori's parents' house.

As they crossed the field, they heard something behind them. There were two lights moving through the brush on the other side of the field.

Charlie could tell it was two people walking closely together.

"Hey, what do you think you're doing?" Charlie yelled across the way.

"What are we doing, what are you two doing?" Instantly Lori recognized Jasper's voice.

They started to head toward them to meet them halfway.

"What is the stream? Make-out point for all the single men in your family?" Lori asked sarcastically as Trevor grabbed her hand then pulled her close to him.

"I have my own place, baby, I don't need a make-out location," he told her very seriously and instantly she blushed, getting his meaning.

Jasper and Maggie approached looking a little embarrassed.

"Hey what are you two up to?" Jasper asked and Dante told them about the noise they heard.

"Did you see anyone come this way?" Charlie asked.

"No, we didn't see or hear anything but we came from the other side. Maybe we should call it a night, bring the ladies back to their place?" Jasper suggested.

"Why don't you two go ahead of us? That way you have some privacy to end your first date properly. We have something to discuss with Lori," Charlie told Jasper and Maggie, and before they could respond, he was pulling her toward his parents' place.

"Where are we going and what is it you have to discuss with me?" Lori asked as Charlie slowed down his pace and casually walked with her.

Dante and Trevor chuckled.

He stopped at the gazebo on his parents' property. He opened the screen door and inside was a small table for four, a mini refrigerator, and a radio.

"Do you know what was missing from our first date?" Charlie asked Lori as he retrieved a lighter from the built-in cabinet against the wall and lit the assortment of candles that were displayed on the table. Instantly the gazebo was flickering with candlelight, exactly how he planned it would be on the way over.

"Nothing was missing from our date. I enjoyed every part of it. Especially the bracelet." Lori lifted her wrist, letting the bracelet dangle back and forth.

"It was pretty perfect except we didn't get to dance." Charlie found a station he liked. Then the beginning of a slow song came on. Lori didn't know the artist or the name of the song but she loved it as Charlie took her hand and asked her to dance.

"What about Trevor and Dante?"

"We're next, but be warned, Trevor likes to dance dirty," Dante said then winked as he crossed his arms in front of his chest as he sat on the chair.

* * * *

"Honey, you have to see this. Looks like Charlie, Dante, Trevor, and Lori are dancing in our gazebo," Phil said to Terry and she got out of bed to see for herself.

"Oh my goodness, they've got it bad," Terry told her husband.

"And fast, don't you think?" Phil replied as he placed his arm around his wife's waist.

"That young woman is special, as special as our sons. They

deserve happiness after all they've gone through in their lives."

"That they do. I can feel the romance in the air, can you?" Phil asked his wife.

"I think it's stronger over there...in bed." She smiled wide, grabbed his hand, and they headed back to bed.

* * * *

"So I guess this is good night?" Jasper asked as he stood by the porch steps holding Maggie's hand.

"I suppose so. I had a wonderful time, Jasper. Thank you."

"I had a wonderful time, too. Would you like to do it again sometime?"

"I'd love to."

Jasper pulled Maggie toward him into an embrace. "You're so lovely, Maggie, until the next time." He gave her a kiss on the cheek then walked away toward his truck.

Maggie waved good-bye and wondered when Lori would be home. She couldn't wait to tell her sister about her date with Jasper.

* * * *

Charlie held Lori closely against him. He could feel her breath against his skin and her hair was tickling his chin. She smelled wonderful and her perfume was all over the shirt he wore.

"You smell incredible, edible actually." He cradled her head in his hand and placed his lips then teeth gently against her neck.

"Charlie!" Lori giggled as he tickled her. She tried to pull away but it was no use, he was determined to keep her in his arms a bit longer.

"I really should get home now. My sister is probably wondering where I am."

"She knows where you are and who you're with. Just because

their night ended early, doesn't mean ours has to." Charlie kissed her neck again this time sending chills through her body.

"That was your idea remember?" she reminded him as she grabbed his face, pulling it away from her neck then grabbing his hands. "Come on, tiger, let's call it a night." Lori pulled him by his hands toward the door.

"Wait! Just one more kiss." Behind her Dante and Trevor started blowing out the candles that illuminated the gazebo and instantly the darkness surrounded them. She didn't see it coming as Charlie turned her around and moved her forward. She couldn't see a thing but then felt Trevor's hands on her waist pulling her toward him. He kissed her lips, making love to her mouth, pulling more desire from her body. His hands explored, moving up her shirt. She felt the palm of his hand move over her breast as she moaned into his mouth. Her entire body heated up and then she felt the second set of hands on her shoulders.

"Just a little taste before we say good night." Dante moved her hair off her shoulder and began to scatter kisses against her skin, her neck, and cheek. Trevor released her lips as Dante cupped her face and turned it sideways so he could gain better access to her mouth. He stroked her tongue with his tongue and they battled for control of the kiss. When she felt the zipper of her pants go down, she tried to pull from Dante's mouth but Trevor was too quick.

"You smell incredible. Just a little taste, angel. Just one."

She wanted to feel him, let him and them do whatever they wanted. She felt Trevor's fingers press down her pants and immediately they were over her pussy lips.

"Oh." She pulled from Dante's mouth and moaned.

"Shhh, we don't want to wake our parents," Charlie reprimanded. She gasped and Dante chuckled.

"Please, Trevor, it's too much," Lori whispered and then she felt his fingers rub her pussy. She grabbed his wrist. "I'm not ready. Not like this," she whispered, and Trevor lowered to the floor, leaned forward, and licked her cunt.

"Oh. My. God." She held on to Dante as he wrapped an arm around her waist.

"Feels good, doesn't it?" Charlie asked as he appeared in front of her. He took her face between his hands and kissed her deeply.

Her pussy dripped with cream from their touch, their kisses, and being here in the dark like this with Charlie, Dante, and Trevor. She wanted to tell them that she was a virgin, but with every stroke of Trevor's tongue she could care less about her virginity. She loved the feel of it and couldn't believe she was allowing him to do this to her with his brothers watching.

At that thought came the realization that she wanted to have sex with the three of them. She was going to have sex with three men.

She must have tightened up or something because Trevor released his hold on her pussy with his mouth and Charlie released her lips and kissed along her mouth.

"We want you so badly, baby. One night very soon, you're coming back to our place and you're staying there," Charlie whispered.

"Definitely, one night soon," Dante added then kissed her neck.

Trevor was zipping up her pants then leaned forward next to her lips.

"You're delicious. I'd never get enough of your cream, baby." He kissed her and Lori could taste herself on his lips and his tongue as he deepened the kiss. It was so erotic, so wild and filled with passion and experience. She thought she would freak out. She begged her body and mind not to lose it. She could lose it later when she was all alone in her room analyzing every moment of tonight.

"Come on, baby. Let's get you home." Dante lifted her up into his arms, shocking her as he carried her out of the gazebo with Charlie and Trevor flanking her on either side. For a moment as they walked through the darkness, she wondered about the noise they heard. Could someone have been watching them? She shivered then hugged Dante tighter as his strong arms embraced her body.

Chapter 12

Charlie, Dante, and Trevor were at Tom Cantrell's house all morning going over the possibility of a partnership. Charlie had been thinking about it for the past few days. He had to admit that Lori influenced his decision. She made him realize how much building and designing meant to him. This partnership could be the perfect opportunity for him to get back into the swing of things again and help out his own community. Plus, Tom confided in him and his brothers about the threatening phone calls and pressure to sell. There was more of a need than ever to hold on to the land and develop it themselves.

"So we can have Barry Johnson write this all up for us nice and official like. Then you can get started on some designs," Tom told Charlie, Trevor, and Dante as he walked them outside.

"Sounds like a plan, Tom. We'll get together once the papers are drawn up and signed and we'll pull together our ideas."

"Thanks again, guys, this is gonna work out perfect," Tom added as they left.

"I'm actually excited about this new project and going into business with Tom and you guys," Charlie stated as they headed back to their house.

"I am, too. I'm a bit annoyed that Tom was receiving threats. It makes me wonder about those dead animals and the barn fire, too," Trevor added.

"I thought about that as well. Perhaps J.R. should make more rounds at night around here," Dante said, emphasizing the *J* and the *R* like Lori did.

Charlie chuckled. "It's crazy, but the first person I thought of as we left Tom's place was Lori."

Trevor wrapped an arm around his brother's shoulder.

"That's not crazy, that's awesome, because I was thinking the same thing."

"We should go to Carl's and see her. We haven't seen her all week because of the extra hours she's been working," Dante said.

"I'm not going there. I hate that fucking uniform," Charlie stated.

"I hate it, too, and watching other guys drool over her," Dante added sounding just as angry as Charlie.

"I don't care for it either, but thinking about peeling it off of her, is a better fantasy, don't you think?" Trevor said with a smile. Charlie shook his head at his brother. He was looking a lot happier lately and Charlie knew it had to do with Lori.

"I'm glad you can joke around about it." Charlie leaned against the hood of the truck. Dante and Trevor crossed their arms in front of their chests and stared at him.

"I'm just trying to deal with it like you two are," Trevor replied.

"Well it's crazy how jealous I've become over her and so quickly. When I think about what she went through, it upsets me."

"It upsets us, too, Charlie, but I really care for Lori. I think this is going to work out perfectly. I admit, I've had difficulty imagining the life she led the past five years. The shit holes she worked in, the men that tried to get into her pants. Fuck, that really pisses me off, thinking about another man touching her," Dante said then stared off in the distance.

"Lori is so strong, so incredibly attractive and independent. I think she's made a change in us for the better, don't you, guys?" Trevor asked.

"She made me see how important my own gifts are, my degree, my talent for building things and my love of designing I gave up because I was depressed."

"Depressed? Charlie, you've been nothing but an ornery bastard these last few years," Trevor stated.

"Like you've been any better?" Dante challenged Trevor.

Trevor chuckled.

"We've all been pricks," Trevor said and Dante raised his eyebrows at his brother.

"You know what is bothering me? I don't like Lori working all these hours. I don't like the way guys are talking about her and checking her out. I've been trying to ignore it but I can't. I don't know how to handle these emotions. Sometimes I feel possessed. I'm afraid I'm scaring her," Charlie said as he stood up straight.

"She's working hard, taking extra shifts at the bar, and even waiting on tables just to make more money to put herself through school," Dante stated.

"We could easily pay for her to go to school. We've got plenty of money saved and will be making more if this project with Cantrell is a success," Trevor added.

"Maybe we'll talk to her about it tonight. If we see her," Charlie said then headed into the house. He was acting like a fucking baby. He missed her and that angered him. He was jealous and that made him think about her and some other guy or guys trying to move in on what was his and his brothers'. He was possessive of her already and they hadn't even had sex yet. That was another thing. Why was she holding out? She had a sexy body, and they'd each expressed their desire to have her. What was she so afraid of? Had someone hurt her? Did she have a bad experience? His heart ached at the thought of her feeling any pain or sadness. He certainly didn't want to be the cause of that in any way. But he and his brothers wanted her so badly it did kind of hurt. Sometimes, when she wasn't with them, he felt a twinge of pain in his chest and even anxiety. They worried about her. He wanted Lori in their bed and the sooner it happened the better off they'd all be.

* * * *

"What do you mean he's not selling? A partnership? With who?" Jerry Connor yelled into the receiver.

"I'm looking at a copy of the deal right now. The attorney they're going to is an old friend of mine. He said everything's being split evenly and they're going to build a whole community up there. My friend sounded pretty enthusiastic about the project, he was all for it. I guess your plans for that land aren't going to happen, Connor," Steve Henshaw told him over the phone.

"We'll just see about that," Connor said then hung up the phone.

Connor opened his cell phone and hit number four on his auto-dial.

"Yeah."

"It's me, there's been a change of plans. I need you to put on the pressure. Find out about this guy Charlie Henley and anyone close to him and also I think it's time to get a little more aggressive, if you know what I mean."

"No problem."

* * * *

The stranger walked over toward the mirror in his hotel room and stared at the picture of the blonde he had taken.

He lifted it to his mouth and gave her a kiss.

"You'll pay for cheating on me the other night. I saw you with them. Their hands all over you. Soon, darling, very soon." He spoke to her picture, fantasized about having her, and knew he wouldn't be able to hold off too much longer.

Chapter 13

"Why does your sister always have to make that damn meatloaf of hers? I don't like the way she cooks those hard-boiled eggs in the middle. It kills the meat," Tom complained as Lynn laughed.

Tom and Lynn were headed back home from town. They just had supper at Lynn's sister Bet's house. It was just starting to clear up after an early evening rainstorm.

"You always say that, Tom, but you eat it."

"That's because I'm polite but not your sister. I've even told that woman I don't care for eggs in meatloaf and she still cooks it that way anyhow," Tom told Lynn who just smiled and patted his leg.

Tom was heading up 9W and there was hardly anyone on the road. They made their way to Valley Stream when suddenly out of nowhere a car with its brights on came swerving toward them. Lynn screamed and Tom slammed on the brakes as the car ran them off the road then slammed on the brakes.

Tom released his seat belt, asked if Lynn was all right, and was about to get out of the car to see if the other driver was okay. Suddenly he saw the flash of light in the side mirror and instantly the glass bottle of flame hit the windshield, then another one hit the back window.

Molotov cocktails! He knew immediately this was bad as Lynn screamed and he pulled her from the seat. He couldn't make out the license plate or the make of the car as the person sped off and both Tom and Lynn ran as far as they could from the vehicle.

Moments later the car exploded into a great ball of black smoke and fire as Lynn cried hysterically and Tom held her tight. The fire could probably be seen from miles as they heard sirens and fire trucks making their way to help them. The heat from the fire reached them from where they stood. They kept backing up but Tom was shaking profusely.

Tom didn't even realize he had cut his arm badly and was bleeding until he released Lynn as the police responded and the paramedics came toward them. He could hardly speak he was so shocked. *Did that really happen? Did someone just try to kill me and Lynn?*

* * * *

Lori arrived home late that night and had heard about what happened to Lynn and Tom. She saw Sheriff Morgan's patrol car still outside their house so she headed over to see if the Cantrells were all right.

"I just got home from Carl's. I heard about what happened. Are you all right?" Lori asked Mr. Cantrell whose arm was bandaged up.

"Oh we're fine, honey, just a little shaken up. Come on inside, Charlie's here and J.R.," he told her as she tried unsuccessfully as usual to pull down the short black uniform skirt.

Lori entered the living room where both J.R. and Charlie stood up to greet her. Immediately she went over to Lynn and gave her a hug as she said hello to Charlie and the Sheriff.

"I heard about what happened. I just got home from work. Are you okay, Mrs. Cantrell?" Lori asked as she stood back up.

"Lori, please, I told you to call me Lynn and it was very nice of you to stop by and see us. You've been working double shifts I've heard. That's tough work you're doing, your feet must be killing you." Lynn motioned Lori to take a seat in the chair next to her.

"I'd love to but this uniform isn't exactly made for sitting down."

"Carl has all the girls wearing that uniform?" Lynn asked.

"Yes, unfortunately this is it," she said, making it obvious that she hated it.

"But not everyone has the body to pull it off," J.R. stated as he rose from his seat. Before anyone could respond he was saying good night.

He gave Lynn a kiss on the cheek, shook Charlie's and Tom's hands, then gave Lori a good-night kiss on the cheek as well.

* * * *

Charlie noticed how the sheriff nonchalantly placed his hand on Lori's hip as he kissed her cheek good-night. He winked at her as he walked with Tom toward the front door.

Lynn and Tom picked up on the whole thing as Charlie stood from his seat and took Lori's hand.

Lori asked Lynn what had happened and she explained the story to her.

"Who would want to do this?" Lori asked.

"That's what we hope to find out," Tom stated as he sat on the arm of the chair his wife was sitting in.

"I'm sure J.R. will come up with something. Maybe after they question people around the area where it happened? Perhaps someone saw something," Lori said and Charlie hoped so.

"We'd better get going, too. I'll come check on you guys first thing in the morning," Charlie said as he kissed Lynn good-night and shook Tom's hand. Lori did the same and they left the Cantrell house.

Charlie had a lot on his mind. It was obvious to him that someone was after Tom's land and was trying to intimidate him. Tom told Charlie about it earlier today but he didn't think the person would seriously try to injure Tom or Lynn. Now he knew better. Charlie was concerned about partnering up with Tom but the more he thought about it the more he wanted the land to stay in Tom and his name. He was starting to get back into that all-business mode and attitude. He had worked against scoundrels like Connor before. He had even participated in business transactions that he wasn't proud of, but this was different. Tom and Lynn were like family and he would do whatever he could to help protect them.

Now, here was Lori, attractive, intelligent, and sweet. She hadn't even responded negatively when J.R. touched her. Charlie couldn't figure Lori out. He couldn't control his feelings, the anger was enormous, and there was too much going through his mind. He looked at Lori as she got into the driver's seat. She worked a double shift today yet she looked refreshed and gorgeous, and that uniform she wore both excited and angered him.

"My God, Charlie, they must have been so scared," Lori said as they got into her car. She gave Charlie the short ride to his house. They got out and Lori stood by the car door.

"What did J.R. say about it? Does he think something will come up?" she asked.

Instantly Charlie was in front of her. "I think he lost his concentration when you walked into the house." He wrapped his arms around her waist, leaning her against the driver's side of the car.

"What is that supposed to mean?" she asked Charlie as she placed her hands against his chest to block him from moving closer.

"We've all known him for years and call him 'sheriff.' You've known him for a month and call him J.R." Charlie let the letters roll off his tongue.

"He told me to call him J.R. What's wrong with that?"

Charlie looked at her face a moment, staying silent, just thinking. He couldn't help the jealous feelings he had. He wanted to keep Lori all to himself and his two brothers. She had no clue what she did to him. She seemed to basically ignore or be blind to the reactions she received that he'd witnessed firsthand. She hadn't even felt the sheriff's hand on her hip. He put it there as if he had every right to.

Lori reached up to touch his cheek with her hand, and he moved his face into it, instantly kissing the palm of her hand.

He stepped away from her car, pulling her with him as they

embraced. His hands slowly slid down her back to her waist. He could feel her hip bone in his hand, the same hip bone only minutes ago the sheriff touched.

He took a deep breath as if trying to breathe away the intense feelings he had. Lori seemed to sense his angry exhale as he cradled her head, held her hair in his hand, and covered her mouth with his. He grabbed hold of her backside as she moved closer against him. The moment was intense and their breathing rapid as Charlie reached his hand under her shirt.

* * * *

"Let's go inside, baby," he whispered and she wanted to so badly but she knew something was upsetting him as she grabbed his hand and stopped him.

"Charlie, no, it's getting late. I should really head home."

"Stay here tonight." He pulled her against him by her waist.

"I'd better not. You seem kind of upset, like something is on your mind."

"You're on my mind, baby. I just want to be with you, to hold you."

"I want to be with you, too, Charlie, but I need to slow things down."

"Is this some kind of game? What do you take me for, some kind of fool? Maybe this just isn't going to work out."

Lori didn't know how to react. This wasn't Charlie. This was a side of him she didn't want to know. She was offended, angry even though her gut told her he was overreacting for a reason. He acted so tough, so confident in front of everyone, but in actuality he was afraid. Afraid of getting hurt and now he was pushing her away.

"You know what, Charlie, I'm going to forget what you just said and head home right now. It's late and I don't want to fight with you."

"I'm sorry, baby...I...I've got too much on my mind and I'm

taking it out on you." Charlie took Lori's hand as he walked toward the front of her car and sat on the hood. Lori stood in front of him. Again he was silent as he embraced her.

"You don't realize what you do to me, how you affect me. Did you notice the way the sheriff spoke to you, kissed you good-night on the cheek, and put his hand on you? My blood was boiling over that."

"Yes, Charlie, I felt him do that and I didn't like it but some men just think they can grab a woman when they want to or make a move if they feel they have a chance. You don't have to be jealous, Charlie. I'm here with you right now. I've been out working all day, a double shift that continued into the night, later than what I expected. I'm here with you because I was worried about the Cantrells and I missed you."

"You did?"

Lori took Charlie's hands and wrapped them around her waist, and then she took his face into her hands, staring very seriously into his eyes.

"I'm going to tell you this only once, so listen up. I'm not going to hurt you or your brothers! I'm not a flirt, I don't like a lot of attention, and the other night when we went out, that was my first real date, Charlie, and it was with three men. A date that I imagined would never take place because of the crazy life I've led thus far. I've never felt like this before, I'm scared and I'm worried because you, Dante, and Trevor are way more experienced than I am. The three of you are so good looking and sexy. I can't get you out of my head. I can't think of anything else but being in your arms and in your company all the time. It's wild and, God, I'm blabbering." She lowered her head to his chest as he caressed her back and her hair.

"Lori, I'm sorry for what I said before. I just want to keep you all to myself. I don't want to share you with anyone else. I want to be with you more than I've ever wanted to be with anyone. I've made a lot of mistakes because of my own fears. You've changed all that. With you I want more. I know you can make Trevor, Dante, and me happy. You already have. I want all of it. I want all of you," he told her as he kissed her softly.

That kiss grew deeper and Lori knew she needed to tell him why she was afraid. He softly released her lips.

"Charlie, there's something you need to know…to understand why I'm hesitant."

"You've been hurt before?" he asked before she could tell him. This was so difficult but she knew she had to get it off of her chest.

"No, Charlie, the other night was the first time I ever went out on a date, you and Dante and Trevor are the first men that I've ever been this close to…I'm…"

Charlie looked into Lori's eyes. He could see the worry, he put together what she told him, registered his thoughts, and then it hit him. He was cautious as he spoke, unsure what to think or say.

"Baby, you mean—"

"Our woman's a virgin."

Lori was shocked at the sound of Trevor's voice. She turned and saw him and Dante approaching and they both looked so good, her heart soared with adoration for them.

She lowered her eyes until Trevor and Dante stood next to her and Charlie. Dante placed his fingers under her chin, tilting it up toward him.

"Is this true? Is this why you've been holding out on us?"

She loved the way Dante's voice sounded and she loved his sexy words. She nodded her head.

Dante smiled then leaned down and gave her lips a soft kiss. "Then we'll be your first and your only," he whispered.

* * * *

Charlie sighed deeply as he held her tight, shocked by her confession, amazed and strangely enough, almost proud. His whole perception of her was wrong from the start. He had never been so wrong about someone in his life. So close-minded and stuck in anger and sadness like he had been before Lori came along. She was amazing, beautiful, and theirs.

* * * *

Lori was relieved to have told them the truth.

Dante took her hand and pulled her slowly toward him. He placed his hand on her waist and she loved the weight of it against her hip. He towered over her, standing at least six feet three inches. His dark, crew-cut hair looked damp, as if he had just gotten out of the shower. As he pulled her closer, she inhaled, smelling the soap, confirming her thoughts.

"Can I ask you something?" he whispered and she nodded her head. He clasped his hands behind her lower back and she placed her hands against his chest. They locked gazes as he spoke.

"Why did you wait? How did you do it?" Dante asked. "I mean, you were on your own. You didn't have any parental supervision and things sounded rough for you, Maggie, and Ben."

She took a deep breath then ran her hands softly up and down the material of his T-shirt. The feel of muscle beneath her fingertips nearly got her to forget his question.

He gave her rear a little squeeze and she immediately refocused.

"I wanted to save myself for the right person. I didn't want to make a mistake and regret it or perhaps not have enough experience in identifying a sincere enough man to give such a large part of me to."

"And does it feel right, to be with us?"

She smiled up at him.

"You, Trevor, and Charlie are the best part of my new life. I want to be sure that is going to work. I want to make certain that you won't fight or get jealous of one another. I want to understand how you see this ménage relationship working."

"You mean it can't solely be about sex?" Trevor asked, coming up to her from behind and rubbing the palm of his hand across her ass. Dante and Lori gave him a firm expression.

"I could determine if this will work based solely on sex," she said, and Trevor pressed the palm of his hand over her skin from her ass, up her spine to the back of her head. As he gently grabbed a handful of hair and tipped her head back, she smiled and said, "But I won't," right before he kissed her.

She felt her heart soar and her nipples harden at Trevor's slick, sexy move. The way he restrained her and held her hair in his hand as he tilted her head back to kiss her breathless did just that. She felt high when he finally released her to Dante.

Dante hugged her to him and caressed her body.

"I hate this uniform and I love this uniform." He moved his hands across her ass, giving it a squeeze.

"Dante," she reprimanded, but the truth was, she loved his hands on her. She loved their hands all over her, but the fear of a broken heart, of getting hurt still lingered in the back of her mind. It was a good time to end the night and head home to rest. Her double shifts all week were weighing a toll on her and making a decision she feared regretting may not be smart.

"Well now that we've gotten that very awkward subject out of the way, I'd better head home. I'm exhausted, really," she told Dante, and he could tell she was a bit embarrassed.

"Before you go I just want you to know I think you're amazing, Lori," Charlie said. "You've been out on your own, supporting your sister and Ben, working in God only knows what kind of places and you still kept it together, held on to your morals and values. You valued yourself, held on to your most intimate possession. It's not something to be embarrassed about. It's something to be very proud of. I'm sorry if I upset you. I'm worried about Tom and Lynn and I can't help but be jealous of another man touching you, but there's nothing I can do about that."

"Forget about it, Charlie. You're the only men who are on my mind. I thought about all three of you, all day today. I couldn't wait until tomorrow. We'll do something, right? We'll get together?"

"Definitely."

They each took a moment to embrace her again before Lori headed home.

* * * *

Lori was screaming in her sleep. She couldn't breathe, she was suffocating, and her whole body was struggling to survive. The pain in her chest and lungs was enormous as she wrestled against the substance that was filling her nostrils and her throat for the last bit of air. There was no one around, no one to save her. This was it. She was going to die.

Suddenly she felt her body rocking back and forth. Someone was shaking her as she screamed and cried to live.

* * * *

"Lori...Lori...Wake up...Please, just wake up!" Maggie was yelling at her sister. She could see Lori's coloring change. She wasn't breathing, she was fighting for air and she seemed to still be asleep.

"What's wrong?" Diana screamed as she and Lou entered the bedroom in their night clothes.

"I don't know, I think she's dreaming but look at her coloring. Mom, is she breathing?" Maggie screamed. Diana told Lou to help lift Lori up.

As they did, Lori jumped up from the bed grasping her throat and chest as if fighting for air to breathe. Lou was about to call 911 when Lori seemed to come out of it, inhaling deeply, over and over again as Diana and Maggie calmed her down. Maggie was crying now as she hugged her sister.

"Oh thank God. Thank God you're all right. I don't know what I would ever do without you." Maggie continued to cry.

"Lori, my God, darling, are you okay?" Diana asked her.

Lori's breathing was still rapid as Lou called Dr. Andrew Henley instead of an ambulance.

"She's still having trouble breathing but she's awake now," Lou told Dr. Henley over the phone as he placed the call on speaker.

"It sounds like she may have had a panic attack while sleeping. Does she remember what she was dreaming about?" he asked.

"The doctor wants to know if you remember what you were dreaming about? He thinks you had a panic attack," Lou repeated as Lori began to comprehend what was going on.

"I'm fine, Dad, just hang up that damn phone. I'm fine, I said!" Lori yelled as she jumped up from the bedroom rug and walked toward the bed. Lou, Diana, and Maggie were shocked at Lori's response. She was never so abrupt with them and it was obvious she was scared.

"I heard her, Lou. Tell her I said to meet me at my office in an hour. If she has trouble breathing again, bring her to the emergency room and call me. I'll meet you there."

Lou hung up the telephone. He gave Lori the message as she sat on the edge of the bed.

"Well we're all up so why don't I make some coffee and start breakfast. It's around five or so. Lou come on and help me," Diana said, hoping that maybe Lori would confide in Maggie and calm down a bit.

They left the room and Lori covered her face with her hands.

* * * *

"Lori, talk to me, what's going on? That was so strange and I'm worried. You couldn't breathe. You lost the color in your face as you were gasping for air and grabbing your chest and throat. What's going on?" Maggie rambled on as Lori tried to calm herself down and process her thoughts. She knew this was dangerous. She knew she couldn't breathe. In her dreams she was being buried alive. She thought about Dante, Charlie, and Trevor and how safe and good it felt in their arms. Lori squeezed her eyes shut as she brought her knees to her chest. The tear escaped and immediately Maggie was alarmed.

She grabbed her sister and hugged her tightly as Lori held on to Maggie. She continued to fight the tears, blocking any others from escaping. Her sister Maggie needed her. Ben and her parents needed her. She was supposed to take care of herself and them not the other way around. Lori let go of Maggie and pulled away.

"That was crazy. I was dreaming and in my dreams I couldn't catch my breath no matter how hard I tried. How did you know I was having trouble?" Lori asked as she pulled herself together.

"I could hear you screaming from the other room and I ran in here and you were gasping." Maggie continued to tell her the whole story.

"Thank goodness Ben didn't hear me."

"That boy should be exhausted from yesterday. We were out playing all day with Jasper, Andrew, and Michelle. Are you sure you're all right? You are going to meet Andrew in an hour, right?"

"I'll see. Maybe. I don't know. It was just a bad dream. I'm tired, working a lot and I—"

"Was out late with Charlie, Dante, and Trevor last night?"

"I stopped by the Cantrells' to make sure they were all right after the accident and Charlie and I wound up talking for a while."

"Talking, huh?" Maggie teased.

"Yes, we talked. I care a lot about him, Dante, and Trevor, but this may not work out."

"What do you mean? You guys are perfect for one another. Plus they're so in love with you. Is it the ménage thing? I know it's crazy and you were just as shocked as I was to learn that these relationships exist, but it seems so right. I've met a few couples in town. Friends of

Jasper's, who were in the military and are now home settling down. Their ménage relationships seem amazing."

"I guess that's part of it. I've never had a boyfriend and definitely not three. With Charlie, Dante, and Trevor it's like I have to bypass the dating thing and go for the big move. They're older and set in their ways. I'm still trying to figure my life out."

"That's my fault. I made you miss out on things that I had the opportunity to do as a teenager. I screwed up and got involved with Derrick. You lost everything including your freedom to live when we left."

"No, Maggie. It's not your fault. You're my sister and I love you. I went with you because I love you and I wanted to keep our baby safe."

Maggie smiled. "You always think of Ben as your own instead of your nephew."

Lori felt the tears reach her eyes. "I love him as if he's my son. That's the special bond we have. But in regards to the Henley brothers, things are moving kind of fast and I have so much to do. I need to focus on making more money for college. I've been working double shifts. Today's my only day off. I'll be working every night this week. Plus I picked up a few waitressing hours as well. I don't want to get sidetracked. College costs money and money doesn't grow on trees."

"I know that, Lori, but you're going to get burned out. You won't be able to keep this schedule up after the summer and when your classes start. Plus you deserve some free time for yourself and your heart."

"I don't know what I'm going to do. I plan on taking it one day at a time."

"I wish you would slow down and let Mom and Dad help you."

"No. That's not an option. I want to handle this on my own. I prefer to do things on my own."

They talked a little longer. Lori was certain Maggie was still worried but she couldn't focus on that now. She had too much on her mind.

They got dressed and met their parents downstairs.

Lori left the house and reluctantly headed into town to see Dr. Henley. Her parents insisted and her mother even threatened to accompany her. There was no use in arguing with their mother. Ever since Lori and Maggie came home, their mother had been making up for lost time.

Lori drove her car down the road, thankful that she hadn't seen Charlie, Dante, or Trevor. She was feeling confused suddenly. They were older, more worldly and sophisticated than she was. They had been involved with some Special Forces unit in the military and achieved their college degrees. They had accomplished so much and she had accomplished so little.

Dante, Trevor, and Charlie were confident, unafraid to say what they felt, and she couldn't help but be intimidated. It was obvious how much more experienced they were, and even Michelle told her. It was public knowledge and Lori knew many women were after them. Even Shelly from Carl's was interested in Charlie, Trevor, and Dante. She hated when they undressed them with their eyes and made lewd comments about what they would do if they got the Henley brothers naked and all to themselves.

Lori's stomach ached and she felt a twinge of pain in her chest. Lori tried to push the thoughts from her mind. She was suddenly losing it. She was losing her grasp on life.

She knew what the doc would tell her. If the nightmares kept up, if this pessimistic way of thinking took over her thoughts, she would be headed to a nervous breakdown.

As much as she wanted to push away her feelings toward the men, the more she felt she needed them and especially right now. Every negative thought that was running in circles through her mind eventually ended with thoughts of Charlie, Trevor, and Dante. In her dreams, on good nights, they always saved her from harm. She couldn't confide in the men she loved so deeply. And she did love them and she wondered if she were stupid and naive to feel so strongly about them so soon.

She would be giving in to her own weaknesses, sharing her every fear and thought with them. Could they be trusted? Would they turn out to be the biggest mistake of her life? Then she thought about their smiles, their embrace, the smell of their cologne and each of their personalities. Handling one would be difficult but handling three could be disastrous. The emotions didn't lessen in their absence. It seemed to grow stronger and soon led her to thinking about their lips and the way they felt pressed against hers. When they kissed her, she was lost in the moment, the sensations that heated her body, ignited something huge inside of her that she never knew existed.

"Grrrrrrr." Lori shook her head and banged her fist on the steering wheel. She was driving herself crazy. Why couldn't she just put the past behind her, look ahead to the future, and see the positives in life?

I'm scared. Damn it, for the first time in my life, I'm scared for myself. Any decision I make will affect me.

She had been so worried about everyone else. She never had time to worry about herself. She had Ben and Maggie, even her parents to worry about while she was on the run. Now there was nothing and no one to be hiding from and still Lori wanted to run. Just keep running, hide, and be safe.

She parked her car in front of Dr. Henley's office. He was at the door waiting for her, welcoming her inside.

"I made a fresh pot of coffee, want some?" he asked her, and she watched him as he poured some of the hot beverage into a dark green mug. He was wearing blue jeans and a T-shirt and Lori realized it was Sunday, his day off.

"I'm sorry my father called you. We didn't have to get together today, it's Sunday."

"Nonsense, Lori, it sounded like a pretty serious situation. Your father said they were about to call for an ambulance. Come into the examination room and let's check you over."

Lori followed him into the room as he put the green mug down onto the counter and grabbed his stethoscope and proceeded. Then he took her blood pressure and everything seemed to be fine.

She explained how she finally woke up and what Maggie had told her.

"Has this ever happened before, Lori?"

"No, Doc, I told you this was a first. I don't think it's anything to worry about really. I'm fine, I woke up, I'm breathing, and it's Sunday, your day off with your family."

Lori slid down off of the examination table as if saying the discussion was over and that was final. Andrew didn't allow it as he took Lori's hand.

"Not so fast, kid. I'm concerned. This could get worse, Lori. Do you think you're too young to have a heart attack, a mental breakdown, or something? Because I'll tell you, you're not too young. You have had various stressful events in your life. Do you know that when a police officer or someone in law enforcement shoots someone, they're taken off of active duty and given a desk job for a while as they receive counseling?"

She shook her head.

"Don't. Don't talk to me about that and about remembering. I don't want to." She tried to walk away but he stopped her.

"Lori, please, hear me out. I'm going to tell you what I think. You need to get your feelings out. You're holding too much inside. The emotions, the guilt, the pressure of succeeding in college, the fear of getting close to someone and becoming accessible and susceptible to getting hurt. These events and circumstances are what life is all about. By just simply acknowledging that they exist, admitting that you're afraid, welcoming these events as a challenge, a fact of life, then you'll survive. Some things you'll ease on through and others you'll go 'bumpety, bump,' the whole way through. But, by holding them inside, by always trying to stay in control of everything in your life, you are going to flat out lose it. Do you understand what I'm saying? I'm not just your physician, I'm your friend and your neighbor, and I care about you."

"How could you get all that from a bad dream and a loss of breath?" Lori asked, trying to lighten things up.

"Honey, it's more than that. You are more than that. Do you realize how many lives you have already touched in this town alone? You're a sweet, kind, gentle, and strong person. You give constantly of yourself to others. You know just the right thing to say and it's all natural. Now this is what I suggest you do. Take some alone time. Just organize your thoughts and feelings. Prioritize everything that is going on in your life and eliminate the stress. There's always counseling, Lori."

"I don't think so. Listen, Doc, I know and understand what you're saying and I'll try, I want to try, I don't want to be afraid."

"There's nothing wrong with that. There's nothing wrong with being afraid. If you keep everything inside and you keep this pace up, eventually you're going to burn out."

"Do you really think what happened to me this morning is serious?"

"It could be if you don't slow things down. There are multiple culprits here."

"I know that, I really do. I appreciate you meeting me here on your day off. I really didn't want to go to the emergency room. I guess I scared everyone, huh?"

"You sure did, but I'm glad you're feeling better, and as far as I can tell, you're physically fine. If you feel stressed and you're having trouble breathing, just try to relax and stay calm. Sit down or get a brown paper bag to breathe into."

"Doc, it only happens when I'm sleeping. I've been able to wake up before on my own."

"So this has happened before?"

Lori looked away and clasped her fingers together.

"Lori?" Andrew said as he covered her hands with his to get her to acknowledge him.

"Only one other time. I'm fine, Doc, really and I promise to take the alone time. As a matter of fact I'm going to start right now."

"Where are you going to go?"

"By the stream. It's peaceful there and relaxing."

"Okay, that sounds good. Be sure to tell your family where you are going. Just in case."

"I'll be fine. Thanks."

Lori shook Andrew's hand and he gave her a hug in return. He was a caring and empathetic physician and she was glad she met him at his office today. She was feeling a bit nervous about what happened and his advice gave her peace of mind as she headed outside to begin her day of relaxation.

* * * *

"What have you found out so far?" Connor asked the stranger over the phone.

"Charlie Henley is no one to mess around with. He's Special Forces, has a degree in engineering, and worked for a firm a year and a half out of the military. Made a lot of money, great reputation, enjoyed playing hardball and one day just threw it all away. He's an amazing architect and engineer, so are his two brothers. Together the Henleys and Cantrell will make big money."

"Not if I have something to say about that. We need to get to Henley, hit him where it hurts, get close to him and make him end his partnership with Cantrell."

The stranger was filled with fury. He had his eye on Lori. She would be his prize, his reward and souvenir after the job well done. Now she would play victim earlier. Connor would want him to harass Lori to get to Henley. Just maybe he would go a little further to appease his personal desires.

"There's a woman he's involved with. I know how to get to her."

"Tell me more," Connor said. The stranger told Connor one plan, but the stranger had plans of his own.

* * * *

"What happened?" Dante asked Jasper all concerned.

"Maggie said Lori couldn't breathe, she wouldn't wake up. Lou and Diana were about to call for an ambulance," Jasper told Charlie, Dante, and Trevor as they stood outside his cousins' house.

"Where is she now? Is she all right?" Trevor asked.

"She went to see Andrew and get checked out. Maggie said she just got home about twenty minutes ago and was headed to the stream for some alone time. Andrew thinks she had an anxiety attack. She's been through a lot, Charlie, and her work schedule is insane. Maggie's real worried about her."

"So are we. I'm gonna go find her and make sure she's all right. She shouldn't be alone or far from help. What if she has another attack?" Dante asked.

Charlie was concerned. "Let's grab some things first. Wait for Trevor and I." Charlie ran inside the house to retrieve some drinks and a few snacks in case Lori needed them. Jasper headed back to the Shays' house to spend the day with Maggie and Ben.

* * * *

Lori walked through the fields by the stream. She drew in a breath as she closed her eyes. She envisioned the patches of multicolored wildflowers scattered around the area and she inhaled their fragrances.

This place was so peaceful, so calm, and the fact that she didn't have to work today gave her enormous relief.

She strolled back toward the secluded area where she had spread a large blanket out earlier as she glanced toward the bouquet of wild flowers. She was startled to see Charlie, Trevor, and Dante sitting there waiting for her.

"I hope you don't mind that we came. We heard you might be here," Charlie told her as he rose from the blanket and greeted her. He was about to embrace her when Lori turned away and sat down on the blanket.

* * * *

Charlie was shocked by her reaction. A glance at his brothers and they seemed to be, too. She was shutting them out. That was obvious. For some reason she didn't want to face them right now.

He never backed down from a challenge. He was a soldier.

Charlie moved in front of her and blocked the sunlight.

"What else did you hear?" Lori asked as she looked straight at him, following his eyes as he knelt down on the blanket in front of her.

"I'm not the enemy, baby. We're worried about you. Should you really be out here all alone?"

"Jesus! I don't need a Goddamn babysitter."

"Watch your tongue," Trevor stated from the side of her.

She exhaled in annoyance, closed her eyes, and started taking slow, easy breaths. He was freaking out with concern. Could she be so upset about her life and so stressed that she had a panic attack? She could have been hospitalized.

"Baby, we just wanted to make sure you're all right," Dante stated.

"I'm fine, Dante, even Andrew said so. It's happened before, I'll get control of it," she told him with great confidence as she leaned back, letting her arms stretch to support her upper body as she closed her eyes and absorbed the sun.

"Now could the three of you please let me be alone? I just want to be alone."

Charlie knew she was trying to act tough but he knew better. She needed them and he would make her see that no matter what.

"I thought we were getting together today?"

* * * *

Lori held her eyes shut, afraid to speak, to answer him because her throat was full. She wanted to cry. She needed to just cry and the thought of doing so right at this very moment didn't frighten her. It actually made her giggle a little. She had read about this feeling before, had even heard other women speak of it. "I need a good cry" is what they would say.

She knew the three men watched her and waited patiently. They weren't patient men. Not by a long shot.

Lori opened her eyes then turned onto her side, lying on the blanket and propped up on her elbow.

"I'm sorry. I thought I needed to be alone but that's not true. It's the complete opposite of what I need."

Charlie fell into the same position beside her, propped up on his elbow, staring at one another, face-to-face.

"Tell me what I can do, baby. Just tell me how I can make you feel better." He was so sincere, so loving and empathetic. Dante moved in behind her and Trevor sat down above her head. They brought her instant peace and comfort. This was exactly why she thought of them this morning after the panic attack. She could easily learn to lean on them and need them. She already was.

Still she fought against speaking, her voice felt shaky.

Stay silent. Just stay silent.

Lori reached over and touched the gray cotton T-shirt that lay loose against Charlie's chest. She wrapped the material around her fingers and moved her body closer against his. Instinctively he embraced her. Behind her she felt Dante move his hand over her waist, and above her Trevor touched her hair.

There was no stopping the tears as she held on tightly, sobbing, as all the events that had occurred over the past five years finally weighed their toll on her.

* * * *

Dante felt his heart ache. It actually ached from hearing his woman sob. She was strong, she was beautiful, but she had done more than her share and kept everything inside. He knew from experience that bad memories alone can do some serious damage. Charlie and Trevor knew that as well.

Dante moved her hair from her wet cheeks as she remained holding Charlie. Trevor caressed her hair and now Dante kissed her bare shoulder. The tank top she wore had very thin straps, and he kissed along the strap then to her neck. Eventually, Lori rolled to her back as she wiped her eyes.

* * * *

Lori didn't feel embarrassed. She felt relieved. All three of them remained with her as she cried. They touched her, comforted her and whispered to her. She glanced at Charlie who kept a hand over her belly on her right side. Then she looked at Dante, who kept a hand on her belly toward the left side and then she tilted her head back toward Trevor who continued to caress her hair. She chuckled at the sight.

"What's so funny?" Trevor asked. She smiled.

"Three extra-large, sexy, good-looking men, squished around a small blanket. You all look very uncomfortable."

Dante moved his hand up and cupped her breasts. She squealed as she reached for his hand but he was too quick. He pressed a thigh between her thighs and held her face between his hands.

"I'm comfortable now," he said, lying over her. Then he kissed her softly.

Very quickly that kiss turned hotter. She felt his hand ease from her cheek, over her shoulder, then back to her breast. He massaged the mound as his tongue explored her mouth. She gripped his shirt, pulling him snugger against her.

He maneuvered his hand down lower and reached under her tank top.

She shifted her position to give him better access to her body. He had her all fired up. As Dante released her lips, he pressed the palm of his hand over the cup of her bra and to her breast. Holding his gaze, she saw the hunger in his eyes and she wished they were somewhere more private. Dante continued to spread kisses along her neck and collarbone then to her breast as he pushed the material of her tank top upward.

She grabbed ahold of his head as he licked the nipple then pulled it between his teeth.

Lori moaned then opened her thighs wider, thrusting her pussy against his ribs.

"We want you, Lori. We want to make love to you," Charlie whispered, brushing his thumb ever so slightly against her cheek.

Dante nipped her breast and she jerked.

"Oh, Dante, what are you doing to me?" She could hear her erratic breathing.

She felt his mouth release her breast. Then he placed the bra back into position along with her top.

"Getting a little sample. But I want more."

"So do I. Let's go. We need privacy," Trevor stated as he rose and began to pack up the stuff.

Dante got up and offered a hand to Lori. She stared at it a moment. She knew that if she accepted his hand and their proclamation of wanting her, then she was going to make love to them.

Charlie gave her a wink.

"Come on, baby. Trust us to take care of you."

She took a leap of faith and placed her hand in Dante's. As he pulled her up and against his body, he held her tight.

His palms moved down her back to her rear, using her—what she believed to be—big ass as leverage to press her body snugger against his.

"You're going to be ours forever. We're going to take care of you, the way you deserve to be cared for."

* * * *

Such a large burden was lifted from her chest. She didn't realize how much of a difference it made letting her feelings out and literally crying on Charlie's shoulder.

Lori acknowledged these feelings of need running through her system. She needed Charlie, Trevor, and Dante in so many ways. In such a short period of time they had become important beyond anything she could ever imagine. She needed their presence in her life. She felt it in her heart as well as deep within her soul. But ultimately, right now, as they walked flanking her like guards of her body, she needed them physically. She'd saved herself out of fear, inopportunity, and hope that one day she could get that happily ever after she heard existed.

As they entered the front door to the men's custom-built, two-level ranch, Lori absorbed her surroundings. She was surprised at how modern the design of the house was and how open the layout. There were two living rooms and one was decorated more elaborately than the other. She assumed that they considered that one the formal living room despite their use of a cowhide print rug under a glass-top, wrought iron table.

The dining room wasn't as formal with rather large, bulky red maple furniture. The china closet spread across one entire wall and was more like three times the size of a traditional china closet. It seemed that they had very few items in it from what she could see and she wondered why they had chosen such a large piece.

As if reading her mind, Charlie explained about finding the piece at an old estate sale. He admired the detailed artistry of the etched woodwork that decorated the frame above the china closet. He purchased the matching hutch as well. Although it was very large, Lori could tell the detailed decoration was unique as she walked out of the dining area and into the kitchen.

It was gorgeous with its dark cherrywood cabinetry and fancy trim moldings. Some cabinets contained etched glass revealing crystal service ware and wine glasses.

The dark black-and-brown-speckled marble countertop was rich and sleek looking. She had never seen anything like it as she slid her hand over the top of the island.

"Do you like it? We installed it ourselves, as well as the cabinets," Dante stated.

"You mean this is all custom made? The cabinets and everything?"

"It was a lot of work but we enjoyed doing it and I'm pleased with the end result," Charlie told her. She was amazed at their creative ability and woodworking skills.

"You three should be more than pleased, Charlie. This is the most beautiful kitchen I've ever been in. It makes me want to cook. Create a culinary masterpiece," she told them as she twirled around the island.

Trevor laughed, grabbed her hand, and pulled her against him.

"You'll do no such thing. I want you to relax while we prepare a little lunch, and promise me that you'll stay for dinner. We had planned on inviting you and now we can spend the entire day together. How does that sound?" he asked.

"Perfect!" Lori told him as she laid her head against his chest.

Trevor held Lori close as he placed his hand behind her neck then through her hair to the base of her head where he began to massage.

His fingers were strong, thick, and capable as he aroused her body and relaxed her at the same time.

Lori closed her eyes a moment, absorbing his touch and looked up toward Trevor, then to Charlie and Dante. Trevor took her face in his hands as he bent his head down to kiss her. Lori wrapped her arms around his neck and their kissing became more intense. Their tongues met softly at first. Then the battle began for control of the other's territory began.

Their breathing became rapid as Lori's hands moved under Trevor's shirt. She wanted to feel his skin against her hands as she slowly ran her nails up and down his back. Trevor was kissing her neck, sending goose bumps all through her body.

"I don't think I can stop this time, baby." He pulled her leg up against him rubbing his hands against her skin from ankle to hip.

Lori didn't want him to stop. She didn't want the sensations he gave her entire body to ever end.

"Don't stop, Trevor. I'm ready! I want to!" she told him and he paused a moment as he took her face into his hands.

"Are you sure, baby? The three of us want you so badly, but we know this is a lot to digest and you've waited for the right moment."

She felt the tears sting her eyes. Trevor didn't want her to have any regrets later.

"Yes, I'm sure, Trevor. I want all three of you to be my firsts. This is the right moment. I know it, in here." She placed her hand over her chest where her heart beat rapidly beneath her skin.

Trevor smiled instantly. Then he picked her up and she wrapped her legs around his waist as he carried her upstairs to his bedroom.

"Let us go get the room ready," Charlie said as he and Dante passed them by. They each caressed her thigh as they passed.

Trevor stopped and pressed her against the wall. He lowered his mouth and kissed her deeply as she wrapped her arms around his shoulders.

* * * *

"I'm shaking, Charlie. I'm fucking shaking," Dante admitted to his brother as they lowered the lights, pulled down the shades slightly, and then lit some candles. "Where the hell did you get those?" Dante asked about the candles.

"I picked them up last week. I thought a romantic setting would be nice when we made love to Lori for the first time. I'm just as nervous as you are, Dante. This is happening," Charlie admitted.

"It is and we're gonna make her so happy, Charlie, and she's perfect for the three of us. I didn't realize you were such a romantic. First the bracelet, then the gazebo, and now the candles."

"I'm not. It's Lori that brings it out in me."

Trevor carried Lori into the room.

Trevor gently lay her down on the bed, caressing her face and hair with his hand.

* * * *

"I want this to be perfect," he told her and she felt the nerves making her hands shake. She avoided eye contact with the men as Charlie pulled off his shirt then Trevor's. She swallowed hard then let her hand glide across the dark navy-blue comforter as her eyes spanned the room.

It was very bold and masculine looking with dark, rich colors of navy, burgundy, and hunter green. The furniture had four large, wide, maple wooden posts supporting a king-size bed. The room itself was very large and contained its own sitting area with a love seat and lounge chair as well as a master bathroom. Lori could see the beige marble flooring from where she lay. But then she felt the set of hands on her shoulders and the tall, large presence behind her.

"Relax, and just feel," Charlie told her.

She closed her eyes and allowed his touch to soothe her nerves.

She absorbed his cologne as he moved in front of her and Dante moved in behind her. She opened her eyes and looked up into Charlie's eyes.

"You look amazing in this light."

Charlie adjusted his stance then kissed her softly on the lips then her cheek and onto her neck. His hands fell to her hips, and as he caressed her hip bones with his hands, he grabbed hold of the bottom of her tank top, lifting it over her head and tossing it onto the floor.

She instantly assisted. She had stared at these men for far too long, admiring their bodies and their muscles. She was about to have sex for the very first time in her life with three sexy, hot soldiers. A fantasy come true.

She responded by helping him remove his gray T-shirt so she could see his tan, muscular chest and belly. It was odd, but she felt self-conscious as her hands glided across ridges upon ridges of pure muscular flesh. The tattoos, the depth of each large muscle made her mouth water, and then she felt the second set of hands on her hips, pulling her pants and her panties down.

"Damn, woman, you've got an amazing body," Dante said.

"Sure do, sweetness," Charlie whispered, then smiled at her.

"I love your muscles and the tattoos," she told Charlie. It seemed to touch him in some deep way. His eyes looked darker and he stared down at the cleavage of her breasts and the swell of her belly. Then, all the way to her pussy.

As he began to reach for her hips, she heard Dante behind her next to Trevor.

"Allow me." He unclipped her bra and let it fall to the floor.

"Sweet mother, you're perfect," Charlie said, sliding his palms up her ribs to her breasts. He cupped them and she tilted her head back and moaned.

"She sure is responsive to our touch," Dante whispered. Then she felt the tongue against the crevice of her ass, then teeth.

"Hey!" she exclaimed, grabbing onto Charlie.

He covered her mouth and kissed her deeply, all thoughts of the sneak attack on her ass cheeks by Trevor disintegrated by Charlie.

They removed the remainder of their clothing and Charlie pulled down the covers. Once again their kisses became rapid as they squeezed and grabbed every part of one another.

* * * *

Charlie wanted Lori's first time to be amazing. Saving herself for them was more than worth it as he let his tongue glide across her chest, capturing a nipple as her body responded. She tilted her pelvis and looked toward him then his brothers who joined them on the bed. Charlie wasn't the least bit uncomfortable having his brothers naked in front of him and Lori. They wanted this type of relationship and all its benefits. They wanted Lori and today was the day they would seal their fate with her and hers with them.

He held her wrists gently by her side with his hands as he moved his tongue lower and lower. She was built to please a man and was going to make this memorable for her. The scent of her arousal nearly set him moving faster for the ultimate goal—his cock deep in her pussy and her belonging to him and his brothers. He licked across her skin, tasting the sweetness of her body spray moving along her curves, past her firm stomach, and straight to her bare pussy.

"Oh, Charlie," she whispered, but then Dante kissed her from above as Trevor leaned down to cup her breast then have a taste.

* * * *

Lori closed her eyes, absorbing Charlie's moves, his every touch. He teased her, tantalized her, touched her as he claimed every part of her body with his mouth, his teeth, and his fingers.

Trevor latched onto her breast, sucking and stimulating her body. She never knew that breasts were directly attached to her pussy. But there seemed to be some sort of imaginary string, and as he sucked and nibbled, her pussy clenched and released her cream. She worried that she may not taste good, but as Charlie suckled and moaned then continued to feast on her pussy, she felt relief.

Dante thrust his tongue into her mouth. She didn't know what to do. Charlie still held her wrists by her sides, restraining her, and she wanted to touch them. She wanted to feel all of them and look at all of them up close.

As the men continued and Dante released her lips to kiss along her neck and shoulder, she widened her thighs and thrust upward.

"Please, Charlie. Please." Her body shook and she came.

As she tried to recover, she opened her eyes in time to see Charlie pulling on a condom. She felt her legs shake and then she looked at all three men. Dante stared into her eyes as he pinched her nipple, making her moan. Trevor licked across her nipple and pulled it between his teeth. She was in awe of their bodies, and their thick, long cocks.

She stared from the condom-encased cock, up over the perfect, twelve-pack and to the chiseled chest then into the eyes of a very hungry-looking Charlie.

"I'm ready, baby, and I want in. Please tell me we're a go."

She smiled at him as her heart soared.

"It's a go, soldier."

This was it, the moment Lori had dreamed about and held off from indulging in, saving herself for the perfect person. Now here they were, so unexpected, like a twister out of nowhere, stealing her heart, possessing her body, leaving nothing untouched or unaffected, never the same after today.

"I love you, baby, you know that, right?" he whispered in her ear. His breath alone drew her body against him, never mind what the words did to her heart.

"I love you, too," she replied, her voice shaking, her body moist with anticipation.

Slowly he entered her and simultaneously they moaned with pleasure and instant satisfaction. Their emotions and desires took control as they rocked in sync and Lori held on to Charlie's shoulders as he kissed her, and made love to her.

Time stood still as they continued to make love for the very first time, lost in the moment and in one another. Every stroke of his cock into her pussy brought them closer together. She wanted to hold on to this feeling forever. She wanted to bottle it up and keep it in safekeeping. She loved the feel of his heavy body over hers and how lost she instantly was beneath him and him inside of her.

"Oh, Charlie, it feels so good. You're so big."

"I'm going slow, baby, but I'm glad you feel it. You feel how close we are? You feel the connection when we're like this and I'm inside of you?"

She felt the tears reach her eyes.

"Oh yes, Charlie. I want more. Give me more."

He lifted up and stroked back in a little harder. A little deeper.

"More," she added, liking the sensation of his cock thrusting against her inner muscles.

"She looks amazing," Dante whispered.

"I can't wait to make love to you, too, Lori," Trevor admitted. She smiled then began to kiss along Charlie's neck. As she licked and sucked, she felt his cock actually grow bigger inside of her. It was some sort of reaction to her nibbling and sucking. As if unsure, she did it again, then again, and suddenly Charlie moaned then began to increase his speed. He was thrusting in and out of her, moving fast and deep, making her lose her breath.

She gripped his shoulders and felt something deep within her begin to tighten and ache. "Oh God, I feel something tight. I feel something," she said aloud.

"Go with it, baby. Let it all go," Dante instructed as Charlie grunted and now pounded into her in quick deep strokes.

She widened her legs and thrust upward as the orgasm overtook her body. She collided with his flesh. Their pubic bones crashed together and she screamed her release as Charlie moaned his. She actually felt the explosive orgasm and the heat of Charlie's cock. He breathed in against her neck, releasing her wrists and hugging her as he pulled her to the side so he wouldn't crush her.

They were perspiring and catching their breath as Charlie began kissing her all over.

"So good. Baby, that was amazing. You're amazing." He gave her a squeeze as if to reassure himself that it was her, she was there, and that he didn't want to let her go.

* * * *

They lay facing one another, legs entwined as Charlie gently dragged his hand across her breast, down her ribcage, and onto her thigh. "I can't stop touching you. You're perfect, do you know that?" he asked and Lori touched his lips with her finger.

"You're perfect. That was...unbelievable," she whispered and he pulled her closer to him.

When she felt the bed dip, she turned to see Dante and Trevor.

"Go to them, Lori. Let them make love to you and bring us together as one."

She swallowed hard as Dante lifted her up. They were kneeling in front of one another. Their knees touching as Dante cupped both her breasts.

"So voluptuous. You're incredibly passionate when you make love, Lori. I need you," he whispered then moved one hand up her chest to her shoulder then neck, cupping her head.

She tilted back as he moved forward to kiss her. It was an amazing feeling. She acknowledged the fact that she felt just as much arousal and attraction to Dante as she did for Charlie. She knew it would be the same for Trevor, as Dante released her lips and kissed along her neck.

She looked toward Trevor and he was kneeling there, too, his long, thick cock in his hands. She shuddered at seeing him naked and beautiful. Both men had tattoos. Both men had bodies like works of art.

Shyly she lowered her head, and that was when Lori noticed the little red spot on the white sheet. She was suddenly embarrassed, and as she tried to cover the spot with her hand, it was too late.

Dante and Trevor saw it. Her heart beat rapidly in her chest as she felt Dante cover her hand and then gently move her fingers.

She felt Charlie lean over behind her. His erection hard against her ass as a mix of emotions consumed her mind and body. She was still embarrassed but she was also aroused. She wasn't sure how they would react. Was it appropriate for them to see this? Many questions went through her mind.

Charlie took Lori by her shoulders and turned her toward him. If there was any doubt somewhere deep in their minds that she had lied about her virginity, it immediately disappeared at the sight of the sheets. He was Lori's first, it would always be that way.

Dante placed his fingers under her chin, tilting her face up toward his.

"Baby, don't be shy with us. We're a team, a unit, a family now. Trevor and I are going to make love to you, too. This is so amazing. You're so amazing." He kissed her lips then released her as Trevor ran his hand up her thigh.

"We're honored to be your first and only lovers, baby. Honored." He leaned forward and gently kissed her shoulder. That was when she felt Charlie's warm breath collide against her bare neck and shoulder.

"Don't be embarrassed, baby. You've given me something so valuable that I could never forget, never mind ever reciprocate. You're going to be mine, be ours, forever." He laid her back down onto the bed.

* * * *

Dante moved between her thighs, spreading them with the palms of his hands. He felt overwhelmed with emotions. One look at Lori, her naked body, and the treasure she just gave them, and he was in awe of her. His heart was racing. He never expected to fall so hard, so fast for another human being ever.

"I love you," he whispered as Charlie moved out of the way and Dante lowered over Lori with his hands above her shoulders and next to the sides of her head.

She reached up and caressed her palms over his chest muscles, causing his cock to react.

"I want to make love to you. I need you now."

"Yes, Dante. Please make love to me."

He lowered his body, pressing his cock between her wet, tight folds. He kissed her lips and plunged into the deep unknown, following his gut and, he hoped, his destiny.

Dante sat still once he was fully seated inside of her. Their bodies locked, their lips and tongues battling for control of the passionate kiss, fueled his desire.

He loved the feel of her dainty feet pressing into his ribs as she tried to rock her hips to get him to move.

He pulled slowly from her mouth and leaned above her on one elbow while he caressed a stray hair from her cheek.

"You're going to learn fast that I like being in control. Especially in bed." He thrust his hips, making her gasp. She caressed his upper arms and the feel of her hands, her plump breasts against his skin made him feel needy.

He pulled slightly out of her then thrust back into her. He used his upper body muscles to hold himself above her body, being sure not to crush her even though he wanted to be part of her in every way. These were foreign emotions as he stroked her pussy, increasing his speed and the thrusts.

He couldn't hold back. He loved the feel of her vaginal muscles clinging to his cock, milking him with every inch.

"Damn, baby, you're so tight and you feel incredible. I need more. I want everything. Come on, baby. Give it to me. Give me more." He pulled up and thrust into her hard and fast. He grabbed a hold of her hands and wrists, placed them above her head, then thrust into her over and over again. She rolled her head side to side and called his name as she counterthrust.

"So good. I can't hold back. Come with me, Lori. Come now." She moaned then shook beneath him as the sloshing sound filled the room, and he thrust three more times before exploding, too.

He remained inside of her and hugged her tight, pulling her to his side as they calmed their breathing.

Dante caressed the damp strands of hair from her cheeks and gripped her chin gently.

She stared at him and he licked her lower lip then nipped it gently.

"So delicious. You're perfect."

Dante kissed her until Trevor moved in behind her.

* * * *

Trevor thought Lori was so beautiful. Her body a work of art, her skin creamy soft. As hard as his cock was and as needy as he felt to make love to her and become one, he also wanted to relish in what belonged to him. And she did belong to him and his brothers. He would never let her go. There would never be another man. No one but he, Dante, and Charlie would touch her, make love to her, or possess her.

His words encouraged his actions as he kissed along her ankle, up her outer calf to her thigh then hip. He used his free hand to roll her to her back, and when she looked at him, his heart soared in adoration some more.

"You're sexy, baby. I just want to lick and taste every inch of you."

She reached toward his head, ran her fingers through his hair as he adjusted his body between her thighs before licking across her hardened nipple.

He twirled his tongue around the areola then pulled the ripened berry between his teeth. He felt the gush of cream from her pussy instantly against his belly.

"I could lie here with you, exploring this body for hours." He licked between her breasts then adjusted his cock against her folds.

Lori raised her thighs up.

He lifted up so that he was kneeling between her legs.

"Your pussy looks so beautiful and wet. It's glistening with your sweet cream, baby." He touched a finger over her folds. She moaned then thrust her hips upward so that his fingers could stroke her more deeply.

He desired her so much and wanted everything from her.

"Tell me who you belong to."

Her chest rose and fell with every shaky breath.

"You, Charlie, and Dante," she whispered then licked her bottom lip.

"That's right, baby." Trevor pressed his thumbs against her pussy lips.

"This body is ours now. You're our woman and we're going to take care of you."

"Yes, Trevor. Oh God, yes. Please don't stop touching me." He pressed a digit up into her pussy and let his other finger press against her puckered hole.

She grabbed for his wrist when his fingers breached her two holes. "Trevor."

"Move you hand. This pussy and ass are mine to explore."

"Oh God, this is crazy."

He felt the gush of cream collide against his fingers.

"Take your hands and place them under your knees and pull back."

She stared at him, looking so uncertain and turned on.

"Do it," Dante ordered and Trevor hid his chuckle. Charlie and Dante were seated on the bed on either side of Lori now and watching her.

"What are you going to do?" she asked as she slowly ran her feminine hands down her thighs to under her knees.

"See what belongs to us." He assisted her in spreading her thighs up and wide. "Oh yeah. That's it." He pressed one finger into her pussy and one through the tight rings of her anus.

"Oh!" she moaned as she thrust her hips down against both fingers.

Trevor smiled, feeling content in his exploration and her acceptance.

"That's it, baby. Just relax and feel."

He moved over her and kissed her mouth as she held her thighs wide.

"You're such a good girl. You want my cock, baby?"

"Yes. Yes, please now."

He chuckled as he pulled his fingers from her ass and cunt. He grabbed his cock and aligned it with her pussy. She was about to release her thighs and he stopped her.

"Hold them wide for me."

"Oh." She moaned another release as Trevor shoved into her in one smooth thrust.

* * * *

Lori was on fire as she convulsed beneath Trevor. Her arms were shaking, her thighs ached and her pussy was on fire. With every stroke of his hard, long cock she lost her breath. His words, his sexual demands fed some inner sex goddess inside of her. She couldn't help but wonder if this was what sex was like for everyone or just her and her three men.

"Oh, Trevor, I can't hold on. I'm shaking."

"I'm almost there, sexy. You hold on and you let me in. Let me claim you, every part of you."

He thrust again and again and Lori felt her body tighten up to almost feeling achiness when she felt his cock grow thicker. She screamed her release and shook beneath him.

Trevor thrust into her deeply, grabbing onto her shoulders as he tilted his hips and exploded inside of her.

"Oh, sexy woman of mine, that was fucking incredible." Trevor hugged her tightly and rolled to his side, caressing her body everywhere.

She released her thighs and now held him close and kissed his shoulder. When she felt his fingers graze over her anus, she tightened up.

Trevor pulled back and looked at her.

She instantly knew that was a look of determination, power, control, and possession in every sense. It heightened her affection for him and his brothers. She nearly lost her breath and felt as if her heart skipped a beat.

"This ass is ours, too." The intensity in his voice matched his facial expression. It was reflected in his eyes, and she accepted every bit of it, as he pressed his finger harder.

Somehow, his naughty touch aroused her body again and he smiled knowingly.

"Soon. Very soon." Then he stroked her as he kissed her and once again she opened up for her lover, giving him all of her.

Chapter 14

"Oh, Jasper, we have to slow down. This is crazy," Maggie said as she sat up on the blanket and rebuttoned the first two buttons of her blouse.

Jasper propped himself up on one elbow and put his hand on Maggie's thigh. She was so beautiful and he just couldn't stop himself.

"I'm sorry, darling, don't get mad. I can't help myself, you smell so delicious."

He rubbed her thigh with his hand.

"Really, Jasper, stop that," Maggie said as she shyly turned away from him.

He sat up beside her, gently taking her face between his hands.

"I'm serious, Maggie, I can't get enough of you." He kissed her lips. She closed her eyes and once again their kisses were deeper and longer. Neither of them would release the other one's lips. Their legs were entwined as Maggie held a handful of Jasper's hair.

Maggie felt on the edge of being out of control. She wanted so much, but fear was a captivating and powerful emotion. She ran her hands along his shoulders and neck as he continued to kiss her. Even his neck was muscular and despite the fact that he was a little hefty around the stomach and waist, Maggie found him sexy and attractive. He was bulky, solid, not fat, and it kind of intimidated her, too. She never thought she could ever feel this way. Although she was young and thought she loved Derrick, he never made her feel this intense. Her whole body was shaking and she wanted Jasper more and more.

She had no right to be in this position. She had promised herself long ago that Ben was her priority in life. She made a huge mistake that could have cost them their lives and she wouldn't take a chance of that happening again.

She abruptly turned her head away from him.

"No, Jasper. I can't do this…it isn't right."

* * * *

Jasper was caught off guard at her sudden change of emotion as he watched her get up off the blanket and walk toward the water's edge.

He took a deep breath trying to think of the right words to say to Maggie. He recognized fear when he saw it. She was shaking.

He slowly joined Maggie, standing beside her when all he really wanted to do was embrace her.

"Maggie, what is it? Are you scared? Did I…" He didn't complete his sentence as Maggie quickly looked toward him.

"Yes, I'm scared! I'm so damn scared it's not even funny."

He took her hand and brought her fingers to his lips. He kissed each one then brought her hand to his chest. He laid it flat against his shirt, over his heart.

"Do you feel that? Can you feel my heart racing?" he asked her, as a tear rolled down her cheek.

"Baby, it's you. Maggie, you do this to me. You make my heart race, my palms all sweaty, and my entire world is turned upside down over you. I know you're scared, Maggie. God knows, I don't blame you one bit for what that asshole put you, Ben, and Lori through. But with God as my witness, I am not Derrick. My mamma raised me better and the United States military enforced it all. I've seen people die, Maggie. I know pain, and when I'm with you, all those bad memories fade away." He cupped her cheek with his free hand while he still held her palm against his chest.

"You're special to me. You've become so important and so has

Ben. Give us a chance, Maggie. One chance for me to prove to you that true love can heal any scar. No matter how deep."

She stared into his eyes and he waited, heart racing, hoping that she would accept his request. She closed her eyes, took a deep breath then turned her face to kiss his palm.

"I'll try, Jasper. Please help me and take things slow and I'll try."

He pulled her into his arms and squeezed her tight. He prayed to God that he could be the man to make her happy, because he already knew that Maggie completed him.

Chapter 15

Lori awoke instantly feeling the warm body against her back and the strong, solid arm she held against her breasts. She blinked repeatedly, realizing that it was dark. Had she fallen asleep all afternoon and into the evening?

Strong, warm lips kissed her shoulder.

"You're safe, angel. I've got you." *Dante.*

She sighed in appreciation of waking up with such a sex god holding her. The man was a perfect image of a soldier. Even now, in the darkness as she closed her eyes she could see him naked. Ridges upon ridges of muscles, the man was his own arsenal.

She gripped his forearm which was pressed snugly below her breasts, and she felt her pussy awaken.

"What time is it?" she whispered, and he moved his arm, taking a new position over her, with one thigh wedged between her thighs. As he moved his thigh again and rubbed slightly against her pussy, she knew he was aware of her arousal.

"Dinnertime." He leaned up on his elbows, placing her body underneath him in such a way she felt both encaged and protected. She didn't know if she wanted to escape from the empowerment of his possession or close her eyes and exhale in relief of him being here, keeping her safe and secure. She closed her eyes and took a long, calming breath.

Dante pressed his thumbs gently over her temples, massaging her hair from her face. He cupped her cheeks between his hands and stared down at her. She anticipated opening her eyes to see his gorgeous, serious hazel ones, or to relish a little longer in the security of his hold. She had not awoken in a cold sweat, fearing her life or the lives of Ben and Maggie. It was obvious how dependent she was becoming on Dante, Trevor and Charlie, but she worried about rushing things. She wanted forever, but they were experienced and a lot older, maybe they had more patience than her.

"What's wrong, sweet angel?" he asked. When she opened her eyes and saw his sincerity, his strong, chiseled face, and pure masculine beauty, she smiled.

"I'm afraid to say."

He adjusted his body so that he encased hers completely with his own. He kept his forearms down, surrounding her shoulders, neck, and head as he slowly thrust his cock against her wet folds.

In a breathless sigh and response to his nonverbal insistence that she tell him what was on her mind, she exhaled her words.

"I need you. I've instantly become reliant on you, Charlie, and Trevor. I don't feel anxious, scared, or fearful of the nightmares that bring on the attacks when one of you is with me. Like this." She tilted her body upward, best she could with such an extra-large man covering her.

He smiled then caressed a finger across her cheek to her lips. He continued a pathway down her ribs and hip before grabbing her tightly and maneuvering his cock into her pussy.

"Good," he said through clenched teeth as he stroked into her. She opened her thighs wider to give him better access to her cunt but his bold expression and dark eyes bore into hers.

"I need you in my life, every moment of every day. I don't want to let you go. I don't want you out of my sight," he stated firmly, making her heart soar in relief.

She straddled his waist, and he maneuvered his hips then leaned down and kissed her hard on the mouth. His hands gripped her arms and pressed them up above her head as he lifted his torso. He was now above her, thrusting his cock into her over and over again as their fingers entwined above her head. Her breasts pushed out, her pussy ached with soreness and desire for more cock. It was outrageous.

Moaning and trying to catch her breath with his heavy strokes, she felt the tears roll down her cheeks.

"Dante, you complete me, too."

They locked gazes as he continued to thrust into her, imprinting his love on her body and in her heart forever.

Over and over again he thrust until she exploded around him, calling his name. He pulled from her body, hugging her close while he exploded against her stomach.

Even in the heat of passion, he took care of her and she loved him for it and would love him, Charlie, and Trevor forever.

* * * *

Charlie and Trevor walked into the bedroom. They were showered and dressed. Trevor turned on the light by the bedside table and took a seat on the bed.

"Hey, gorgeous." He caressed Lori's shoulder as she hugged Dante close.

Charlie and Trevor had heard Lori and Dante making love. It got his dick hard and the need to see Lori and hold her became nearly unbearable. He felt a bit on edge and he didn't like it.

"What's going on?" he asked as he noticed their bodies were locked. Dante slowly pulled away from Lori and he saw that his brother wasn't wearing a condom.

"We need to take a shower," Dante said.

"I can see that. What the hell were you thinking not using protection, Dante?" Charlie asked.

"It's okay. He pulled out," Lori replied ever so sweetly and innocently. She may have lived a life in danger and on the run for five years, but she was still inexperienced and it was their responsibility as older men, her lovers, to take care of her at all times.

"You can still get pregnant."

"I was careful, Charlie," Dante said, sounding annoyed at Charlie for acting as if he were the leader of this arrangement. Well he was the oldest and he was going to make certain that this ménage relationship worked for everyone's benefit and especially Lori. She needed love and protection.

"If this relationship is going to work, Lori needs to come first. Her protection and her safety are priority."

Dante slowly pulled up from the bed and Lori immediately grabbed the sheet to cover her body. The sight of her nakedness got him all aroused again and he wanted nothing more than to jump into that bed and make love to her again. But she was probably sore, from having sex multiple times for the first time in her life.

"She needs to soak in a tub. Trevor, get it ready for her." Charlie barked out orders.

"Dinner will be ready in twenty minutes."

"I should call home and let them know where I am," Lori said, sounding completely scared. Charlie didn't mean to bark out orders. It was just the way he was.

He walked over toward the bed and gave Dante an annoyed expression. Dante grabbed his upper arm.

"I would never hurt her or put Lori in harm's way." He released Charlie's arm then walked out of the room.

When Charlie looked down at Lori, she was gripping the sheet tightly against her chest and staring at him in shock or maybe fear. Had he scared her?

Trevor walked into the bathroom to get the tub ready. Charlie sat down on the bed, his thigh touched her thigh.

Charlie reached out to press a strand of her blonde hair away from her cheek. He cupped it as he stared into her green eyes.

"Are you sore?"

She nibbled her bottom lip and shook her head slowly side to side.

"Don't lie to me. The bath will help."

She squinted her eyes at him in annoyance. That was obvious.

"This type of relationship is special and unique. It takes a lot of self-control and sometimes one of us may mess up, but if we talk about it, we can work it out."

"Charlie, no one messed up."

He brushed his thumb along her lower lip.

"We have a lot to talk about. You need to take a hot bath and you're probably starving. Let me help you up."

Charlie stood up then went to lift Lori and she swatted his hand away.

"I can do it. I'm fine," she said with an attitude. He controlled his temper. He knew she was tough but they all made love to her and then Dante a second time. She would definitely be sore. They were big men and she was a feminine and petite woman. He didn't want her to associate sex and pain with them.

As she went to stand up, she cringed slightly.

"You see, Goddamn it. Listen to me when I tell you something." He scooped her up into his arms and began carrying her across the room.

"Put me down. I am more than capable of walking."

He was pissed off instantly at her inability to allow him to care for her. She couldn't walk. He didn't want her to feel any pain, and if she soaked in the tub and then stood up, she would surely feel better.

"What's going on?" Trevor asked as they approached the tub.

"She's sore."

"We didn't hurt you, did we, sexy?" Trevor asked then caressed her cheek.

"No, damn you. Charlie is being ridiculous," she snapped. Trevor widened his eyes in shock then immediately vacated the bathroom.

He knew Charlie had a temper. Everyone who knew Charlie knew that when he gave a direct order, you'd better listen and do it.

"I'm going to set you down slowly."

As he began to set her feet down, Lori pulled from him, nearly tumbling into the bathtub.

He grabbed her upper arms to steady her.

"What are you doing? Stand still and let me take care of you."

"Charlie." She said his name so loudly it shocked him. As he looked down at her, realizing once again how petite and sexy she was, he saw the anger in her eyes.

She placed her hands on her hips, causing her beautiful, full breasts to bounce slightly with the movement. He couldn't help but stare in appreciation for what belonged to him.

"I am more than capable of taking care of myself. Stop patronizing me."

Her attitude and abrupt retort got under his skin. He wasn't used to anyone answering him back. He was used to being in control and in command and this wasn't going to change. He stepped closer, making her step back until her lower thighs hit the tub. The steam from the water rose up behind her making her look even more seductive and beautiful.

He reached out to place his hand on her hip and she jumped ever so slightly. So she wasn't as tough as she claimed to be.

He gripped her hips with both hands and pulled her hard against his body. His cock flush against her belly and chest, he stared down at her.

"I am not patronizing you, I am caring for you. I don't want you to associate making love with three men and pain together. We're big." He thrust his cock against her naked body and she widened her eyes, getting his message. "I want to make sure when you're with us, there's nothing but love and happiness."

She took a deep breath and stared at him with such indignation, which then turned to tenderness.

"Then stop pissing me off and ordering me around,"

He felt his blood pressure rising.

He immediately lifted her up, she straddled his waist, and he kissed her hard on the mouth. There wasn't anything more for him to say. He wanted to tell her to get used to his orders and to realize that he was going to take care of her and protect her from anything that could possibly upset Lori or make her have an anxiety attack. But instead he placed his emotions into the kiss and before long, she was tearing off his clothes and he was helping her.

They were breathing heavy, nipping at one another's mouths and chins.

"You need discipline," he told her, now standing in front of her naked.

"You need to lighten up and stop being a drill sergeant."

He lowered to take a nipple into his mouth and suck hard.

She gasped, and when he released her breast, she leaned forward and pulled his nipple into her mouth giving as good as she was getting.

Charlie lowered down, lifted her ass cheeks, and turned her toward the counter. He aligned his cock with her pussy and shoved into her hard.

Lori gasped as her nails dug onto his arms where his elbows bent.

In and out he thrust into her and she counterthrusted back. He realized what a hypocrite he was fucking her without a condom like Dante had. This was exactly what he was doing. He was fucking her, trying to enforce his command into his woman, and damn it to hell, she was giving it right back to him.

He licked and sucked into her neck as he pushed harder into her cunt.

"You will learn to listen to me."

"Not a chance in hell," she retorted and that was it. She exploded and he was close behind.

"Damn stubborn woman." He growled out then pulled from her body and hugged her to him as he exploded against her skin.

The feel of her toned thighs against his waist and her wet pussy made him feel like an animal that claimed its mate.

"Never like this. I've never felt anything like this," he whispered against her neck. When he felt her fingers caressing his crew-cut hair, he knew he was obsessed with Lori.

He squeezed her ass tighter.

"Mine," he told her, and the damn wise-ass woman squeezed his ass back.

* * * *

They all gathered around the kitchen table. Charlie insisted upon carrying her downstairs after they took a shower together since the bath water had grown cold while they had sex. Lori felt her cheeks warm at the memory. These men were so alike, yet so different. Charlie insisted upon being in control at all times. He was bossy and commanding, but she loved it. She realized that the best way to deal with him when he pissed her off was to give it right back to him.

She looked at Dante as he sliced into his rare steak and he winked at her. She was getting used to his little pet name for her even if she didn't see herself as being sexy. He was definitely a flirt and had a bit of wildness in him. If he grew his hair long and grew a beard, he would appear almost savage like. Her own caveman to make love to. She giggled at the thought. Then there was Dante. Sweet, calm, passionate Dante who thought of her as an angel. She felt like one when they were making love. However, making love to three men seemed to make her feel more like a naughty devil. Especially as thoughts of Trevor's allusion to anal sex actually interested her.

"What exactly are you thinking about, sexy? Your cheeks are a nice shade of pink," Trevor asked then nudged her knee underneath the table.

"Nothing. Just enjoying dinner. I should call home and check on them," she said, changing the subject.

"They're fine. I talked to your dad earlier and let him know that you were with us. For the night," Charlie stated then bit off a thick piece of rare meat from his fork.

She dropped her fork and widened her eyes at his statement.

"You what? You talked to my dad? You told him that we, that I'm staying the night? Are you insane?" She was so embarrassed.

"Calm down, Lori. Everyone knows that you belong to us now," Trevor stated.

She looked at him in shock.

"You don't understand. I've been away for five years. Five years on the run, without my parents around. They'll worry."

"No, they're not worried because they know that you're with us," Dante said.

"Your dad understood and agreed that staying with us was best," Charlie added.

"What?" She covered her face with her hands. She was mortified that Charlie alluded to the fact or perhaps came straight out and told her dad they all had sex. Her father?

She jumped up from the table and began to pace. She felt her breathing hitch. She felt the instant tightness in her chest.

"Lori, calm down." Dante grabbed her hand but she pulled away and paced.

"Charlie, how could you do that? I can't believe you just called up my dad and told him that I was staying here with the three of you. Did you tell him we had sex, too?" she asked, raising her voice.

He slowly wiped his mouth with the napkin then placed it down on the table. She stared at him, enraged at his dominant, controlling behavior. Was this normal behavior for an experienced older man? Did he really think nothing of telling her father they had sex and that she was staying the night? *Holy shit!*

Charlie pulled his chair out, his thighs were wide and he placed his hands on his knees in a relaxed stance.

"Come here," he told her.

Holy fuck did my pussy just say "hell yeah" and prelubricate for cock?

She crossed her arms in front of her chest and he raised one eyebrow at her. How did he do that?

"Go to him," Dante told her and Trevor placed his hand on her lower back and began to move her toward Charlie. As soon as she was close enough, he began to run his hands back and forth along his iron thighs. She swallowed hard.

"Come closer."

Of course she did as he told her. He was a sex god and she was a four-hour-old ex-virgin surrounded by three sexy, hot soldiers with enough testosterone to take over the universe.

As soon as she was between his thighs, he began to rub her thighs the way he was caressing his. His fingers only made it to the lower part of her ass where that extra flap of ass cheek lay and connected to her upper thighs.

"Look at me." She did. He was so tall and large that even with him sitting, she was nearly eye to eye with him.

He squeezed her ass and she grabbed onto his shoulders to support herself.

"Your dad understands about ménage relationships. He's worried about you and your safety and health just like the rest of us. I explained to him how much we care for you and love you. He was thrilled not upset. You have nothing to be embarrassed about. Everyone saw this coming. Accept us, baby."

She took a deep breath and absorbed the feel of his large hands touching her, arousing her.

"I was away for so long, Charlie. I am freaked out by your call to my dad and your directness. After all, I was a virgin not so long ago."

He smiled at her.

"We'll never forget that you gave that to us. That you trusted us and that we are bound together now. I want you to sit down and let us explain how this relationship is going to work. I want you to share any questions or concerns you may have immediately."

He grabbed hold of her chin and stared directly into her eyes.

"I mean immediately. At any point if you have questions or concerns, you tell us. Got it."

She nodded her head.

"Now, sit down and finish dinner. We all skipped lunch today." He released her.

She took her seat and Dante chimed in. "Yeah, my poor arm was asleep from her holding on to it. I was starving." He took a bite of steak. She felt her cheeks warm and was a bit embarrassed but knew he was teasing. So she took a piece of steak, and before she placed it into her mouth, she added a comment of her own.

"You three shouldn't have been hungry, after feasting on me." Trevor chuckled as she took the bite of steak and realized that this was part of the relationship they were beginning. There were going to be arguments and there were going to be disagreements. She just hoped that what she read about once was true. Makeup sex being the best.

* * * *

Charlie watched Lori as she ate. She had gotten awfully quiet and he was concerned. Not that he was a talkative person or liked to get mushy over things, but she needed reassurance. She had been hurt in the past and trust wasn't an easy thing to give. It wasn't for him either. He worried that someone so young and attractive might grow bored of him in the years to come. He wasn't certain why that thought hit him, but as it did, he felt angry, jealous, and ready to explode in a possessive combustion. He tried to stop the negative train of thoughts.

"You said I can ask you guys anything. I want to know why such individually attractive, perfect, strong, intelligent men, like the three of you, want to share me? Why one woman?" Lori asked. His chest tightened. Figures the woman would go for the big question right off the bat.

Before Charlie could respond, Trevor spoke.

"Well, first, you should know that the three of us are not perfect. In retrospect, that's why we feel a relationship like this with you would work."

"Yes, what Trevor says is true and where one of us is lacking, the other two can make up for it."

Dante added.

"You'll always be provided for and never left to feel uncared for or unappreciated," Charlie said as he held her gaze. When she chuckled and shook her head, he felt insulted. Did she not think them capable of such devotion?

"I hate to tell you guys this, but even if the three of you tried your hardest, we're all human. We're all individuals. One of you is liable to upset me or insult me. Perhaps one more than the others." She looked straight at Charlie. Dante and Trevor chuckled. Charlie didn't find her comment amusing at all.

"Charlie, we butt heads because we're a lot alike. I care for each of you individually right now, but yet, together as a unit. It's weird, but I think I understand what you mean about providing where one might be lacking. But no one is perfect, as I said. You don't need to be. Hell knows, I'm not. I have so much going on in my life right now and it would be a relief to know I have the three of you to lean on if I need you. So if that's what makes this relationship begin to work and head in the right direction, then I'm in. I can use all the support I can get."

Trevor reached over and took Lori's hand and squeezed it.

"You've got all three of us."

"Which leads me to my other question. Will I be enough woman for the three of you?" She swallowed hard. They stared at her.

"You are perfect in every way," Dante told her.

"You've already proven that you can love three men and give them all your heart," Charlie stated.

"Sweetheart, with tits and ass like yours, we'll be happy men for the rest of our lives."

"Trevor!" Lori, Charlie, and Dante yelled, and Dante threw his napkin at Trevor's head.

Trevor smiled then winked at Lori.

They all laughed, but Charlie stared at her in appreciation for the woman she was. He knew she was the one and it made him happy and scared the hell out of him.

She smiled as Charlie watched her and was amazed at her maturity. They sure were lucky, so why was he feeling on edge still and why was that instinctual little tug in his gut holding his undivided attention?

Chapter 16

The stranger watched her as she worked the bar. No one really flirted with her anymore. They knew she was taken. Not by one man, but surprisingly three. It disgusted the stranger and he thought about changing his plans. But as he spoke to the man that hired him to harass the Cantrells, Lori's role seemed to become more important. Plus, he told the stranger that her life really didn't matter, just as long as the Henleys pulled from the deal.

"I think if you start sending the Henleys some threats then hint toward hurting Lori, we might get what we're after. In fact, maybe giving the woman a bit of a fright, might be a smart move," Jerry Connor had proposed. But the stranger didn't think that would work too well. Lori was always surrounded by friends or relatives of her three lovers. The only time she was alone was when she jogged in the early-morning hours.

She did have a big heart and offered regulars a ride home if they had too much to drink. He could try that angle. Set a trap and if she didn't fall for it, whoever did would be his temporary prize to hold him over. That other bartender was kind of sexy. She flaunted her tits, though small, left and right to get the guys' attention. She would do.

There was that kid of her sister's, too. Perhaps doing something to him, or having him deliver a message after the stranger got close enough would do.

He smiled to himself and continued to watch Lori. She sure did have a great body. Why would any man want to share her? If she were his woman, he'd kill anyone who even came sniffing around her. He chuckled. *When she's my woman, she'll be too busy pleasing me. No one else will ever matter and they'll never lay a hand on her again.*

* * * *

Lori had been working her third double this week. The guys weren't too happy about it, but Sunday was only forty-eight hours away. She wiped down the bar and noticed the one guy in the corner who watched her like a hawk all night. He was seated under one of the fake palms so she couldn't quite see his face fully, but she knew he was there. He kind of gave her the creeps, but she never walked out to her car alone at night, so she wasn't worried.

The bar was hopping and didn't look like it would clear out any time soon.

She looked toward Sylvia, her fellow barmaid.

"Is it me or does this bar get busier every Friday?"

"It's not you, it's the season. Plus there's a big rodeo show going on at Brukner's. They'll be more and more cowboys next weekend here," Sylvia informed her.

"Well, I hope they tip well. I have to save every penny I make for college. I register tomorrow morning."

"That's great. I've been taking a few courses here and there. I need to split what I save for rent. So does Jenny. She's been looking for a new apartment, too."

"Well I'll keep my ears open." Lori went back to focusing on the new group of guys who just arrived. She was getting used to seeing men in Stetsons with Wrangler jeans and large belt buckles that showed off their bull-riding abilities.

"Hey, darlin', you have got to be the sexiest little bartender I ever laid eyes on. What's your name, girl?" one cowboy asked, and she was taken aback by his forwardness as much as his good looks. She swallowed hard.

"Leave her alone, Channing. She's taken." Sylvia gave the cowboy a wink.

"What are you drinking, cowboy?" Lori asked then gave Sylvia a smile. Sylvia gave her a playful bump and the cowboys started hooting and hollering.

Lori shook her head at their wildness but was glad for the crowd. It would make the next three and a half hours go quicker.

* * * *

The stranger watched as the lights went out by the tiki bar. His beautiful blonde bombshell had to practically beat the cowboys off of her tonight. She was headed his way when the other bartender stopped her.

"I'll finish up. You head out."

"Are you sure?"

"Yes. Plus, Sheriff Morgan is here. He asked me to tell you that he's inside."

"Oh, I hope everything is okay," Lori replied.

"Ah hell, honey, I think he's got a thing for you."

"Naw, he knows that I'm seeing Charlie, Dante, and Trevor. I'll talk to you tomorrow," Lori said then headed inside.

A sinking feeling hit his gut. He had envisioned the blonde's long, tan legs wrapped around him tonight. He even had the rope and ties in the trunk in case he needed to restrain her fully before reaching the motel.

Instead of Lori, the brunette with the red highlights approached his table.

"Come on, honey, the bar is closed. Time to head out."

"One more drink," he slurred and so his act began. A glance toward the brunette's eyes and he saw her sympathetic expression. She would be the substitute tonight. She was going to be his playmate.

* * * *

Lori headed into Carl's to grab her purse from the small locker. Carl said that someone was waiting on her. She knew it wouldn't be Charlie, Trevor, or Dante. They were sound asleep by now because the construction crew was headed to the new property by 6:00 a.m. She knew immediately that it was Sheriff Morgan.

She glanced at her watch. It was three twenty. Looked like her morning jog would turn into an afternoon one. She couldn't wait to hit the pillow.

As she took her purse from the locker, she dropped her keys as she closed the door and bent over to pick them up.

She felt the eyes on her and swiftly turned to find Sheriff Morgan standing there.

"Hi, Sheriff." She pulled the skirt down best she could as she headed toward him.

He was dressed in casual wear, not his uniform.

"Long night, huh?" he asked.

"Sure was. I can't wait to get home. What are you doing here?"

"Well, I do have a social life, Lori. I'm not always on duty," he said then winked.

She placed her hands on her hips and stared at him. The older man lived law enforcement.

"You live and breathe the law. What are you really doing here?"

"Actually, I was hanging out with Carl and some old army buddies of mine. We were in the back area near the boat docks."

"Oh, I saw a bunch of men heading over there. One came by the bar to smoke a cigar."

"That was Switch. He's quite the character. You're heading out now, right?"

"Yes, I am."

"I'll walk you out. Carl's got a situation in the kitchen."

Lori walked along with J.R. As they entered the parking lot, Sylvia was pulling out in her car.

"Pretty rowdy bunch of cowboys hanging around the bar tonight. I hope none of them were giving you a hard time?" J.R. asked, as Lori unlocked her car door.

"They were harmless. Sylvia said that there's a rodeo going on nearby?"

"Sure is. Pretty fun event actually."

"Well I've never seen a cowboy ride a bull, but some of the guys said that they'll be there this Sunday."

"It's a sight to see."

She smiled then opened the car door.

"Well, thank you for walking me out. You have a good night."

"A good morning. I don't know how you pull these doubles all week. Bet you can't wait to get through tomorrow to be off on Sunday."

"What, does everyone know my schedule?"

He gave her a wink. "Can't lie about it. If a man's going to go to a bar for a few drinks, he's going to pick the nights when the prettiest bartenders are working. Careful driving, Lori." He tipped his hat, gave her a wink, and walked toward his truck.

Lori felt a little bit guilty inside. Not that it meant anything with J.R. walking her out of Carl's or that he gave her a compliment. She felt like she hadn't seen her men in so long and with all the cowboys flirting with her and then the sheriff walking her out, she missed them.

Lori climbed into her car, locked the doors, then texted the three of them so they would get it in the morning.

Miss you…Love you…Good night.

Chapter 17

"Do you believe this shit?" Trevor asked as he ran his fingers through his wet hair.

"Three fucking thirty in the morning. She can't go on working like this and not there," Dante added as he poured himself a cup of coffee.

"I know. It pissed me off, too, but she did say she missed us and loved us. She's trying real hard to handle things on her own. Maybe we can talk to her about it this morning?" Charlie said as he cleaned off his plate and prepared to meet the construction crew on site with Tom Cantrell.

"How can you be so calm?" Dante asked in annoyance, taking his plate and cleaning it off.

"I'm not going to freak out and start making crazy demands on her. She's working and trying to save money for college."

"We can give her the Goddamn money," Trevor barked at them.

"No, we can't. She would never allow that," Charlie whispered as he stared off toward the door as if thinking about the possibility as well.

"Well we need to think of something. I heard the damn rodeo guys are hitting up Carl's big-time. I got three texts last night before Lori's text about how the guys were totally hitting on her," Trevor stated.

"From who? Jackass Will? He's always trying to get you going. He knows that Lori belongs to us. Most of the fucking town does by now," Dante added with attitude.

"Either way, it pisses me off. I want her here. Where I can keep an eye on her and keep her safe." Trevor raised his voice.

"You need to calm down. She's ours. We'll see her tonight. We need to get out to the property before the bulldozers start digging up the land," Charlie said, but even his heart felt heavy. He was worried just like Trevor was.

* * * *

Lori registered for her classes this fall then headed back home. When she arrived, taking the road that led past the Cantrells' property and the Henleys', she saw all the orange flags and some of the large holes being dug as construction vehicles started digging.

What had started out as a meeting of partnership between the Henleys and the Cantrells turned into immediate construction in less than three weeks. She was really impressed.

As badly as she wanted to stop in to see Charlie, Trevor, and Dante, she had a splitting headache and needed to talk to her parents. Registering for the classes was overwhelming and there were a few extra concerns now.

She parked the car then got out and climbed the porch stairs. They were making lunch.

"Hey, there you are. How did it go?" her mom asked as her dad, Maggie, and Ben looked up at her smiling.

She felt kind of guilty now, moving on with her life. The thought hit her hard and her smile faded.

"What's wrong? Are you feeling okay?" her father asked then placed an arm over her shoulder and walked her toward the table.

"I'm fine, Dad. Just stressed out." She inhaled his cologne and embraced the feel of being held by him. Even though the years had passed and she missed out on physical contact with her mom and dad, it was as if she and Maggie had never left.

She turned into his shoulder and hugged him.

"I love you, Dad."

He hugged her tight and released an uneasy breath. He was

concerned for her.

As he released her, he smiled.

"It can be quite overwhelming to register for college and pick the classes you need. I bet there were some extra costs you weren't anticipating, too."

She nodded her head.

"I'll handle it though."

"We can help you, Lori. We've got money saved."

She shook her head as she held the top of the chair. "I can handle it, Dad. I still have a month of working and saving to do."

"And what about once school starts? You'll need time to study," Maggie stated.

"I'm going to work it all out. I just need to confirm the schedule of classes."

"And what about the job with the school district?" Maggie asked.

"Michelle has to get me the interview first and then I actually have to get the job, Maggie. It may not be feasible."

"She said that was a way into the district so that once you achieve your degree they can hire you as a teacher. Your chances are better."

"I know that. I have a lot to think about. I think I'm going to go for a run."

"What about lunch?" her mom asked.

"I'll get something later. My stomach is in knots right now."

Lori left the room to go change. A jog always helped to clear her head, and as she headed out the door, she did her stretches then took off for her regular route.

* * * *

"Tom, there's nothing anyone can do about this now. We're in contract and no threats are going to stop us from achieving our goals," Charlie told Tom Cantrell as he handed over yet another threatening letter from an unknown source.

"I told the sheriff about these. I don't want anyone getting hurt on this construction site. If what you believe to be true is in fact true, then Jerry Connor will not stop trying to take this land even now that we have begun breaking ground," Tom said.

"We'll take the extra precautions," Dante said.

"Here comes the sheriff now." Trevor nodded toward the roadway.

As they all watched the vehicle approach the small hill that brought the land into view, the sheriff slowed down.

Charlie felt the anger hit his gut as Lori jogged by the sheriff's car and the sheriff appeared to be talking with her and making her laugh.

Charlie had awesome vision and could see a good distance clear in front of him. When Lori waved then ran down the small path that led toward the swimming hole without even looking their way, he felt like running after her.

"She didn't see us. His car was blocking her view," Dante said as if he read Charlie's mind.

"She's meeting us at our place in an hour," Trevor said through clenched teeth. Then the sheriff pulled up.

"Howdy, looks like you've got a lot done in a short period of time," Sheriff Morgan said after he got out of the patrol car.

"Yeah, it's impressive, isn't it? Charlie, Trevor, and Dante know a lot of people and they're all gung ho about working this summer and fall," Tom told him.

"Was that Lori who ran down the path?" Trevor asked with his arms crossed in front of his chest as he stared down the sheriff. Charlie felt the same way.

The sheriff looked back toward that direction and smiled.

"Sure was. I saw her heading this way and spoke with her a bit. Was real surprised that she had the energy to do her jog today."

"Why's that?" Dante asked him.

"She worked late."

Charlie wondered how the hell the sheriff knew that. Before one of them asked the sheriff, he offered the information.

"I walked her out to her car around three thirty or so. The place was really crowded, all night long."

"Lori's trying to save money for college, but I think she works too hard," Tom stated and the sheriff agreed.

Charlie felt a twinge of jealousy knowing that the sheriff was with her, but he was a lawman, and would protect her from harm.

Tom started telling the sheriff about the threatening letters and phone calls. The sheriff wrote everything down and continued to ask Tom questions.

"I did check out that abandoned vehicle you guys called in this morning. It belongs to the son of a couple in town. He ran out of gas and left the car there, then walked all the way back home for help. They should be here shortly to fill it up with gas and get it out of there."

"Well, we appreciate you looking into things. I want this construction to go well," Tom added.

"You two talk. We're going to wrap things up for the day. We'll see you tomorrow morning, Tom. Same time," Charlie stated.

"Sure thing," Tom said as Charlie and his brothers headed over to the men who were gathering together preparing to leave for the day.

* * * *

Lori pulled on the shamrock-green strapless sundress that hugged her curves and landed just above the knee. It was a classy, yet casual look, and she topped it off with low-heeled white sandals. She wanted to look good for Charlie, Dante, and Trevor. She missed them and with all the stress she was feeling, she looked forward to getting lost in their arms.

She had filtered through her drawers, pulling out the little bag with the new set of thong panties she brought. They were black and all lace, which didn't really cover much at all.

She had showered using a special bodywash she picked up at the same store and felt that it was fresh and appealing.

"Wow, you look great and smell good, too," Maggie said as she entered the bedroom, closed her eyes, and inhaled.

"What is that stuff?" she asked as she took a bottle off the bureau and began opening it.

"It's not that one. It's a bodywash I bought the other day."

"Hmmm." Maggie placed her hand under her chin and looked Lori over.

"Do you think I can borrow some?"

Lori chuckled.

"Hot date with Jasper?"

"I haven't slept with him yet." She sat down on the bed.

"I didn't say that you did. How is it going anyway?"

Maggie grunted then fell backward on Lori's bed. She threw her arm over her eyes and made noises.

"What's wrong?"

"Everything, nothing, ah hell, I don't know." Maggie pulled her arm away from her eyes and sat up, leaning on her elbow. She played with a strand of fabric on the comforter.

"Jasper is so incredibly sexy and macho and manly and everything I ever wanted in a man and everything I ever feared in one."

Lori fixed her dress as she sat down on the bed.

She crossed her legs and looked at her sister.

"Tell me about it. Whenever I think about what Charlie, Trevor, and Dante are capable of, being soldiers, I start to panic. I know they won't hurt me, but then the fear starts up. I just don't want to screw it all up, so I place some distance between us. Yet, here I am, missing them terribly and I can't wait to see them and none of the fear matters. I don't get it."

"That's because you're in love with them."

"Yes, I am. And you have strong feelings for Jasper, but you're allowing your own fears and the past to rule your future and your decisions. You can't keep doing that, Maggie. It's time to move on and Jasper is a great man. Plus, Ben likes him a bunch."

Maggie smiled.

"They get along well and you're right, I like Jasper a lot. Sometimes, when we're making out, I feel like I should just let him continue and just go with the strong feelings I have, but then Derrick pops into my head. I can't afford to make any more bad decisions in my life, Lori."

"Maggie, you're human. We all make mistakes no matter how hard we try to avoid them. You can't think like that. You have to focus on what you feel inside here." Lori covered her chest where her heart was.

"I love you, Lori. I'm so happy for you. The guys are amazing. You'd better get going."

Lori stood up and looked at herself in the mirror one more time.

"Do you like the dress?" Lori asked.

"I love it and so will the men. Too bad it won't be on you that long," Maggie said as she walked toward the doorway.

Maggie!" Lori called after her and Maggie chuckled.

Lori looked at the dress and the blush to her cheeks.

I hope they like it.

* * * *

Trevor opened the front door and felt his chest tighten and his dick instantly hardened. Lori looked incredible.

"Hey, beautiful," he stated after staring at her for a few seconds too long because he noticed her lower her eyes as if he wasn't impressed with her.

Trevor reached for her, wrapping an arm around her waist and moving his other hand under her hair and against her neck before kissing her.

She smelled incredible. The feel of her dainty hands grabbing him tight and rubbing along his waist drove him wild with desire. But he had to calm himself down. The woman was only in the front entryway to their home.

He slowly released her lips and smiled as they touched foreheads.

"I missed you."

"I missed you, too, Trevor," she told him and he smiled then took her hand and led her through the house and onto the side-enclosed patio. It was screened in.

"It looks like we may be getting a storm any minute."

"I know. I saw some lightning in the distance on my way over here."

"Saw you jogging today," Trevor said as he led her deeper onto the porch where they had set the table and lit some candles.

"This looks so nice. You did all this for me?" she asked.

He pulled her against him and held her face between his hands. Trevor stared down into her eyes. He had so much to say. Plus he wanted to demand why she let the sheriff walk her out from work and why she stopped to talk and laugh with him? Then came the feelings of guilt. He was being insecure. Never in his life had he felt incapable or not good enough. But with Lori, he felt his own insecurities getting in the way of the more important task at hand. He should be loving his woman, and securing a good, healthy relationship with her, instead of focusing on his fears of losing her.

"All three of us did," Charlie sated as he and Dante entered the room.

Trevor released his hold as Charlie approached, leaned down, and kissed Lori softly on the mouth. He took her hand and looked her over. "I like it," he said. She smiled and Trevor saw her eyes light up.

Dante approached and he looked stern.

"You look gorgeous. That color is almost identical to your eyes." Dante kissed her softly. Trevor stared at Lori, and now Charlie and Dante looked at a loss for words.

Lori clasped her hands in front of her and then looked at each of them.

"What's wrong? Something is wrong," she whispered.

They were silent and then Trevor couldn't wait.

"I don't know why this is bothering me so much. What the hell were you doing letting the sheriff walk you out from work last night, or should I say this morning?"

He was trying his hardest to not sound angry, but concerned. The moment the words left his lips, he felt guilty and realized how insecure he was. This was his first serious relationship. He wanted to give Lori every part of him, and especially his heart. He knew the culprit to the insecurity and reservations. He was scared. Scared to love. Scared to trust and scared of losing the best thing that ever happened to him. Lori.

"Trevor, he was there with friends and waited for me to leave so I wouldn't have to walk out alone. Carl was stuck inside with some sort of kitchen situation."

"What about the conversation on the hill? We were standing right down the road and you didn't even wave to us. The sheriff made you laugh and stole your complete attention," Dante added.

Lori took a deep breath.

She stared at all three of them and for some reason she felt like laughing and like crying. Laughing over the fact that three very dominating, sexy men like these three were jealous of the sheriff and crying, because she was so touched by their care for her and their love. She needed to make them understand that she wasn't going to hurt them, just as she needed them to show her the same.

"First of all, there was no hidden meaning about J.R. walking me to my car. You guys are the ones that demanded I remember to take precautions always. Secondly, I love the three of you and I don't have any romantic feelings for J.R., and third, if I didn't love the three of you, then I wouldn't have missed you so much, I wouldn't have looked forward to seeing you and talking about the stress I'm under and I surely wouldn't have gone out and splurged on this new dress.

Nor these sexy panties." She lifted her dress and showed off the black lace see-through panties for emphasis on her entire statement.

Her three stubborn men stared at her, so she pulled her dress back down into place, smoothed her hands down the front then stared at them.

"Get over here," Dante ordered. Her belly tightened and, oh boy, did she feel wet as she slowly walked closer.

He didn't touch her. Dante didn't pull her into his arms and kiss her breathless as she anticipated. No, not this macho, take-charge soldier of hers. Instead he made her shiver with arousal and anticipation.

"Unzip that dress, slowly."

Oh Lord, Maggie was right. This dress didn't stay on long at all.

She stared at him, giving him the same stern, hard expression he gave her as she reached back and unzipped the dress. Moving her hand in front of her bodice, she held it in place.

"Off, I said."

She stared at him, made him wait a moment until she saw that vein by the side of his temple pulsate. She moved her hand away from the bodice of the dress and the material fell to the floor, leaving her bare-breasted and only wearing the black lace panties.

"Hot damn," Trevor stated from behind her.

She felt empowered and sexy. It was like she instantly fell into the role of seductress as she stepped closer.

"I want something," she whispered and Dante's eyes widened.

"I don't think you're in any position to ask for anything," he stated.

"I think you're angry, and I don't want you to be, Dante. Let me show you how much I love you." She licked her lower lip, noticing his eyes following her tongue.

She slowly reached for his belt buckle, undid his pants, and shoved them down.

After a glance up into Dante's face, she saw the blush across his cheeks. Her hands were shaking, and she hoped she could do this. As she inhaled his scent, soap and outdoors, she licked her lips and pressed her hands into his boxers.

"Ah hell, Lori." He grunted and closed his eyes. She cupped his balls, and stroked his long, thick cock with delicate fingers. She felt empowered as the thick muscle thickened and grew beneath her palm.

Lowering to her knees, using her dress to cushion them, she pressed his boxers down and locked eyes on Dante's huge cock.

As her tongue licked the tip, Dante grabbed hold of her hair and head and stepped closer. His male scent consumed her as she opened her mouth and Dante slid inside.

"That's the sexiest thing I've ever seen," Trevor stated.

"Sure as shit is," Charlie added, and she knew they were watching. That fact gave her the courage and desire to please Dante and make this first time sucking cock memorable and exciting.

Up and down she moved her mouth, swirled her tongue, then sucked him to the tip.

"Tell me I'm your first, Lori. Tell me my cock is the first cock you've ever sucked," he demanded in a wild tone. She didn't want to release him to say yes so she nodded her head. "Fuck yeah." He thrust a little into her mouth. She was caught off guard and afraid she may gag, but then Dante caressed her hair.

"Sorry, baby. You got me so excited and hard. I fucking love you so damn much. So much." He grunted his words and she moved faster, sucking him up and down. She had a steady pace going, her lips were growing numb and her tongue tired but she wanted to please him so badly. She hoped she was doing this right when suddenly he roared as he held her head tight and thrust into her mouth. She panicked only a second then felt him explode down her throat. She swallowed and swallowed then hugged him around his ass and gave his cheeks a squeeze as she released his cock.

"You're amazing, woman. Sweet Jesus, you're mine forever." He caressed her hair then lowered to his knees. He hugged her then pulled back and kissed her hard on the mouth.

* * * *

"Let me see these new panties you splurged on," Charlie whispered as he bent down and lifted her up to her feet.

He ran the palms of his hands over her hip bones then leaned forward to kiss her belly.

"Trevor and I have plans for you. Ain't that right, Trevor?" Charlie pushed his shoulder forward, causing Lori to tumble over his shoulder as he stood up. He carried her from the room, caressing her ass and pussy as they headed upstairs.

Charlie felt his heart racing. He loved Lori so much and her words, her directness just set any fears of jealousy out of the picture.

As he lowered her to her feet, he cupped her breasts, then leaned down to lick across the tips.

"You taste so sweet. What are you wearing, baby?" Charlie asked as he stood up and pulled off his shirt.

"Something new I bought when I got these here panties." She winked at him. He chuckled at her sassiness.

Charlie undid his pants and stepped out of them. She reached for his cock and he moaned as he relished in her touch.

"You're feeling awfully frisky, baby. I think you need to know who owns this body and who sets the rules around here," Trevor said as he leaned over her shoulder and shoved her panties down and off of her.

Lori gasped and released Charlie's cock.

He stepped to the side and placed a condom on before he lay down on the bed.

"Come on up here," Charlie said and Trevor turned Lori around then lifted her up so she could straddle Charlie.

Charlie stared into her jade-green eyes and nibbled his bottom lip.

"I missed being inside of you. Come on up here and ride me,

baby."

* * * *

As Lori adjusted her body so she could attempt to ride such a big, thick man as Charlie, she felt Trevor's fingers caress down the crack of her ass.

She gasped but Charlie moved a hand up over her shoulder to the back of her head and pulled her down for a kiss. He simultaneously fisted his cock and aligned it with her pussy so when she lowered, his cock pushed right between her wet folds.

"Charlie," she said, mouth open, and he thrust up into her as his mouth collided with hers.

Up and down he pumped his hips while Trevor massaged her ass and played with her back hole.

She attempted to counterthrust to Charlie's thrusts as he devoured her moans, but then she heard Trevor's voice and felt his fingers press then pass over her anus.

"My brothers got their 'firsts.' Now it's my turn, sugar. I want this ass. I want to fuck this perfect round ass of yours first. How does that sound?" he asked and Lori moaned as she tried to nod her head. She felt on fire as Charlie released her lips and she panted.

"Yes, oh God, be careful, Trevor. I'm scared." She panted and Charlie thrust his cock up into her.

Charlie caressed her cheek and then nipped her chin as Trevor massaged her ass over and over again.

"I'll be careful. You've made me so happy, baby," Trevor said as he pressed something thick and cold to her anus. She felt his finger push in and out.

She gasped and Charlie covered her mouth with his as he thrust upward and held the palm of his hand against her lower back, keeping her in place.

"Nice and easy, baby. I'm going to stretch this ass and get it ready."

She felt Trevor pull his fingers out then squeeze something cold and thick against her anus. It felt odd and then his fingers pressed into her again. Her groin tightened and tingled, her pussy spasmed and she began to rub her pussy and hips back and forth.

Charlie moved his hand lower and squeezed her ass then moved it back up as Trevor pulled his fingers from there.

"Here I come, baby," Trevor said and then she felt the tip of his cock, thick and round, press through the tight rings. She felt the burning and the restriction as he attempted to push into her. Then he grunted and pressed all the way in.

Dante sat down on the bed. "Incredible. You're so beautiful, Lori. My God," he said as Charlie released her lips and she moaned.

Charlie pulled out as Trevor pulled out then pressed into her. Then Charlie pressed up into her and Trevor shoved in.

"Raise those thighs," Trevor demanded and she moaned and shook her head.

"Do it," Dante commanded. She slowly pushed both thighs upward, giving Trevor greater access to her ass and causing Charlie to press all the way up into her.

"Fuck, she's so tight. I'm there. Fuck." Charlie exploded inside of her. Lori pressed back against Trevor and then he grabbed her hips, lifted her midsection up so she was on her knees and he thrust balls deep into her ass.

"Oh!" She screamed her release as Charlie moaned, moving his cock from inside of her. Charlie cupped her breasts and pinched the nipples making the aftershocks of her orgasm almost excruciatingly uncontrollable.

"Oh God," she stated over and over as Trevor thrust into her ass. She thrust her hips back and it earned her a hard slap to her ass, which somehow made her pussy erupt again.

"I'm there, baby. Holy shit." Trevor shoved in all the way and exploded in pleasure. She felt his thighs shaking despite her own thighs' need to cave in.

She felt the kisses to her spine, the squeeze to both ass cheeks right as Trevor pulled from her sacred hole.

She collapsed against Charlie and he chuckled as he held her in his arms and caressed her hair.

The three of them leaned down and kissed her at once, then whispered, "I love you."

Chapter 18

Charlie slammed his fist down on the table as he looked at the pictures inside the envelope.

His stomach ached. He stared at Dante and Trevor who looked ready to kill.

"First the fucking phone calls and now this?" Trevor stated.

"This is fucking crazy. Who is doing this? They're going to hurt her. They're making their threats known," Dante stated.

"I know that. Three fucking pictures. Lori at Carl's, Lori playing with Ben on the swings," Dante stated.

"Lori half fucking naked on the porch from the other night. Fuck, he was that close. So fucking close he could have taken pictures of her naked body and her sucking—"

Trevor ran his hands through his hair and growled.

"We need to think. We have to catch this shadow guy. He's ballsy enough to come around here at night and to threaten us like this," Charlie stated.

"What about Lori? Do we tell her about this?" Dante asked.

"No. She's got enough on her plate right now. You heard her two nights ago when she was here. She's stressed over registering for college, working and making money while going to school and taking the online courses. She doesn't need this shit, too," Charlie replied.

"She needs protection. If anything were to happen to her..." Trevor said.

"We should inform the sheriff," Dante added.

"And show him these pictures? This one of Lori only wearing her black panties from behind? She'll be mortified. Hell, you guys and I know that the sheriff likes her," Charlie said.

"He knows she's ours." Trevor raised his voice and looked furious.

"Calm down. I know he does but still, it's better if we just tell him. He doesn't need to see this one. The others justify the threats."

"Okay, let's call him and I'm going to text Lori. She's at work now." Trevor pulled out his cell and texted her.

"Trevor, notify the men in the family and the ranch hands. Have them be on the lookout for any strangers walking around."

"You bet, Charlie," Dante said then headed out the door.

* * * *

The bar was so crowded Lori couldn't keep up with the orders. Carl was helping her because Sylvia was a no-show and they'd just reached Jenny twenty minutes ago. She was on her way to Carl's to help out.

"I don't understand this. It's so unlike Sylvia," Carl stated as he shook the metal mixer then poured the sex on the beach into the glass. He added a special fruit flower then served it up.

"Me either." Lori hit the blender as she poured the mug of beer from the spout. Thank God she was ambidextrous and could make just about any drink out there. It was a warm night and the favorite was margaritas.

"I'm a bit worried. Jenny said she never came home Friday night."

"Friday? She was working here with me. I left at closing and saw her car leaving the parking lot."

"I called Sheriff Morgan. He's looking around and asking other friends and Sylvia's ex-boyfriend if he saw her. He said he'd stop in tonight."

"God, I hope she's okay."

Just then Lori felt her cell phone buzz, but she was too busy to answer right now.

She continued to make drinks until it finally slowed down around eleven.

She was leaning against the bar. Now that Jenny was there to help, they'd caught up and were less busy.

Lori glanced at her phone. Five messages from Trevor?

She quickly dialed his number as the country music blasted in the background.

"Trevor, is everything okay?" she asked.

"Why didn't you answer your phone?"

She was shocked by his attitude. As if she purposely ignored his calls? God, this man was like a yo-yo with his emotions. He was kind of insecure she figured, to think she was up to something after what they shared two nights ago.

"Trevor, I'm working. It's crazy busy."

"It's a fucking Monday night."

"I know, but with the rodeo in town and then Sylvia was a no-show, Carl and I had to work the bar alone. It was nuts. Now Jenny is here, too."

"Carl was working the bar with you alone? Did he try anything?"

"Trevor, please. Like that would actually happen? I think everyone knows that I'm taken and by three very threatening types of individuals."

"Threatening? I don't threaten."

"Right, so what is this all about? Is something going on?"

"No. Just worried about you. What time are you getting off?"

"I don't know yet. I think I'm closing because it was Sylvia's night, but like I said, she was a no-show. I'm worried about her. Carl is, too, and Jenny. She didn't come home Friday night."

"I'm sure she's okay. Did anyone notify the sheriff?"

"Yes, he's looking into it. Listen I need to go. It is insane here. I'll call you tomorrow."

"No, call at the end of your shift. One of us will meet you and walk you out and follow you home."

"Trevor that isn't necessary. Plus, you need the rest. You're working on the new construction site and trying to finish the last details to my apartment. Remember that I'm off tomorrow, if Sylvia shows that is. I want you to help me register for that online course I read about."

"Okay. I love you. Call me when you're almost done so I can come meet you."

"Good night, Trevor," she stated then disconnected the call. As she did, she noticed someone sitting at the table under the palms. It looked like the same guy from the other night she felt was staring at her. She couldn't be sure though. She couldn't see his face, just his stocky build. She had an uneasy feeling in her gut, as someone asked her for a draft beer, and as she glanced away then back again, it appeared as if the guy under the palm was staring at her.

She refocused on the customer and then another man who asked for two margaritas. When she ran the blender, she looked back at the table under the palm and now a man and woman were sitting there.

Did I just imagine that?

She damned Sylvia for being a no-show and she damned Trevor's overprotectiveness and phone call demanding she call him when she was done with her shift. What was going on around here?

She decided to focus on finishing her shift as that uneasy feeling continued to eat at her gut.

* * * *

The sheriff never made it by Carl's and never called. Carl walked her out and expressed his concern over Sylvia's disappearance.

"I just don't get it. I've treated her well. I think she's been happy here."

"Don't worry, Carl. I'm sure she'll show up and have a good explanation. Thanks for walking me out and for the help at the bar tonight."

"No problem. It was kind of fun. I missed doing that. I used to bartend when I was in college. Anyway, good night and say hello to those men of yours. Lucky bastards," he said then gave her shoulder a squeeze before he headed back inside.

Shit. I was supposed to call Trevor.

Lori got into her car, pulled out her cell phone, as she started the engine, then noticed the bunch of wild flowers and a card on her passenger seat.

She knew she locked her car doors, but she looked in the backseat and got a funny feeling as she hit send on her cell.

It was two thirty in the morning. The phone rang several times as she stared at the flowers. They looked like they came from the bushes near the swing set where she played with Ben. The bushes were wild and the flowers beautiful. She had complimented them as she played with Ben.

She swallowed hard.

"Hello," a groggy voice answered.

"It's me. I just finished working now."

"Oh, great. I'll just get my shoes on and head over," Trevor stated.

"Don't be silly. By the time you get here, I could be home and showered."

"Wait, is everything okay? Any word on Sylvia?"

"None. The sheriff didn't stop by either so I don't know what's going on." Lori pulled out of the parking lot.

She stared at the flowers as she drove down the road.

"Oh, thanks for the flowers. When did you drop these off and how the heck did you get into my car? The doors were locked. Oh, wait, was it Charlie?"

"Flowers? We didn't leave you any flowers. What kind are they?" he asked, and she started to tell him when she noticed the set of lights behind her, another car was coming closer and kind of fast.

"I didn't open the card, Trevor. I thought they were from you."

"Don't go home, come straight here, Lori. Where are you now?"

he asked and as she answered the car behind her hit her car bumper in the back.

She screamed as she held the wheel tight and tried to maintain control.

"Lori, Lori!" She could hear Trevor yelling her name. She couldn't reach for the phone.

It had fallen onto the floor. "Trevor, someone just hit me with their car. I can't reach the phone."

"Fuck, Lori, are they still following you?"

"Oh God, they're coming closer. What do I do?" she asked as the car hit her back bumper again. She screamed as she lost control of the car and ran into the ditch on the side of the road. The tire blew out, she hit her forehead on the steering wheel and felt dazed.

"Lock the doors. Lori, are you okay?"

She looked up and saw the car heading straight for her. Her seat belt was stuck as she tried to undo it. The sound of the engine revving told her that the driver wasn't going to stop. It was a truck of some sort. She got the belt off and climbed to the passenger seat as he struck the corner of the car.

Lori went flying into the passenger door, and glass hit her shoulder. She was screaming.

Her head throbbed terribly as if she had hit her head or something and she turned to look for the vehicle but it was gone. The road was dark except for her headlights that shone straight ahead. She could hear yelling and she remembered the phone. Her hands were shaking. She couldn't even pick it up. She dropped the cell phone once then pulled it to her ear.

"Trevor," she said in a very shaky voice.

"Lori. We're on our way. We called the highway patrol. Are you okay?"

She was shaking profusely and she felt the burning pain and throbbing in her arm and shoulder. Her head hurt.

"Lori?" Trevor yelled.

She dropped the phone and stared out the window, she could hear the rumble of an engine and she lowered against the side door. With eyes barely open, she played unconscious as the truck slowly passed by. The driver was looking to see if she were injured. She just knew it as her heart felt like it would leap from her chest. Tears filled her eyes and she begged herself not to show consciousness and not let the tears roll down. He wanted to kill her, whoever it was. Then suddenly he turned around and took off, speeding down the roadway.

* * * *

Sheriff Morgan felt sick to his stomach. He couldn't believe something like this could happen in his town. He looked at the dead body of Sylvia Masters. She was so young and beautiful before this sick bastard had his way with her. J.R. hadn't wanted to call Lori and Carl or stop by just yet. He'd waited and figured he'd explain things in the morning, and then Lori was run off the road and nearly killed.

He ran his hands through his hair. He was grateful that Lori survived and there was an all-points bulletin out on the dark pickup truck who ran her down. There were numerous reports from homeowners who saw the speeding truck minutes after the accident.

"That truck was reported stolen yesterday morning in Bruxton, Sheriff," his deputy told him, and J.R. was pissed off.

"Have the state police look it over with a fine-tooth comb. Maybe this asshole left prints in there. He had to. I'm going to head to the hospital to see Lori."

"Your Texas Ranger friend, Gunner McCallister, is here."

"Great. Send him in."

Gunner walked in and shook J.R.'s hand.

"Is there a chance my friends' woman is in trouble?" Gunner asked as he leaned his hand on his holster. J.R. thought he looked downright mean and ornery. But he also knew he was good friends with Charlie, Dante, and Trevor. They had become friends, too, over the past few years and worked cases that crossed his desk.

"I'm afraid there's something going on here. Let me explain what I have and what my gut is thinking, and then we'll head over to the hospital."

"I just spoke with Charlie. He has some things to discuss and something about threats to him, his brothers, and the land they're excavating for construction."

J.R. widened his eyes.

"He thinks this is connected to it? Sylvia's murder, too?" J.R. asked.

"That's what we're going to figure out," Gunner said as J.R. rose from his chair and felt his gut clench. Thank God he had the Texas Ranger to assist him with this. He would need every law enforcement resource he could get to help him keep Lori and her loved ones safe.

* * * *

Lori kept opening her eyes and seeing little images. Trevor's concerned face, Dante's hand squeezing hers, flashing lights, the sheriff and then Charlie, his head surrounded by white light and people in white.

When she finally opened her eyes, feeling groggy and achy, she saw her mom and Maggie.

"Oh God, she's waking up," her mom said and instantly she saw her loved ones.

She shook and shivered.

"It's okay, baby. You're safe now," Trevor said as he leaned down and kissed her cheek.

"The driver. The driver," she repeated.

"Don't talk. Don't worry about a thing," Charlie whispered.

She tried to sit up when she felt the pain in her shoulder.

"Stay still, sweetheart. You have some injuries from the crash," Dante told her.

"Injuries? Oh God, he was going to kill me. He came back and hit the car. He looked right at me. I pretended to be unconscious. Oh God." Tears rolled down her cheeks.

"Shh, baby, just rest. Don't talk about it right now. We don't want you to get more upset," Maggie whispered.

The door to the room opened and the doctor walked in. "Sorry, folks, but there are way too many people in here. Could y'all step outside, so I can speak with the patient?" An older nurse stood right next to him holding the door open for Lori's family to leave.

"We're not leaving her," Trevor stated firmly.

"Trevor, let's go out in the hallway. The doctor will tell you everything when he's done," Lou said.

"I will talk with you once I'm finished with Lori," the doctor added then smiled.

Lori started to panic. She grabbed onto Dante's hand and squeezed it.

"Relax, sweetie, just relax," Dante said as he helped Lori sit up. She wanted to tell the doctor to keep the men there. She didn't want to be away from them.

"Stay…stay," she blurted out in between trying to catch her breath and remain calm.

Do not have a panic attack. Remain calm. They're here with me. The driver can't get me.

"We stay and that's final," Charlie stated firmly as he took position on Lori's other side. He placed his hands against her cheeks and stared into her eyes.

"Focus on me, Lori. Calm your breathing and just focus on me."

She stared into his hazel eyes. She absorbed the firm tilt of his chin and the way his eyes crinkled when he gave a calm, yet stern order. She blinked a few times, felt the tear roll down her cheek and then the second set of hands on her back. They were caressing her, and as Charlie brushed his thumb lightly back and forth across her lower lip, she closed her eyes and just breathed. In and out, her chest opened up and the airway felt less constricted.

"Stay with me," she told him and he smiled.

"Not going anywhere without you." He leaned forward and kissed her.

* * * *

Once the doctor checked her over, he was preparing to release her. She didn't have a concussion, nothing was broken, and Lori was insistent that she would be better off at home with her family.

Trevor wasn't sure if she were minimizing the pain she was in out of fear of him, Dante, and Charlie leaving her here at the hospital. The doctor prescribed some painkillers that would help the bruising he said she had on her shoulder and ribs. Plus it would help her to sleep. As he stared at the cut on her forehead, he felt his own blood pressure rise. Someone was really trying to hurt her on purpose to get them to stop building on the land with Tom Cantrell.

"Excuse me, can we come in?"

Trevor turned toward the door and saw Sheriff Morgan. His chest tightened immediately. They had heard about Sylvia's body being found in some piece-of-shit motel outside of town. She had been raped, beaten, and murdered. Trevor swallowed the sour taste in his stomach.

Could that have been Lori?

Then Gunner McCallister entered, too, shocking Trevor and his brothers.

"Sheriff, Gunner, what are you doing here, buddy?" Charlie asked as he reached out to shake Gunner's hand. Gunner gave a small smile then glanced at Lori.

"I came to help. How's the patient?" Gunner asked as he moved closer to the bed.

Trevor looked at Lori as she held on to Dante's arm. Dante was sitting there caressing her hair.

Trevor looked at Gunner and saw his concerned expression.

He touched Lori's hand as he bent lower.

"You doing okay, sweetheart? These men taking good care of you?"

"Yes, Gunner," she said with tear-filled eyes, and he smiled.

The sheriff cleared his throat and Gunner moved out of the way. The sheriff approached, holding his Stetson in his hands and caressing the rim.

"Hey, gorgeous. I don't want you to worry about a thing now except for healing up. You let your men take care of you and leave this to me to find the man responsible."

Lori gave a small smile.

"Thank you, J.R. Have you heard from Sylvia yet? Carl is so worried, just like the rest of us. It's not like her to do something like this."

Trevor noticed everyone's expression change. Did they seriously think that Lori, a person who cared for everyone she met, would not ask about Sylvia? *Shit.*

"What is it?" Lori asked as she looked at all their faces.

"What happened?" she asked then tried sitting up and cringed from the pain. The sheriff placed his hand on her leg as Dante placed his hand on her chest.

"Lie back, baby, rest now," Dante whispered.

"Why don't we go out into the hall a minute, Charlie? I want to catch you up on the progress of the investigation," Gunner stated.

"Sure thing. Honey, Trevor and I will be right outside in the hallway. Dante will stay with you."

She just stared at them as they left the room.

* * * *

"How the hell do you know that the person who killed Sylvia is the same one who went after Lori?" Charlie asked Gunner.

"Well, we weren't sure at first, not until we figured out that the flowers left in Lori's car with a note were the same flowers left at the crime scene where Sylvia's body was found," Gunner stated.

"We talked to the restaurant staff at Carl's. One of the kitchen helpers saw Sylvia helping a large man into the passenger seat of her car. The worker said he appeared to be drunk," Sheriff Morgan stated.

"That's something Lori would do. She's done it before for people she knows though. Do you think that Sylvia knew this guy?" Trevor asked.

"We're going to have to question Lori," Gunner whispered.

"No. Absolutely not. Not now, not when she's on the verge of a panic attack. No way," Trevor stated adamantly.

"Trevor, I understand how upset you are and worried about Lori, but she could have information that could help us solve this faster and get the one responsible off the streets," Gunner replied.

"He's right, Trevor. I guess if we're going to do this, then you two should do it here in the hospital in case she needs medical assistance. God, this is going to really upset her. She liked Sylvia a lot," Charlie added.

"You three can be in the room with her when we tell her about Sylvia and then ask her some questions," the sheriff stated, and Trevor and Charlie nodded their heads.

"Hey, I called Sandman, and Big Jay in on this. With their connections we can maybe find out more about this Jerry Connor and his associates. Big Jay is already tailing Connor and Sandman is working on a warrant to tap his phones," Gunner told Charlie.

"That's great. I can't believe these people are willing to kill over land. There's plenty of land elsewhere, what's so big about ours and Cantrells'?" Charlie asked.

"Could simply be its location. It's not far from the city, yet it is still far enough out there to be considered country life. The town is booming fifteen minutes away and the views and the land are appealing. There are numerous natural springs and water supplies, wildlife, fishing, you name it. It's prime land."

"I guess it is. Gunner, we need to protect Lori and her family. We need to protect all the families living on that land."

"We'll do it. Don't worry."

Chapter 19

Lori lay next to Trevor who held her while she slept. As she opened her eyes, surprised by the total darkness she was in, a worried feeling consumed her. Then she felt Trevor's arms tighten around her, and he adjusted his hips.

She tried to relax and absorb the warmth of his embrace and knowing that she was safe, but then her mind started thinking about everything. Flashes of different images swarmed her mind. Sylvia was dead. Raped, beaten, and murdered and it could have been her. If the sheriff hadn't told Sylvia that he was waiting inside Carl's for her, then perhaps it would have been Lori who was taken by the stranger. Surveillance cameras couldn't catch the perpetrator's face, but saw his act as he pretended drunkenness, or at least that is what the sheriff thought. Why would Sylvia give a complete stranger a ride home? Had she known him?

Lori released an uneasy sigh. As she closed her eyes, she thought about the flowers in her car and the card. They were from the man that killed Sylvia. The same man who kept bumping into her car, who ran her off the road and who came back to see if she were dead or at minimum badly injured.

Lori covered her chest with her hand as she clenched her eyes tight. She could see the headlights. She saw the smoke coming up from the right corner of her car where the tire blew out.

The fear, the anticipation as she waited, eyes closed, pretending unconsciousness made her shiver even now. The dark truck rumbled, slowly passed her. She ever so slightly opened her eyes. It was as if she wanted to know if he would kill her, shoot her, take her out, and finish her off. The tears rolled down her cheeks and there he was. She saw his face and gasped.

"Trevor, Trevor, wake up," she said as Trevor placed his hand over her waist and slowly came awake.

"What is it, baby? Can't sleep?" he asked as he sat up. He was bare-chested and she was only wearing a T-shirt. One of theirs.

"I saw him."

"Saw who?" Trevor asked as he rubbed his eyes then reached over and caressed her hair from her face.

She locked gazes with Trevor.

"The man in the truck who tried to kill me."

Trevor's eyes widened and then the bedroom door opened.

"Is everything okay?" Charlie asked. He was fully dressed and he appeared tired.

"She said she saw the driver's face." Trevor got out of bed and pulled on his jeans.

"Are you sure, baby? You said earlier that you kept your eyes closed and pretended to be unconscious."

"I opened my eyes slightly as he came right by the driver's side window. I saw him, but I guess with all the trauma and the fear being in shock, I had forgotten."

"Can you describe him for us?" Charlie asked, taking a seat on the edge of the bed. Dante entered now, too, only wearing dark jeans.

"Yes. We need to draw him or something. I'm not good at drawing."

"I'm okay. What are we drawing?" Dante asked.

Charlie turned to look at Dante.

"The killer."

* * * *

Dante drew the picture, erased parts then redrew it about five times before Lori was satisfied with it. They scanned the sketch into the computer and sent it to the sheriff and to Gunner.

As they ate breakfast and gave Lori as much loving as they could, they heard the doorbell ring.

Trevor went to answer it and returned to the kitchen with the sheriff and Gunner. Gunner placed a picture down onto the island in front of Lori.

"Is that him, honey?" he asked her, very seriously. Dante nodded his head for Lori to take a look. She appeared so uncertain and fearful even now, in their home and surrounded by him and his two brothers.

Lori looked at the picture and stared up at Gunner.

"Who is he?" she asked.

"Is it him, baby?" Charlie asked her and she nodded her head.

"You did awesome, Lori. Really great job remembering his mug. This guy is badass big-time. Sandman got the warrant for phone taps on Connor. Big Jay was watching Connor's place and monitoring the calls. One came in from Fellington, five miles from here and about twenty minutes from where Sylvia's body was found," Gunner stated.

"Oh shit. Is this the guy?" Trevor asked.

"Well, in the recorded conversations between Connor and this guy he calls the stranger. This is the nickname this guy goes by. He's got a record a mile long, no convictions though and no main place of residence. He's a free spirit," Sheriff Morgan added.

"So what do we do?" Charlie asked as he placed his hands on Lori's shoulders and squeezed them.

"Yeah, how do we catch this guy and prove that Connor is responsible for all of this?" Dante asked.

"Well the phone taps are key. Connor blatantly stated to the stranger and to Don Henshaw, that piece-of-shit real estate guy in town, about threatening the Cantrells and upping the pressure. Sandman used his resources to find out what else Connor is involved in and it isn't pretty stuff. He's been doing this kind of shit for years. He threatens landowners, forces them to sell to him, and then builds these shit-ass condos and spas in the middle of nowhere. Except he left a trail along the way and a few battered individuals willing to testify," Gunner explained.

"How do we prove that the stranger killed Sylvia?" Lori asked.

"Hopefully the fingerprints we found at the crime scene and the evidence under Sylvia's nails match this guy's. She put up a fight. Direct transfer of DNA onto the victim," Gunner stated.

"Damn. I'm still in shock at all of this. I hope Connor and this stranger guy rot in hell," Dante said, and they all agreed.

"Now what?" Lori asked.

"You rest, let your men take care of you," Gunner said, "and the sheriff here will have some extra deputies patrolling around the ranch while I round up these two assholes. We're posting the stranger's picture on television indicating how important it is that we question him. Hopefully someone will see him and report his whereabouts."

"Great. We really appreciate your help with this, Gunner. You, your brothers, and the sheriff have been awesome," Dante said then shook their hands.

"We'll catch them and put them away. Don't you worry," the sheriff said then reached over and gave Lori's hand a squeeze.

They said good-bye then left the house.

* * * *

Trevor didn't feel as relieved as he thought he would. Identifying the suspects, locating them, and building evidence against them should be giving him peace of mind, but it wasn't. He glanced at Lori, noticing the bandage on her forehead and part of the large, wide bruise that peeked out from the sleeve of her T-shirt. Her blonde hair was in a low ponytail to the side and she looked so youthful and innocent. He felt the rage at the situation getting the better of him.

"Trevor?" Lori said his name, and when he looked up, her eyebrows furrowed and her lips puckered up in such a cute, yet serious manner.

"Come here." Immediately his body responded to her voice, her command, as he walked toward her.

"Hold me?" she asked, and he immediately embraced her, wedging his thigh between her thighs. She pulled him tight as she laid her cheek against his chest. He could feel her warm breath penetrate the material of his shirt.

"Everything will be okay. Gunner and J.R. will catch these men."

He caressed her hair and then looked toward Dante and Charlie. Their expressions had to have mimicked his. They looked just as angry and unsure as Trevor felt.

God, help us keep Lori and the others safe. Please.

* * * *

A few days had passed and the judge issued a warrant for Connor's arrest, but he evaded capture and was on the run. The stranger had indeed left prints at Sylvia's crime scene. On top of that, Charlie told Lori that the detectives Gunner and the sheriff were working with linked the stranger to five other homicides. He apparently left some form of flowers and a note on the victims' bodies. The notes said the words, "now you die." Gunner also said that people the stranger threatened for business contracts for Connor also received notes. Theirs said, "today you live."

Gunner was confident that they would find Connor and the stranger. But the men still took precautions.

Lori was feeling cooped up and as if her plans for the future were suddenly going to come to an end. She was warned about not going jogging and she wasn't allowed to go to Carl's to work. Now she was sitting around, making no money, and feeling lazy.

Maggie and Jasper went out for an early dinner and Lori's parents headed to Casper's to have lunch with the McCallister brothers and their wife Eve.

Lori looked at Ben who was completely bored.

She glanced at her watch.

Dante would be over in an hour.

"Aunt Lori, can't we please go outside on the swing set? I'm bored," he stated and she felt bad. He had asked her five times in the last hour. She was trying to spend extra time with Ben. He had been very upset about her car accident. She picked up her cell phone and called Dante. He didn't answer his phone and it made that funny noise as if he were on another call so she hung up.

"Okay, how about we go outside for just a little bit and wait for Dante? We can go in the backyard."

Ben jumped up and down then grabbed her hand and pulled her toward the back door.

* * * *

"So, what you're saying is that guy 'the stranger' as he calls himself, is wanted for questioning in Dallas and Austin on three separate murder investigations?" Dante asked Gunner as he spoke on his cell phone to him. Charlie and Trevor were standing next to him in the sheriff's office. They had come down to press charges against Connor officially for threatening them. The sheriff had suggested they do everything they could to document what happened and to protect them for when Connor was caught.

"Do they think that he actually committed the murders?" Dante asked as he placed the call on speaker. They all listened.

"It seems to me that he is their prime suspect. It gets worse, guys. The stranger worked for two businessmen. One in Austin and one in Dallas. Both men disappeared. Sandman calls me and tells me that through his connections in the government, he gets some extra information from a friend of his. This investigator who has been working the case for two years now believes that this guy, 'the stranger,' is not only responsible for the murders but also believes that he is linked to several missing women. He has signed statements from multiple civilians stating that the stranger was either seen with the missing women hours before their disappearance or in the vicinity of their workplace and home."

"Shit, Gunner. What are we dealing with here, a sexual predator besides a killer?" the sheriff asked.

"It's not looking good. I suggest you guys get back over to your place and keep all the women, especially Lori, under your constant protection. Even though a couple of weeks have passed, this is far from over. I don't like it and I don't like that this guy can evade even government agents," Gunner said.

"I agree. Tell Sandman we said thank you. We're going to head out right now," Charlie stated.

Dante disconnected the call.

"Fuck, Lori called while we were on the phone."

"Call her back, let her know that we're on the way," Trevor stated, and he looked antsy and nervous. "Come on."

Dante felt his desperation to get to Lori. In their arms, she was the safest.

* * * *

Lori heard her cell phone ringing. She was about to go back to grab it as Ben headed outside and then she heard him yell.

Lori ran through the open back door and gasped as the forearm hit her throat. She fell onto her ass, gasping for air. As she tried to catch her breath, there was some big man holding Ben. Ben was crying and calling her name. She started coughing as she held her throat.

"I was going to keep you for myself, but it seems that the boss has other plans for you. Get up. We're going for a ride."

The man had dark, evil eyes and as Lori looked at Ben, she feared for his life.

"Leave him. Please, he's just a baby."

The guy looked at Ben then back at her.

"He dies with you. That will be the best revenge from Connor to your men. Get up." Lori could hardly stand, her legs were shaking so much. The man gripped her by her hair and kept a tight hold on Ben's shoulder.

"Where are you taking us? Please just leave the kid. He didn't do anything."

The man squeezed her hair harder.

He leaned closer to her and sniffed her hair. She felt the bile rise in her throat. This man was the one who tried to kill her. He killed Sylvia.

"Lori, I'm scared," Ben said in between crying.

"Shut up. You and your aunt are going to die together."

"Stop it. He's just a kid."

"Not for long. He's going to be dead and buried right on the construction site your men and the Cantrells are building. Perfect way to die. Slowly as the dirt caves in around you like quicksand."

Lori wanted to fight the man and scream for help, but now they were in the wooded area between their house and land and the Cantrells' and the Henleys'. Ben knew the way to the men's house and to Tom Cantrell's.

"Why are we headed toward the Cantrells'?" She looked down toward Ben. He locked gazes with her and she winked at him. He instantly stopped crying and put on a tough face. She knew that he expected her to save him, them, but she wasn't certain how. All she knew was that she needed to get Ben to safety. Her life didn't matter as much as his.

As they came to a rocky area before the clearing and where his car sat, she made her move and hoped that Ben had the quick thinking and fast legs he needed to get to help.

Using all of her momentum, she sidestepped in front of the man's legs and shoved her hips sideways into him. As she tumbled to the rocks and the man released Ben so he wouldn't fall, she yelled to Ben.

"Run, Ben, run and get help!" she screamed. As the man tried to grab Ben, Lori jumped up and hit him in the ribs and jumped onto his back. She wrapped her arm around his neck and squeezed as he coughed. She looked quickly to the right and saw Ben running, little arms pumping and heading toward the Cantrells'. That was her mistake. She was so focused on making sure that Ben got away that she must have loosened her hold because the man bent over and threw her from his back. He then proceeded to lift her up by her shirt, and struck her repeatedly. He was practically growling and she thought she saw stars as she tried covering her face. She rolled into the fetal position and he lifted her up by her belt buckle as if she weighed nothing at all and tossed her like a rag doll. Her already-bruised arm and shoulder hit the ground. She heard the crack and felt the pain in her forearm. He was going to break her bones one by one and bury her alive. The fear, the recollection of her panic attack–induced nightmare was going to become a reality. She would never see Charlie, Trevor, and Dante again.

She screamed in pain and anger as she tried to crawl and stand up. He struck her again, punching her in the side of the head and causing her body to roll to her back. She couldn't move her arm. She couldn't even feel it.

He was over her, straddling her waist, crushing her with his weight.

"I knew that you would be a good fit for me. The others didn't put up half the fight that you're putting up." He took uneasy breaths and stared down at her face then over her breasts. Her top was ripped and he stared at her cleavage. She couldn't make a move. She was throbbing in pain.

She watched him control his breathing then trail a finger over her lips and chin then down her neck to her breasts. He licked his dirty, filthy lips then pulled his lower lip between his bottom teeth as his nostrils flared.

"I think I'm going to fuck you before I bury you alive." He cupped her breast and squeezed it hard.

"You like sex. You're doing three men at once, you little whore."

The anger and hatred hit her hard and she didn't think, didn't care about her own life.

"Fuck you!" she yelled then hit him with her good arm.

He grabbed her throat, squeezing the air from her lungs. She kicked and struggled beneath him as she stared wide-eyed at the man who was going to end her life. This was it. She was going to die right here and never see Charlie, Ben, and Dante again, nor Ben, her parents, and Maggie.

She felt herself losing the fight as she closed her eyes and he released her throat with a thrust downward.

She tried to remain conscious but she could hardly breathe or swallow and then he was lifting her up, throwing her over his shoulder.

As her body bounced on top of his shoulder, she felt his hand on her ass as she stared at the ground. Her vision blurred, and with every blink of her eyes she felt herself losing consciousness. Everything hurt. She coughed and the sound, the movement from her body brought her mind back to focus again. This was it. Her life was going to end.

"What the hell took you so fucking long and who was the kid?"

She heard the voice but couldn't look to see who it was. He had a partner. *Who the hell is that?* She thought the voice sounded familiar.

"The kid doesn't matter. We'll dump her like Connor wanted," the big guy stated.

"She's so sexy, it's too bad really," the other man said, and she felt the hand move up her thigh to her ass under her shorts and squeeze.

"Fuck, she's got a nice ass."

Who is that?

"If anyone is going to fuck her, it's me, Henshaw. You're just here to tie up loose ends."

Henshaw? Don Henshaw from in town? The guy the men don't like and nearly fought with at the ice cream place? Oh God. He's involved, too?

As the big guy swung her forward, she lost her balance and was so weak she flew back hard against the car door.

"Fuck, what the hell did you do to her?" Henshaw asked. "She's all fucked up."

"She's a wildcat," he said then grabbed her chin and face, leaned forward, and kissed her. Lori struggled to get free but she couldn't move her broken arm. He plunged his tongue deeply into her mouth, making her gag, and as she tilted her head back her throat ached something terrible. She couldn't breathe or swallow or do anything to defend herself. Her body was breaking down as the tears flowed.

"Let me taste her. Just feel her a little," Henshaw said as the big guy released her mouth. He ran his hands down her shirt and cupped her breast.

He shook his head.

"It's too bad. I would have kept you around a lot longer than the others."

She was losing focus again as he shoved her into the backseat and Henshaw joined her there. She wondered who he meant by the others. Her mind was so fuzzy now, she didn't even know if she should fight or just allow the comfort of unconsciousness to free her from the pain.

"You're beautiful, even battered and weak," Henshaw told her.

She stared at him as the tears rolled down her cheeks and he pushed her shirt aside and began touching her. She thought about Trevor, Charlie, and Dante.

"And you're going to die," she whispered then closed her eyes, unable to focus anymore.

* * * *

"Sheriff, it's Tom Cantrell. We've got a big problem here. Jesus, Sheriff, the guys took Lori. Ben is here, crying and scared out of his mind. He ran here from the fields behind Lou and Diana's house."

"We're on our way. We'll be there in two minutes."

Tom disconnected the call as he watched his wife Lynn rock Ben on her lap. He was crying and pleading for them to hurry up and help his aunt.

"The sheriff is on his way, so are the Henleys, son. It's going to be okay. They'll help Lori. They'll find her."

A few minutes later Tom could hear the cars and trucks arrive. He opened the front door and saw the Texas Ranger vehicle and other patrol officers heading toward the Shays' house.

Maggie and Jasper pulled up in his truck and looked as if they didn't know anything was happening.

Tom waved them in, and Charlie, Trevor, and Dante asked Ben what happened.

Tom felt the tears reach his eyes as the little boy explained what happened and where they were taking his aunt and what they planned on doing.

"Ben, honey, oh my God, baby." Maggie came in crying and ran to Ben. He hugged his mom and cried as Jasper knelt down and caressed Ben's back.

"Mommy, Lori saved me again. She fought the bad man. He was going to bury us alive to hurt Mr. Cantrell, Charlie, Ben, and Dante. He's crazy, Mommy, and big and ugly. We have to help her, Mommy." Ben pulled from her arms and took her hand and Jasper's hand to lead them from the house.

"Hold on, buddy. We've got this. You stay here with your mom," the sheriff stated.

"No! Aunt Lori needs us. She needs us to save her this time. She's hurt."

"What do you mean hurt?" Trevor asked.

"The bad man beat her up. He hit her throat and I looked back and he was choking her."

"Oh, Jesus, no. Please, God, protect Lori," Lynn stated aloud, crying with her hands clasped together.

"We have to find her fast," Charlie stated.

"The construction site. He said he was going to bury us there," Ben said.

"Let's move. Call Gunner and have them meet us there pronto."

Tom watched as everyone ran from the house, jumped into their cars, and headed up the road a mile to the construction site.

"We need to go, too, Mommy. Aunt Lori needs us there," Ben insisted.

"I'll drive," Jasper said, and Tom and Lynn left with them.

* * * *

Lori couldn't walk, which earned her another smack and a kick to her thigh. She fell to the ground only for him to lift her up and carry her to a large dirt pile area near a very large hole. She saw Henshaw running toward the bulldozer. He was climbing in and as he started the loud engine she could have sworn she heard sirens in the distance.

As hope of being rescued filled her heart, the big man shoved her into the hole. She screamed as she felt the long fall then slammed onto her broken arm, her head hitting something hard.

Dirt began to fall on top of her. She sensed the crumbled bits of dirt, the intense smell of earth filled her nostrils, initiating panic and fear like nothing she ever felt before consume her. This was it, she was going to be buried alive.

The sound of the engine from the bulldozer above whined high as the first bit of dirt fell from the bucket and slid down the sides. She rolled to her right and tried to get up, but as she lifted her head, it throbbed, filling her gut with nausea as something thick and warm oozed from her head and went into her eye. She couldn't move to stand up. Her mind fought over her body's ability to just get up, stand up, and fight. The sounds of the engine revving, sirens blaring and people yelling sounded muffled in the back of her mind. Was she hallucinating? Was she already dying? She thought she heard gunshots, something as the bulldozer stopped, more dirt came down upon her and she lost her focus and rolled into the fetal position. She reached out with her good hand and grabbed a hold of the dirt wall. The dirt and rock scraped under her fingernails then crumbled. There was no way to climb out, to get free.

I'm going to die.

* * * *

"Fuck, he's right there and, look, someone is on the bulldozer dropping dirt. Fuck, hurry!" Trevor yelled as Charlie skidded out near the bulldozer.

Trevor and Dante jumped out as Gunner and the sheriff exchanged gunfire with some big dude Trevor thought was the stranger.

Dante climbed the bulldozer and threw someone out of it then pulled the bulldozer back and turned it off.

As Trevor reached the side, he saw Henshaw, lifted him by the collar, and punched him straight into the face. He fell to the ground as one of the deputies handcuffed him.

Charlie was yelling down into the hole.

"Oh God, no. No, please be alive. Lori!" Charlie yelled down. Trevor and Dante joined him by the side.

"Wait, let's get some rope or something. It might cave in," the sheriff yelled as he and Gunner joined them.

"No, she needs us," Trevor said then jumped down into the hole, rolled and landed a foot away from Lori.

He felt the dirt falling in slightly around them. They didn't have much time.

He placed his hand against her cheek, the sight of all the bruises, the blood, the gash on her head and broken arm angered him and scared the living hell out of him.

"She's unconscious, barely breathing, and in bad shape."

"The ambulance is here!" Charlie yelled down.

"How bad is she, son?" Tom Cantrell asked.

Trevor looked up at the gathering crowd. He locked gazes with Charlie and Dante then Ben and Maggie.

"Bad," he whispered and felt the tears reach his eyes. He loved Lori so much and he thought his heart was stone and could never feel so much for anyone. She changed all that. She was a hero, a strong person, and a fighter. But now she needed them. She needed her family and friends, and they were all above them, moving into action.

"Trevor, did you hear me? I'm coming. We need to tie her down to the flat board," Charlie yelled to him.

Dante helped the paramedics as Charlie jumped down into the hole and immediately looked over Lori's injuries.

"Fuck, this is bad," he whispered to Trevor.

"I know. If she doesn't make it, Charlie—"

"She'll make it. This is Lori we're talking about here. Come on. Let's do this."

Dante and the paramedic slowly lowered the flat board and the ropes. They took their time gently moving Lori onto the stretcher. As she lay on her back, Trevor absorbed the sight of bruising to her throat, her face, and chest. He clenched his teeth.

"They fucking touched her. Look."

"We can't focus on that now. The stranger is dead. Gunner shot him as he took shots at him and the deputies. Henshaw is in cuffs. She's safe." Charlie clipped the attachments on the board, strapping her in tightly.

It was an effort pulling her up and then pulling up Charlie and Trevor.

Just as they watched Lori being placed into the ambulance, they heard the sound of dirt falling and the hole collapsed. They had just made it in the nick of time. Trevor ran a hand over his mouth as he felt his chest tighten and his body shake in fear as the adrenaline rush began to diminish.

Lori could have been buried alive. I could have lost her forever.

Chapter 20

Lori had a tough road ahead of her. She felt tired, weak, would get dizzy every once in a while, and had blurred vision. The doctors said it was normal after sustaining multiple hits to the head and then landing on that rock in the dirt ditch. Her arm was still in a cast but in another two weeks it would be off and right in time to start school. She hadn't been able to work, but Charlie, Dante, and Trevor insisted that they were going to take care of her and that she no longer had to worry about money. She came upstairs about an hour ago to lie down and she felt that fear and bit of anxiety about being alone. She was trying her hardest to not let the fear control her as Andrew had explained during one of their therapy sessions. She felt comfortable with him and found his counseling techniques helpful.

But it seemed that she couldn't last more than an hour alone. Which was better than three weeks ago when she couldn't stand to be alone for more than a few minutes.

As if knowing she was getting panicky, Trevor came upstairs and joined her.

"Hey, sexy, how are you doing?"

She opened her arms to him and felt the tears reach them, but they wouldn't fall. She was gaining control of that, too. No more crying at the drop of a hat or hiding out, shaking in fear. The nightmares continued but her men were always there to take care of her. It was part of the PTSS she suffered from, just as Charlie, Dante, and Trevor suffered from it, too. But they told her, since she had become part of their lives, their nightmares had lessened and their focus was solely on loving her.

He climbed onto the bed and hugged her. He lay down and she snuggled against him.

"You're shaking, honey. How long before it started this time?" he asked as he caressed her chin.

"An hour. I'm getting better." She squeezed him tightly.

"You'll get through this."

She knew she would. The four of them talked about everything. There were no secrets between them, no fears of sounding weak or off guard. That had taken a lot for Charlie, Trevor, and Dante to do since they were macho soldiers, and they blamed that on her, too.

She smiled as she kissed Trevor's neck then she made her way to his lips.

He smoothed his hand along her shoulder then to her breast. He cupped the mound and she was happy that it didn't hurt anymore. The bruising was almost fully gone, and each time her men feasted on her breasts and made love to her, the memories of that day and being touched by two psycho men lessened.

Immediately the kiss grew stronger, deeper, and she maneuvered her hand to his belt buckle. The damn cast was in the way and he released her lips and chuckled against her mouth.

"Let me." He shifted up and took off his clothes, and she watched him, eager to see what was hers to feast upon.

"Now you." He reached over and she lifted her hips as he pulled her shorts and panties off of her.

Then she sat up and he divested her of her T-shirt and bra, smiling then licking his lips.

"Lie back and open up for me, sexy."

Her heart hammered inside of her chest. She loved his pet name for her and the way Trevor gave his orders in bed.

As she opened wide, the bruising along her thighs still apparent, he climbed up between her legs. Now that she was on birth control, they didn't have to use condoms, and as Dante said, there was nothing to block their connection.

He caressed his hands up her thighs as Charlie and Dante stood in the doorway.

"We should have known what you two were up to," Charlie stated then began to undress.

Trevor lowered his shoulders to the bed and licked across her cunt.

She thrust upward and went to grab his head to hold it as he ate at her cream and caused tiny spasms to erupt and lubricate her pussy.

"Hands up. You know the rules," Dante stated, joining her on the right side of the bed completely naked.

Charlie pulled off the rest of his clothing and joined her on the left side.

They each cupped a breast and Charlie kissed her mouth.

"Do you still feel dizzy?" he asked, filled with concern. She shook her head.

"How long before the feeling hit you?" Dante asked then kissed her earlobe, bringing it between his teeth and making her come a little.

Trevor hummed then pulled his mouth from her pussy.

"She likes that, Dante."

"I know," Dante said then pinched her nipple.

"How long?" Dante repeated.

"Longer than usual."

"Anything else bothering you?" Charlie asked, leaning down and taking her nipple into his mouth. He sucked, swirled his tongue around the tip, then nipped it with his teeth before releasing it.

"Stop teasing me and make love to me already," she stated firmly and they chuckled.

"Someone is getting awfully demanding," Trevor said then sat up, lifted her hips so that he could line his cock with her pussy, and slowly pushed into her.

She started to lower her arms and bumped Dante in the head with her cast as he sucked on her nipple, and Trevor and Charlie laughed.

"I'm sorry, Dante."

He had a scowl on his face as he rubbed the top of his head.

"You should be." He covered her mouth, kissing her deeply.

Trevor continued to thrust into her and spread her legs wider.

"How's the head?" Charlie asked as he ran the tip of his nail across her nipple. Dante did the same on the other side.

She knew why they were asking. They wanted to make love to her together, but feared she might get dizzy or sick to her stomach on all fours with her head down.

She wanted them inside her so badly she actually ached. Which was wild.

"I want you both. I need you always," she told them.

Both men stood up from the bed and as Trevor lay over her, making love to her slowly, licking her neck and kissing her mouth, she heard the dresser drawers opening and knew that they were getting the lube. She felt excited and aroused.

"Fuck, baby, you're so wet. I bet you're thinking about having two cocks in you at once, aren't you?" he asked as he thrust his hips and held her face between his hands.

"Yes." She moaned and he thrust again.

"You're ours forever, sexy. We're never going to leave you. You'll never be alone again."

He kissed her hard on the mouth.

She felt the tears hit her eyes. She believed him. She loved them so much.

Trevor lifted up and began to thrust into her faster and deeper until she exploded, saying his name until he joined her, filling her with his seed.

Trevor leaned down and kissed her lips, her cheeks, and then her breasts as he slowly pulled from her body. "Let's get you ready." He lifted her up into his arms as Dante lay down on the edge of the bed, his long, ironlike thighs spread wide and his cock fisted in his hands.

She locked gazes with Charlie who tapped the tube of lube against the palm of his hand as he stood there looking like a muscular sex god.

Trevor kissed her again then placed her on top of Dante, swiped his finger from her pussy to her anus, giving her the chills as she shivered.

"Come on, angel. I need to be inside of you."

She leaned down and kissed Dante on his lips then pressed her tongue between his teeth. She loved how he called her his angel. As she rubbed her pussy back and forth over his hard, thick cock, she felt the hands on her hips then lips kiss her spine.

"I love this body, these sexy, toned thighs. I want to be inside of you, little runner. I need to feel you."

"Yes, please," she whispered. Then Dante fisted his cock and she adjusted her position, taking him fully inside of her.

She moaned in relief of having him inside of her. She felt most secure and connected like this, enveloped in this way.

Immediately she released his lips and placed her good hand on his chest and began to move up and down. He assisted, holding her hips and lifting then lowering. They knew the cast got in the way and they helped her, always putting her needs first.

"You look so fucking sexy," Trevor whispered then placed his hand behind her head and leaned down to kiss her on the mouth. She tasted herself on his lips and it made her hunger for Dante and Charlie grow stronger.

Charlie pressed her chest forward and she knew he was getting ready to penetrate her ass.

Her belly quivered as Dante wrapped an arm around her shoulders and held her tight against his chest as he thrust upward. His thigh muscles were so rock solid and strong, she was amazed at their capabilities.

The cool liquid hit her anus, and she tensed up as Charlie caressed her ass cheeks open. "I love this ass. I won't last long, honey. You know how I get when my cock is in this tight, perfect ass," Charlie said, and she knew. He didn't last long when he fucked her ass. Neither did Dante or Trevor.

She pushed her ass back against his fingers as they pushed into her anus.

"Fuck, that's hot. She's sucking your fingers right in there, Charlie. She's ready for it." Trevor cheered them on. She felt him caress her back and she loved how all three of them touched her as they made love together. She wanted it to be like this forever.

Charlie pulled his fingers from her ass and replaced them with his cock. He felt thick and hard as he pushed through the tight rings, making her ass burn.

"Oh God, you're so hard."

"Fuck, I am, baby. You do it to me," he said through what sounded like clenched teeth. He thrust into her and she gasped then slightly lifted. As Charlie pulled out, Dante thrust upward, making her lose her breath. It suddenly felt as if both men's cocks grew twice in size and girth. Her chest tightened, her stomach ached, and as they thrust into her she screamed her release. Dante followed, moaning her name and shaking beneath her, and then Charlie surprised the hell out of her as he gripped her hips and began a wild rhythm pulling in and out of her ass. He was moving so fast she felt her pussy pulsate again. Dante moaned as she screamed another release right as Charlie exploded inside of her.

The three of them were lying there motionless for seconds as Trevor chuckled.

"Charlie wins," Dante said.

Lori didn't know what they were talking about. Nor did she care as Charlie caressed her ass as he slowly pulled from her body.

Dante kissed her and smiled as he wiped the damp strands from her cheeks before rolling her to her side. As he pulled from her body, she moaned and Trevor was there caressing her.

He leaned down and locked her nipple then kissed her mouth.

"Feeling okay, sexy?"

"Very okay," she whispered.

She lay there relaxing, hoping to have the energy to shower or at least talk one of her men into joining her as Dante began to get dressed. He didn't look too happy.

"What's going on?" she asked.

Charlie smiled as Trevor pulled her into his arms. "Nothing, baby. Dante just lost a bet," Charlie said as Dante looked at her.

"I'm going to go downstairs and make us lunch. I'll see you in a bit," Dante said then left the room.

"A bet?" she asked as Trevor carried her from the bedroom to the shower.

"A bet," Charlie said then kissed her shoulder and reached into the cabinet under the sink. He took out the plastic wrapping for her cast. Even though she had a waterproof one, she didn't like the feeling it gave her when water came up the fingers. She nudged Charlie as he grabbed a washcloth and cleaned himself up with soap and water. She watched him stroking his cock and nearly lost focus on the conversation.

"Well, what bet?"

Charlie just smiled as he wrapped her cast then walked over to the shower.

"What bet, Dante?" she asked.

"Just a small wager among brothers."

Charlie stood under the spray lifted her up so that she straddled his waist. She felt his erection, hard against her pussy and ass. Then she felt Dante rubbing the soap all over her.

He kissed her shoulder.

"You see, baby, this ass of yours is so fucking incredible. The three of us just can't seem to last when we're fucking it," Trevor said. His words elicited a moan from her as she leaned her head back then felt the fingers caressing her pussy.

"We're having a little wager to see how long we can fuck this ass without coming," Trevor said then pressed a digit against the puckered hole.

She gasped.

"You are not," she reprimanded.

"Are, too," Charlie said. He kissed her then smiled as he thrust his cock against her folds.

Dante lifted her hips up so that Charlie could thrust into her. These men were so much bigger than her and so strong it impressed her to near orgasm.

"Charlie has lasted the longest so far, but now it's my turn," Dante said, and as she looked over her shoulder, she saw him with the tube of lube. He squirted it onto his fingers as the water sprayed over them, and Charlie thrust up into her.

"I love these tits. You've got the most delicious set of breasts, baby. And this pussy, fuck, you feel so tight milking my cock. I won't last long at all," Charlie said, and she felt lube-covered fingers pressing into her ass.

Dante chuckled. "Ain't gonna work, Charlie. I'm on a mission." Dante pulled out his fingers and replaced them with his cock.

"Oh God, maybe this isn't such a good idea," she stated, totally turned on by their words, their actions, their bodies, and their need to possess her ass in such a way.

"You're gonna love it, baby. Hold on to Charlie, sexy, I'm gonna set a record that my brothers won't ever come close to."

She gasped as he pushed into her ass and both men began to thrust into her one after the next.

She didn't know if she should be upset with them or utterly turned on, but her body responded positively. She counterthrust and moaned and cheered them on.

They teased one another relentlessly, thrusting into her, kissing her skin, and making her weak and nearly paralyzed between them. As it became certain that no one was going to beat Dante, Charlie exploded inside of her. Dante continued his thrusts until she gave him orgasm after orgasm. He gripped her hips and thrust deep yelling out her name and then a loud "oorah!"

Charlie and Dante pulled from her body and helped her upright as they soaped her up, rinsed her off, and assisted her in getting dressed.

They headed downstairs where Trevor gave Dante a high five, and then he stared at Lori.

She was utterly exhausted and ready for a nap.

Trevor placed the sandwiches on the table then came up behind her, wrapped his arms around her waist, and whispered, "Don't fall asleep yet. I've got a record to beat, sexy, and you're going to help me win."

He kissed her forehead then took a seat at the table along with her, Charlie, and Dante.

Charlie was smiling as he ate, Dante looked completely confident that Trevor didn't have a chance beating him, and Trevor looked hungry.

Her ass actually felt like it reacted to Trevor's comment, and damn her pussy for getting all uppity and wetting the new panties she'd just put on after the shower.

Was this what a relationship with three sexy military men, who strived to always be the best, would be like? Three huge brothers who wanted to show themselves up and compete to make love to her ass the longest? She chuckled at the thought as the words hit her mind. This was insane. Yet, she found herself feeling hungry for them again even after the double love session only twenty minutes ago. She could surely get used to this life. Always feeling protected, loved in every aspect of the word, and always having three sexy hot military men as her lovers.

They wanted to take care of her, provide for her so she wouldn't have any stress in her life. It all sounded great but she was a worker, an achiever, and there was so much to accomplish. This blue-collar girl couldn't go so easily to a princess being served the world. But she did like knowing they were there for her and that she could count on them.

"What's that face for, baby? Are you feeling all right?" Charlie asked then caressed her cheek.

She looked at the three of them. Suddenly appearing serious, no longer joking and solely putting her needs before them. She decided to lighten things up a bit and play along with them. After all, she wasn't stupid. The men had some serious assets she craved on a regular basis.

She wiped her mouth, winked at Trevor, then looked at Charlie and Dante.

"My money's on Trevor. I think he'll last the longest." She stood up.

She heard the chairs move and then Trevor laughed. Strong arms lifted her up and she locked gazes with Trevor.

"Troublemaker," he said.

"You know what we do to troublemakers, don't you, Lori?" Charlie asked as Dante rubbed his hands together. She didn't get it.

She felt Charlie reach underneath her and caress her ass. He held her gaze.

"Troublemakers get punished."

Her eyes widened.

How the heck did this whole thing turn against her?

"What?" she asked.

"A spanking is in order, I think," Dante stated as he continued to rub his thick, large hands together. She tightened her thighs as her pussy clenched in response.

"Oh boy, I think we need to talk about this," she said as Trevor carried her out of the room and up the stairs.

"First we're going to spank this pretty ass and remind you about not causing trouble with your lovers, and then I'm going to fuck it, sexy. Long, deep strokes that keep you begging to come."

"Oorah!" the three men cheered.

"Oh. My. God." Lori felt so aroused and hungry she didn't have a care in the world except making love to her men and being their love and possession. Life was only going to get more and more interesting with these men. She just knew it.

Now how can I get them back for this one?

As they removed her clothing, her mind thought of multiple ways to play this out. However, once their lips touched her skin and Trevor placed her over his knees, all thoughts were lost. She loved them with all her heart. She was grateful for making it here to a new life where her family and loved ones were protected and safe. She accepted and relished in the excitement of being in love, safe and secure with her wild American soldiers, destined to make every day of her life exciting and fulfilling.

"Open up those thighs for me, woman," Trevor said. "We're about to set a record."

She moaned aloud as she did what he asked and accepted their ministrations, opening up her body and her heart to three men that loved her in every aspect of the word.

THE END

WWW.DIXIELYNNDWYER.COM

ABOUT THE AUTHOR

People seem to be more interested in my name than where I get my ideas for my stories from. So I might as well share the story behind my name with all my readers.

My momma was born and raised in New Orleans. At the age of twenty, she met and fell in love with an Irishman named Patrick Riley Dwyer. Needless to say, the family was a bit taken aback by this as they hoped she would marry a family friend. It was a modern day arranged marriage kind of thing and my momma downright refused.

Being that my momma's families were descendents of the original English speaking Southerners, they wanted the family blood line to stay pure. They were wealthy and my father's family was poor.

Despite attempts by my grandpapa to make Patrick leave and destroy the love between them, my parents married. They recently celebrated their sixtieth wedding anniversary.

I am one of six children born to Patrick and Lynn Dwyer. I am a combination of both Irish and a true Southern belle. With a name like Dixie Lynn Dwyer it's no wonder why people are curious about my name.

Just as my parents had a love story of their own, I grew up intrigued by the lifestyles of others. My imagination as well as my need to stray from the straight and narrow made me into the woman I am today.

For all titles by Dixie Lynn Dwyer, please visit
www.bookstrand.com/dixie-lynn-dwyer

Siren Publishing, Inc.
www.SirenPublishing.com

Lightning Source UK Ltd.
Milton Keynes UK
UKHW02f1457020518
321990UK00005B/675/P